I, NEMO

I, NEMO

J. DHARMA &
DEANNA WINDHAM

*This is a work of fiction. Names, characters, places, and incidents either
are the product of the author's imagination or are used fictitiously. Any
resemblance to actual events or locales or persons, living or dead, is
entirely coincidental.*

Original Cover Art by Jennifer Hood,
www.WeGotHoodzpah.com

ISBN: 9780786752867
eISBN 9780786752874

Distributed by
Argo Navis Author Services
www.argonavisdigital.com

Distributed by Argo Navis Author Services

Acknowledgments

No book or writing career is launched without a team of people working together, and our success is no exception. We would like to acknowledge several people in our lives who have been instrumental in helping us reach this point. Deanna's parents, Jack and Janice Shriver, have been a constant source of encouragement and have helped us to accomplish our goals when others would have given up. Deanna would especially like to thank her Mom, whose lifelong support has been the cornerstone of her success and who believed in her even when nobody else did, sometimes including herself. We would like to thank our agent, Robert Thixton, who believed in our literary vision and was willing to fight the odds with us and who has gone above and beyond the call of duty to help us reach our goals.

We would also like to thank Dr. Julian Whitaker and Whitaker Wellness Institute, without whose medical expertise and treatment Deanna likely wouldn't have survived to write a book. We would also like to thank Jennifer Hood of We Got Hoodzpah, who has tirelessly worked with us to get the covers just right and who has been a constant friend encouraging Dharma on his hardest days. Lastly, with love we would like to remember Deanna's dear friend, Lieutenant John Frye, who believed in anything she did, was a constant source of knowledge and advice, and who helped Dharma with some of the technical aspects of naval life and seamanship.

Prologue

August 6, 2015: 1245Hrs South Pacific Ocean

The ship RV Antediluvian slid across a placid black sea. Not a sliver of moon shone. The only light came from the icy rime of stars coating the inverted bowl of the nighttime sky, the big vessel's running lights, the light coming from the long rectangular windows on its bridge and the round portholes in the sharply cambered hull.

Brierly looked away from the monitor's screen and rubbed his eyes.

Ian laughed at the newbie. "That only makes it worse, Mate." He'd seen dozens of them. Young and idealistic and fresh out of some fancy college and fired up with enough enthusiasm to fill the bellies of any ten men. All that shit changed after an expedition or two: Then the reality set in. Even with the obligatory training and orientation mandated by insurance companies, there were hazards such as nitrogen narcosis. The grandfather of scuba diving, Jacques Cousteau, had once remarked, "I like it and fear it like doom." Ian knew exactly what the Frenchman had meant. At sea level nitrogen was as harmless as pie, but sink a few fathoms and it could render you dangerous to your dive mates, and yourself. Then there was the cold. Even in the tropics the temperature would drop rapidly as the diver descended lower and lower into the murky depths. Water leached the body's heat away from it so hypothermia could become a real problem for a diver in anything less than peak condition. And there were the sharks and the rays, like the one that had killed Steve Irwin. Ian nodded to himself. The aquatic amusement parks had made the ocean look too benign. Wholesome blondes cavorted with killer whales, and the world was cast into a state of extreme shock when one of those wholesome blondes was suddenly ripped apart by one of them. Marine archeologists were easy targets for sharks although some carried bang guns for protection. The only real protection from a great white, which could chomp a Triumph motorcycle in half, was a shark cage. But you couldn't survey a wreck site from a cage. And if the wreck site was too deep the only way to see it was from a mini submersible.

"You won't see anything staring bug-eyed at the screen," Ian said to Brierly. Not that he cared all that much. Let the kid exhaust his bloody eyes. Everyone has to learn to carry their own water. He'd learned his lessons, all hard won, and earned his scars.

Still, sometimes, it was hard to resist the urge to offer advice to a newbie.

Brierly nodded, conceding the Aussie's point. This was his

first expedition and as the new guy he got to pull the second watch- from midnight until four am. The expedition's leader Jacob Ballion was searching for the wreck of the Imperial Japanese battleship IJN Hirohito, a behemoth even larger than the Yamato, which had worried the Allies during Word War II until it was sunk by an American submarine in the South Pacific. They had been searching for two months and still no luck. Tomorrow at 1200 hours they were due to head for home at Pacific Oceanographic Institute in San Diego. The mood on board was one of somber resignation. No one wanted to go home empty-handed. The only one onboard who seemed untroubled by the expedition's failure to find the Japanese wreck was Ian Hawkes. Brierly wondered if anything ever ruffled the Australian's feathers.

"Nothing. There's not a goddamn thing down there," Brierly murmured despairingly, peering with sore eyes at the monitor.

Ian gave a diffident shrug. "Underwater archaeology is a lot like poker: sometimes you have a winning hand, sometimes you don't."

The hours wore on until Brierly thought his eyes would melt and slough out of their weary sockets. He was reaching for the coffee pot on the table to his left when something on the screen caught his attention from the corner of his eye. He turned and stared full on at the flat panel monitor screen. "Now what the hell is that?"

Ian scooted his chair over and peered at the monitor's screen. He looked at Brierly. "Better wake the Skipper," he said.

A moment later the RV Antediluvian's computer room was filled with people. A dozen curious eyes studied the image on the monitor. Everyone was speaking at once.

"What is it?" someone asked.

"A boiler?" someone else suggested.

"Not at that size. It's almost three hundred feet long," Brierly replied.

Jacob Ballion stood with his arms crossed staring down at the image on the screen. He'd dived all the famous wrecks: the Titanic, Lusitania, The HMS Hood, Graf Spee, he'd even found the lost wreck of the little known Confederate iron clad, the Jefferson Davis, in the Gulf of Mexico. When the Russian nuclear submarine Lenin went missing in the South Atlantic, the Russian Navy turned to him—so did the U.S. Navy.

"What do you think it is?" a grad student asked after a long, awed silence.

"Perhaps an ironclad of some kind," Jacob Ballion replied slowly. "But not like any I've ever seen. It's definitely mid nineteen century technology, though."

"Could it be a submarine?" Brierly asked.

"It can't be," objected Smithers, a naval historian. "There were no submarines worth the name other than the Confederate Navy's Hunley, and it was much smaller and powered by a hand crank."

Ballion nodded. "Agreed. So let's go in for a closer look."

0430HRS

The deep sea submersible Chipmunk dropped through the dark ocean. It had been sinking for two hours, piloted by Joe Banning. Inside the titanium pressure sphere, lying on his stomach next to the pilot, Jacob Ballion studied the instruments on the console before him. Capable of diving safely to six thousand meters, the Chipmunk could reach seventy percent of the world's oceans. The submersible was outfitted with an acoustic imaging sonar that not only allowed it to detect the bottom of the sea as it descended but to identify both geological and manmade objects. Inside the little submersible it was cold and the air was filled with the sound of whirring motors and the pumps forcing air through the CO_2 scrubbers. Outside the twelve inch thick view ports, the quartz iodide and metal halide lights illuminated the black sea.

"Bottom in sight," Jacob Ballion announced evenly.

Banning nodded, flipped a switch, released the descent weights and adjusted the sub's buoyancy until the Chipmunk was floating only three feet from the seabed floor. The radio crackled and a voice said, "Chipmunk, this is RV Antediluvian, status check."

Jacob Balllion thumbed the mike. "Roger, RV Antediluvian, this is Chipmunk. All leaks, dumps, and oxygen are normal, CO_2 scrubber is working."

"Roger, Chipmunk."

Ballion nudged the pilot. "Okay. Let's go."

Banning flipped a switch and the Chipmunk's thrusters kicked in and they glided across the seabed floor. They rose to pass over a very low hill and then dropped down onto a flat plain.

Ballion checked the sonar's screen. "Another five hundred meters," he announced.

Banning nodded as he worked the controls and monitored the submersible's systems. "Funny place to find an iron-clad, don't you think?" he commented.

"Especially this far out in the Pacific," Ballion replied.

O530HRS

A dark spindle shaped object suddenly loomed ahead. The pilot applied reverse thrusters and the submersible slowed. The two men stared through their view ports.

"Holy shit! Look at that!" Ballion cried.

"Boss, is that what I think it is?" Banning asked, not believing his eyes.

"It damn sure looks like a sub," Ballion said, his voice awe-filled and quizzical. He cleared his throat and touched the mike. "Antediluvian. Are you getting this?"

"Roger Chipmunk. Pictures are clear and crisp."

Ballion recognized the voice of the naval historian. "But it just doesn't fit with the historical record," he wondered aloud. "This close, it is easy to see the construction technique is mid 19th century."

"I always thought it was just a story, but here it is...." Ballion shook his head, too awestruck to finish the sentence aloud.

"And pretty much as described," Banning added.

"You're not saying...?" Smithers statement trailed off. "History will have to be re-written."

Ballion thumbed the mike. "We're going in for a closer look."

"Roger Chipmunk"

The submersible approached the wreck, its high intensity lights shining like the eyes of a primordial monster. Then as it neared the long low black shape, its reverse thrusters kicked in again and it slowed to a stop, its wide angle digital camera click-ing, its video camera panning over the long spindle shaped object lying half submerged in the seabed.

Three miles above there were sharp gasps and shouts of jubi-lation. True, this was not the WWII era Japanese battleship they were searching for. No, it's something far more significant—a myth brought to life; the equivalent of finding the Loch Ness monster, or Big Foot, or a crashed UFO. Impelled by a command from its pilot, Chipmunk moved toward the wreck, its lights playing over the black hull of the vessel. A curtain of rusticles hung like icicles from the pointy ram jutting from the legendary submarine's bow. The deep sea submersible turned and glided along the length of the wreck, pausing at a huge oblong hole in its side.

"That must be one of the viewing ports," Ballion commented. As if in confirmation, the submersible's lights caught the unmistakable glint of jagged shards of thick glass hanging from bronze bands ringing the port.

The pilot gave the controls a nudge and the submersible moved further aft to the stern where a great bronze four bladed propeller lay half-buried.

"That looks surprisingly modern," Smithers murmured.

Ballion interrupted the excited chatter of the crew above, "Let's head back to the view port. I want to have a look inside the sub."

Hovering over the view port, a small cage under the submersible opened and the ROV Scooby popped out and moved off, tethered to the submersible by a thread of a wire, its six buglike lights resembling unblinking eyes.

Ballion worked the ROV's controls with the precise movements of a brain surgeon. He gave the joystick a nudge and Scooby moved through the wrecked submarine's broken view port, its camera swiveling inside its clear dome. Inside, it turned slowly, its lights playing over iron walls. Jagged fragments of wood paneling leaped out of the dark.

Ballion stared at the screen. The robot's camera and lights swiveled, taking in broken furniture, gold dishes, the tattered remnants of fine rugs worn by the ravages of the water, and display cases filled with oddities and rarities, just visible through their glass surfaces coated with a thick layer of silt. At the other end of the room was a large vault with its door standing open, hanging by one hinge.

Ballion guided the ROV toward it. Scooby's mechanical arms unfolded with one dexterous movement, and out of one of them a surprisingly human-like hand with long, skinny mechanical fingers unfolded and seized the edge of the door as the robot reversed thrust.

The view screen instantly filled with an obscuring cloud of silt kicked up by the ROV's powerful jets. The door opened in a shower of silt and rust and tore off its last hinge, falling to the floor. When the clouds of silt finally cleared up, everyone stared, open mouthed at what was inside. None of them had ever seen so much treasure in a wreck. And on a shelf among heaps of gold coins, jewelry, heavy gold plates and goblets, was an iron chest. Scooby's arms extended, its mechanical hands flexing.

1230HRS: Onboard the Antediluvian

Ballion and Banning carefully placed the iron chest on the table in the conference room. The others crowded around them and watched as Brierly used a lock picking tool to open the lock. The lock clicked open and Brierly stood back.

"You should be the one to open it," he said to Ballion.

Ballion put his hands on the lid. "Here it goes," he said, raising the chest's lid. It was dry inside the chest, which was empty except for a thick black leather bound book with a large gold N emblazoned on its cover.

CHAPTER 1

In My Mind's Eye

Let this chronicle serve as the true and unvarnished tale of my life irrespective of any nonsense penned by that rascal—the so-called professor Pierre Arronax. If ever I have rued an act of clemency or allowed the cold tempered steel of my inner core to be self magnetized toward the nobler metals of the human condition—I say this: mark me well, Sirs, it was this one thing. Nothing do I regret more than ignoring my better judgment and not opening the valves to my beloved Nautilus' ballast tanks and sinking beneath the waves to let that scrofulous Frenchman drown like a rat. So, as I have already declared, these pages will serve as my representative in the all-too-likely event I am unable to speak for myself, in order that the true account of my life may be passed along to posterity.

Captain Nemo
The Nautilus
1873

Even now I hold it a grave offence withal to put down in writing the grief I feel; for words, like the sea, half reveal and half conceal the pain within. Yet, I have cast my line for better or worse. When I embarked upon my career as a naval architect and mechanical engineer in my youth, I was wide-eyed with the first peach-fuzz blush of innocence and felt that I had been tasked by the Creator to accomplish something important and meaningful. Foolishly, I believed that my work for **Her Majesty's** navy would be the means for doing so. How wrong those early assumptions of my life were.

How desolate of spirit once I perceived the true state of affairs. What a blind fool I had been, a fact I discerned soon enough to the accompaniment of much bitter grief. But all that was well beyond the pale of the horizon. All was yet clear sailing in those days, with no intimation of the storms bearing down on me—and us: my beloved Lavinia and I, our daughters Elspeth and Prudence, and my dear bosom companion Harrison.

Aye, there was aught but full-on joy in the spring of my life.

And not a squall line on the horizon.

On the day of what until then was my greatest triumph, I had no inkling of what cruel fate had in store for me. How I have gnashed my teeth and torn my hair in grief over my misfortune since then. Betrayed! Betrayed by my best friend, my country, and the one person most dear to me—even now every fiber of my being cries out in white hot anguish at the memory of what transpired so soon after my triumph. It burns in the pit of my stomach; yea, scalds my flesh with its dreadful scenes ever unfolding in my mind's eye—some events so horrible I can scarcely bear to summon their recollection.

All I had wished to do was render good service to my fellow man. To that end I had conceived of a warship of such formidable qualities and technological innovation that war would become too terrible to contemplate by rational men. For I had lost my father Jonathan Mason Senior and my beloved elder brother Sean William in Her Majesty's service, leaving only I and my dear mother, Rosalinda Edith Mason, to carry on as best as we could in our modest home. But I digress….perhaps from the effects of the creeping years…perhaps from my long self-imposed exile beneath the sea's waves I have lost the gift for cogent interlocution with my fellow mortals. And so, gently laying my hands on the spokes of the free-wheeling helm of my mind, I turn it thus and so to regain the truer heading this tale calls for. Aye, true north toward showy Polaris and not a rhumb line but straight on.

It was on the day of the launch of my creation, HMS Warrior that all my hopes and desires seemed providentially to be fulfilled. It was a sere gray day on the morning of the twenty ninth of eighteen sixty of **Our Lord**, when all the most elect of **Her Majesty's** government: the Prime Minister, Lord Palmerston, and his cabinet, the First Naval Lord, Sir John Pakingham, and the most renowned members of the Admiralty and the Lords and Ladies of the court descended in coaches and railway cars to

Leamouth Wharf at the confluence of the Thames and Bow-creek to witness the launch of England's warship. It was a chill gray day and I was happy for the new woolen scarf, knitted by my wife Lavinia Cotswold Mason, and my greatcoat.

Today the air was not filled as it usually was with the staccato rattle of rivet setting machines, and the sooty fumes from the foundries that turned out the iron plating and cast in viscous white yellow steel the parts for the engines or the whine of the great lathes that carved the propeller drive shafts from blocks of steel. Today the air was filled with band music and the joyful buzz of an excited crowd gathered to see the launch of the then greatest warship ever built. Tens of thousands of people had converged on the Thames Ironworks, most arriving before dawn. Yard workers and schools had been given the day off. Foreign dignitaries had come with their entourages to witness the great event: ambassadors from the European nations, exotic envoys from the countries of the Levant and the Orient. The Americans were there too, of course, despite their looming troubles.

It was an exciting time to be an engineer. We were witness to the most profound developments in naval design and construction as sail began to give way to the more reliable motive power of steam. The bang and clash of steel and iron being fashioned into the components of iron hulled ships had replaced the thud of hammers driving nail into wood and the whine of adzes shaping planks. The sulfurous smell of furnaces and red hot iron had superseded the sweet smell of kiln and air dried oak and pine. A good thing as England's forests were by then nearly depleted, after centuries of shipbuilding—and we no longer had free access to the New World's rich store of lumber. In my lifetime I had witnessed the arrival of the paddle wheel steamer which in turn was now being rapidly supplanted by the more efficient screw propeller. To be sure, both still required the use of a full suite of sails, with steam laid on for the chase or for escape as the case may be.

My wife's soft voice interrupted my ruminations. "Oh Jonathan! What a lovely, lovely ship you have designed!" she said, her breath like smoke in the freezing air. Her grip on my arm tightened and her smile was as sweet in my eyes as a summer evening.

I smiled down into her honest open face with its clear green eyes, her nose delicate and upswept with a beauty mark beside it, lips full and pink as a rose blossom, framed by hair as fiery as an autumn dusk beneath her bonnet. "Thank you, My Dear," I replied. The color mounted to her face in one of her easy blushes. I smiled gently at her and pressed her hand. We were standing in the tall review stand on the shipyard's concrete wharf, our view blocked by the long high black hull with its two tall buff colored funnels and soaring bare masts since she was not yet fully rigged. As I said, the stand was filled with dignitaries and the surrounding shipyard and the streets leading to it were filled to overflowing with the proud workmen and mechanics who had labored these past twenty months to build **Her Majesty's** newest and greatest warship, along with the curious who had come from the City to witness its launch.

"You must be so proud," Lavinia said, beaming at me.

I frowned, and my wife looked at me in earnest. "What has made your handsome face go all cloudy, My Love?" she asked in her lilting voice.

Slowly, so slowly as if testing each syllable for the truth it contained, I said, "Every engineer struggles to bridge the gulf between what he sees in his mind's eyes and what his hands have actually wrought. This vessel before us is no different, Lavinia. She falls far short of what was in my mind's eye when I first envisioned her."

I felt a tap on my shoulder and turned to see my best friend, Captain Harrison Randolph Barrington, standing in his finest dress uniform smiling at me. "Lavinia is right, Jon, she is as fine a ship as was ever built. You ought to be very proud of her."

I inclined my head, but said nothing, being too modest to say anything in reply to such a compliment from my dear friend. Harrison and I, and Lavinia, too, had been close friends since childhood. And Harrison had been the Best Man at my wedding. He pressed his point. "You say she is not exactly what you envisioned, but she will be better than anything afloat. What then have you to berate yourself about?"

I looked at Harrison then. He was tall, even taller than me (and I am six feet), with wavy dark hair and green eyes, a gentleman by breeding and temperament. "That is an over simplification," I replied. "This ship, as advanced as she is, has many inherent flaws in her design. For one thing, she requires vast amounts of coal to move her bulk, and the energy conversion from coal is hugely inefficient. She can never be very far from an ample supply of fuel to feed her ever hungry engines. Also, she is limited to movement in two dimensions. She can neither rise above the level of the seas nor willfully sink beneath them. To protect her vulnerable engines from enemy projectiles I had to place them below the waterline. One day, ships will not run on coal and wind. They will travel over the seas at fifty knots or greater and will submerge beneath the waves—only rising to attack a foe, or they will rise high above the waves to launch their attacks from great heights." I gestured toward the warship. "This is nowhere near what is possible."

"A ship that flies or sails underwater?" Lavinia asked with a ripple of laughter. She looked from me to Harrison. "I fear my husband is having a jest at our expense."

Harrison wasn't laughing, though. His green eyes were locked on my face, hawk-like. "If not coal and wind power, then what motive power would you advocate using?"

"Electricity," I replied lightly. "Only the dynamic power of electric motors can enable a vessel to do the things I just now enumerated. With a properly designed electric motor, one could drive a screw type propeller that would turn at thousands of revolutions per minute and pump life sustaining oxygen into tanks to maintain the crew, as well as fill and empty ballast tanks at will that would allow a vessel to sink and rise as need be."

"Have you designed such a vessel, Jonathan?" Harrison asked evenly, staring at me. His eyes were sharp as two shards of green glass. This was the turning point in my life, but I had not the hard-won wisdom to understand the significance of this moment or of that look. Alas, I stumbled into my demise.

I gave him an easy smile then and tapped the side of my head with my forefinger. "Only in here, but I doubt not the soundness of my design."

Harrison looked away briefly then his gaze returned to my face. "You must put your design to paper and submit it to the Admiralty—through me of course, so that I can see that it gets the proper attention."

I shook my head. "That design shall never see the light of day, my friend. The country that possesses such a vessel, an undersea ship, would be too tempted to use it for evil intent, gaining un-heard of and unjust advantage over the peoples of other nations. No, just because a thing can be done by engineers and men of science is no reason to do it if it results in harm to mankind."

Harrison's hawk-like eyes scanned my face. "So you will not provide **Her Majesty's** navy with this design you just spoke of?"

"No, no I will not," I replied baldly. "I have provided Her Majesty's navy with a formidable ship capable of out-manuever-ing, out-gunning, and out-performing anything else on the seas – enough to make any nation that would go to war with us an unthinkable risk. That is enough. Her navy does not need, nor does any man or nation need, the power to subjugate another. No. This will be a design that I keep to myself unless the time in the world be right for it." Overhead an ominous dark sky bil-lowed and a chill wind blew in from the Thames. Out on the river the pennants of the yachts and warships that had arrived to witness the launch of the great ironclad were snapping angrily in the breeze. A chill ran down my spine, but I attributed it to the cold winter day.

Harrison nodded toward the great iron warship's armored gun ports, tersely changing the subject. "It was wise to use the new Armstrong breech-loading guns. Her rate of fire will be superior to anything afloat, especially that of France's Gloire."

I gestured toward my creation resting in its stocks. "As this ship was to be provided with iron armor plating, multiple gun decks were out of the question. My design called for a broadside of seventeen guns with fifteen feet between gun ports, with the bow and stern added on, I ended up with a vessel of three hun-dred and eighty feet."

Harrison nodded. "A hundred feet bigger than anything ever launched."

"Quite so," I replied matter-of-factly, "but her hull's design with sail laid on and her trunk steam engine will render her faster than even the swiftest clipper ship."

Lavinia looked at me, her eyes gleaming with pride. "Please forgive my ignorance, but I can scarcely credit how such a conglomeration of iron can float."

I gave the easy laugh of a boy finding his first painted egg on an Easter egg hunt. "It's really quite simple, my dear. If one takes a tin pie pan and places it in a sink full of water it will float, will it not?" Lavinia nodded, conceding the point, and I went on. "If one attempts to push down on the pie pan, especially in the center of it, the pie pan will push back. It doesn't want to sink. That is what we marine engineers call buoyant force. It has to do with the volume of the hull and the volume of the water it displaces."

"Very same in principle to hot air balloons," Harrison interjected.

I turned to him in surprise. Although he is a military man he is highly intelligent and very well read. "Well done, Harrison," I replied with a smile. He was my best and oldest friend. How many hours had we passed over the years, boon companions? He was the brother I had lost. Our likes and dislikes were so identical—we often finished each other's sentences because our minds were of similar casts—that we were more like twin siblings than mere friends. How could I know that this scion of one of England's leading families harbored a deep envy of everything that brought me joy? He came from wealth, I came from the middling class; he was a rising star in the Admiralty and was recently promoted to a high position in that organization's intelligence department with nearly unlimited power and prestige, all I had were my nautical designs. But even so, there was more than a little prestige to be apprehended thus, and I was content.

(Lacuna begins)
Note 1: Text here was hopelessly smeared and pages 9 through 16 stuck together.
Note 2: When Nemo's diary was found it was first assumed that it had escaped water damage. Sadly, this was not the case. Some of the pages are stuck together, and in others the ink has smeared badly in sections rendering it nearly impossible to make out the text. We subjected the manuscript to analysis using a Proton Induced X-ray Emission device, which spared the manuscript itself any physical trauma. We discovered that the first third of the diary is written using a common dip pen ink comprised of ferrous sulfate, gall, gum and water. Nemo, cut off from all contact with civilization, then used an ink that our analysis re-

vealed to be comprised of
melanin, and the amino acids ty-
rosinase, dopamine, et al. This
ink is produced as a self-defense
mechanism by several species of
cephalopods who release the ink
to ward off predators.
I should list the salient features of the diary itself: It is
in octavo format, and the pages
are high quality Whatman Wove
paper. The cover is made of
sharkskin dyed black with a gilt
triple ruled gilt border, and a
large embossed N in the center.
Nemo writes in the Spencerian
handwriting style then common
among the educated class with his
uppercase letters sweeping and
ornate, and his lowercase letters
oddly modern looking. His letters
are well-formed and the words and
sentences evenly spaced.
Inside the rear cover is a pocket
that was found to contain hand-
ruled engineering drawings of the
Nautilus. We can now identify the
enigmatic captain Nemo with cer-
tainty as Jonathan de Chevalier
Mason, a highly regarded British

naval architect responsible for
the design of British ironclads
HMS Warrior and HMS Black Prince.
He rose from relative obscurity
to England's leading designer of
cutting-edge warships then suddenly fell out of favor and dis-
appeared from the historical
record until now.

James Ramillies Dunham, PhD
Archaeologist
(Lacuna ends. Text follows)

What happened next could have been predicted by any fool
except the fool who was presiding over the launch of the HMS
Warrior. After Sir John Pakingham, First Naval Lord, had delivered his florid speech and smashed a bottle of good Madeira
against the iron bow, the blocks had been knocked out. The great
warship had begun her ponderous descent down the slipways
when she suddenly came to a grinding halt. I stood there willing
her to move. 'Move goddamn your eyes…get your black iron ass
down into the water where you belong!' But the HMS Warrior
defied my mental urgings.

There was an awkward moment.

An eerie hush had descended over the assembled crowd of
spectators.

The warship hung there, suspended between terra and mare.
The martial strains of the band music tailed off into a desolate

silence and a cold wind blew in from the Thames. I was calm on the outside but my heart was knocking against my Adams apple. I stole a glance at the Lords Commissioners of the Admiralty—a pack of war-mongering sons of bitches as ever I set eyes on. Much head wagging and nodding was going on.

Sir John, decidedly not immune to the court of public opinion, turned to me in irritation. "Confound it, man! Your ship is stuck in the slipway!" he said. I had observed over the months that the First Naval Lord had a pronounced knack for stating the obvious. His face had set like stone. "Some might think this ill-omened," he opined.

My expression did not alter by a flicker. "Only the very ignorant would entertain such a thought, Sir John," I replied more than a little accusatorily.

He fixed his basilisk gaze on me. "Are you calling me ignorant, Mason?"

"No, I am not. I am referring to the unschooled sailors and workers." I went on smoothly in the confident tone of a young man who knows his job. "I am not at all surprised this has happened. Fate has not turned her face against us. Nor are we the victims of silly superstition. We have simply and plainly run afoul of the weather."

Sir John sniffed. "So you say, young Mason. So you say."

Lavinia looked up at me. "What has happened, Jonathan? Why hasn't the ship gone into the water?" she asked in an urgent undertone. She had drawn closer to me in that universal protective gesture of devoted wives the world over.

I smiled at her suddenly concerned face. "The cold has caused the hull to be stuck on the slipway. It is nothing that can't be easily remedied." It was the coldest winter in fifty years. A thick blanket of snow covered the wharf, the shipyard's offices, foundries, and workshops. The Thames and Bowcreek rivers were hidden in places by a silvery white rime of ice. I had taken the precaution of placing braziers along the slipway to ensure the grease did not freeze. Tugboats waited offshore and hydraulic rams were standing nearby in case my ship (Yes, I thought of her as 'my ship') failed to slide down the ways. It sometimes happened that a ship would not smoothly slide down the slipways. History was full of examples of this. On the other side of the Atlantic the Americans' famous frigate USS Constitution had become stuck in her slipway. Of course, most of the time, this had to do with poor planning and an imperfect understanding of geometry. I was certain that my calculations were correct. I had tested them on a model.

I summoned a vice admiral, and quietly gave orders to him. He in turn spoke to an aide who spoke to an aide who spoke to a subaltern who gave orders to a captain who in turn spoke to the yardmaster. Within minutes, blunt bowed steam tugs came chugging toward the warship belching clouds of sooty black smoke from their stubby red funnels. Hawsers were thrown to the warship and made fast to her stern bitts. Then while the band played, the tugs backed away from the warship until the hawsers were tight as overdrawn bowstrings. On my instructions, a couple hundred sailors and dockyard workers ran back and forth on her spar deck to rock the ship.

"Now watch," I said to my wife.

Harrison, standing at my elbow, was staring at the HMS Warrior. He leaned toward me and whispered so that Sir John couldn't hear and said, "This will be a black eye for you if she fails to launch." I think that somewhere in the back of my mind at the time, I thought I detected an ominously dark undertone of what our Teutonic brethren call *schadenfruede*, a secret pleasure at my misfortune.

I dismissed it as an unworthy thought.

Harrison was my friend.

"Never fear. She'll launch," I said confidently. "I daresay that unless the grease on the slipway has turned to some type of super glue, the tugs will get her going."

"You are so calm," Lavinia said wonderingly.

"I have science on my side," I replied.

And as it turned out I was not wrong. So slowly at first it was imperceptible, she began to inch backward then gathering momentum she slid into the Thames with a great splash that nearly swamped several of the tugboats. A great cheer rose from thousands of throats. I drew a deep sigh of relief and thought that that night I would sleep in peace.

(Lacuna begins)
Note: Above, Mason is not referring to the modern adhesive Super
Glue but to any glue with superior adhesive qualities to anything then known. Again, a large
block of text has been hopelessly
destroyed through exposure to
moisture so we do not know what
passed between the launching of
the HMS Warrior and the celebratory dinner at the Douglas Hotel

in London.

(Lacuna ends. Text resumes)

Years later that celebratory dinner ball seems as if it were a pensive dream.

"Jonathan de Chevalier Mason and Mrs. Lavinia Mason," announced the doorman in a stentorian voice. The entire room rose from their seats at their tables and clapped as we entered the glittering dining room. Lavinia and I looked at each other for a brief magical moment, then Harrison came up, and the spell was broken.

My friend was all smiles. "I have it on good authority that you are to be knighted." What a far cry from being told that Warrior's interrupted launch would constitute a black eye on my spotless career to hearing that I was a shoe-in for a title.

I summoned my smoothest smile. "Indeed?"

Harrison, oblivious to my utter disinterest, nodded toward the prime minister sitting at the table at the head of the dining room. "I heard it from the old boy myself."

The dinner was elegant and fine in all respects. Our table was graced with several famous personages: Among others there was Sir John and his bosomy wife, an American naval officer named Captain Mathew Maury, and the celebrated author Charles Dickens.

The writer was holding forth. "A black vicious ugly customer as ever I saw, whale like in size and with as terrible a row of incisor teeth as ever chomped down on a French frigate," he said.

A Frenchman, his name escapes me, sitting beside Mr. Dickens took a sip from his glass of wine. "As our countries are at peace, it is my fervent hope that that boast may never be put to the test. Enough blood was spilled in the last war between our countries."

A cloud of 'here here' rose from the table. Not the least from your humble scribe who even then abhorred war and tyranny in all its forms.

Lavinia turned to Mr. Dickens. "I just finished Bleak House, Sir. I felt so sorry for poor Mr. Nemo. Dying alone of opium poisoning and in poverty must have been horrid."

Dickens nodded, conceding the point. "The main thrust of the story, if you please, is the sad state of our judiciary system and the need for meaningful reform. I drew upon my own experience as a Chancery litigant seeking to enforce the copyright of my work."

The American, a southerner from his accent said, "It is almost magical that your warship contains an apparatus that can convert ordinary seawater to potable water for the sustenance of her officers and crew. It's a strange alchemy almost like lead to gold."

I twisted the slender stem of my wineglass and looked at the garnet hued liquid in the bowl. "Any new technology if sufficiently advanced will appear as magic," I replied.

He nodded, conceding the point. The conversation at the table swirled around me while I sipped my wine and said nothing. I was never one for social affairs.

Harrison whispered in my ear. "About that under sea ship of yours...."

I smiled, sweet as sugar. "That will never happen, my friend."

"I am sorry if I sound impolite," he said evenly. "But I cannot let pass any new technology that will give Her Majesty's navy an advantage over its adversaries."

"Have you forgotten that we are currently in a state of peace on all sides?" I reminded him.

Harrison nodded toward Captain Maury. "That may not be for long. Our American cousins are on the verge of war with each other. Lord Palmerston intends to declare support for the southern states should they succeed from the Union."

I shrugged. "What has that to do with me?"

"You are Her Majesty's chief naval architect."

"What of it?" I looked at him then. "By the by, I always understood Lord Palmerston to be an opponent of the slave trade."

"Don't be so naïve Jonathan. Surely you know that our mills rely heavily on cotton from America's southern states. Moreover, Lord Palmerston harbors a deep animosity toward the United States. He refers to them as upstart crows. In his view, British power would be enhanced by a dissolution of the Union of the United States, and a southern confederacy would be a ready and willing market for British goods."

I drained my wine glass to its dregs then held it up. An African servant in white wig glided forward and refilled it, then I turned to my friend. "For my part, I hope the new American president when he is inaugurated is able to preserve that noble Union. I also hope that if there is a contest between the North and South that the north prevails and that the human beings held in thrall by the south are given their freedom."

The American spoke up. "I personally abhor the practice of slavery but I believe the problem must be solved by the states themselves and not by the federal government. Many of us believe that Mr. Lincoln plans to interfere in our personal affairs."

"It is wrong for one human being to oppress another," I said forthrightly.

"On that we agree, Sir," Captain Maury replied, in a drawl that betrayed his Virginian birth.

"I am an admirer of your oceanographic studies," I said with a smile and a deep unwillingness to ruin the occasion—hence I had passed on to a safe subject. What man of science is ever unwilling to hold forth about his work?

"Thank you, Mr. Mason," the American drawled. "Your ship would make the prefect research vessel. Instead of guns though, I would fill her with scientific devices and scientists."

"Sadly, that is not likely to happen," I said.

"What do you do, Captain Maury?" Lavinia asked.

"I am the superintendent of my country's Naval Observatory," he replied, "in charge of the chronometers, charts, and other navigational equipment."

"Captain Maury is being overly modest," I said, smiling at him over the rim of my wineglass. "His work on ocean currents has all but proven the existence of a northwest passage across the polar circle to the pacific—that there is an area near the North Pole that is occasionally free of ice."

Lavinia smiled at the American. "Really? How so?"

Captain Maury leaned back in his chair. "A whale is a mammal and it must have air to breathe. Logs of old whaling vessels often listed the very individualistic markings of their harpoons. In my research I discovered that Harpoons found in captured whales in the Atlantic had been shot by whalers in the Pacific and visa versa so I deduced the whales must migrate from one sea to another at the top of the globe."

"I own a copy of your *Wind and Current Chart of the North Atlantic*, and *Sailing Directions and Physical Geography of the seas and Its Meteorology*, is in a drawer of my bed stand. It is a masterful work, Captain Maury. Right up there with the works of the French naturalist Pierre Arronax."

"Another commonality of great minds!" Captain Maury said, "We are both admirers of Monsieur Pierre Arronax! Let us raise our glasses to the sea."

"To the sea, our mother, giver of life to our planet," I said before draining my wineglass.

Harrison murmured tightly. "We need that undersea boat, Jonathan."

I set down my glass and turned to him and said, matching him tone for tone. "Never while the sun shines will I turn over the design to such a hellish weapon to any government. Men are not ready for such technology. It would be as if some scientist were to devise a bomb that could obliterate an entire city. Men would not hesitate to use it. I will not be a party to such evil. Do not speak to me of this again."

And that should have been the end of it.

But it wasn't.

CHAPTER 2

The Star Chamber

That night, in the privacy of our room, we discussed the successful launch of my proud vessel, the men and their wives who had been at the fete in its honor, and the continued absence of a beautiful woman at Harrison's side.

"But Darling, you must have an idea as to why Harrison is still a bachelor. He is, after all your best friend." As Lavinia asked me this question that I believed to be innocent at the time, little did I guess the sinister truth behind it. She was struggling with the buttons at the back of her dress and was ready to call for her maid servant to help her, but was still waiting for my answer, ready for any juicy gossip, as I thought, to share with her friends.

I had been gazing at her all night during the dinner party

barely able to contain my wild urges and behave in a socially acceptable way. Now with her alone with me in our room, I was not so constrained and could no longer bear the sight of her clothes upon her body. I longed to see her naked form instead of the luscious suggestion of the curves of her breasts above her bodice. I needed to possess her. My passion and love for her overwhelmed me, but I held myself firmly in check and made my voice firm, although suggestive, as I said, "Darling, I do not know why Harrison remains unwed, and right now I am not all that interested in the matter. But let me help you with your struggle. Surely there are more interesting things we might discuss?" I said walking toward her, removing my cravat and unbuttoning my shirt. As I gazed at her reflection in the mirror I saw the color mounting to her face followed by a slow and inviting smile.

Lavinia dipped her eyes demurely. "It is always my preference to be aided by my Liege whenever it is possible," she told me in the sultry voice reserved only for our bedchamber.

I kissed a hot line of rising passion down her back as I set each clasp free, one at a time, starting at her neck. As I got to the mid of her back, she rose from her chair to make by job easier, not caring when she kicked it to the side out of her way, bending demurely in front of me, her forearms on her dressing table, as if to aide my attempts at her undress. I could see her breath coming faster as she bit her lower lip, tracking the progress of my hands, my lips, and my tongue down her back. I was roused almost to pain when she thrust her hips into me, moving her buttocks against my swollen need for her. I could barely keep from tearing the last clasps free to remove her beautiful form from its constraining garments, but then she stood in front of me in all her glory. I reached in front of her and held both her breasts in my hands as she stood looking at me passionately, also full of need and love, in the mirror. She turned around and I could watch the fullness of her buttocks in the mirror and caress them as she worked to unleash me from my trousers, her breath coming in short gasps as we kissed with increasing desire. Free from its painful constraints at last, she took my tortured manhood brazenly in her grasp and moaned as I kissed her full lips. I picked her up in my arms and took her to our bed, taking just a moment to admire the exquisite beauty of her womanly form before I descended upon her willing body. She arched toward me as I entered her, giving a small gasp of pleasure, as she often did, when I filled her with my length. We moved together rhythmically, in a pleasure and confidence that only long time passionate lovers can attain. I watched her face, full of desire and the most exquisite pleasure as she climaxed over and over. When I could take the torture no longer, I turned her onto her stomach, and she arched her hips into the air to make herself more accessible to me. We came together in an ecstasy of release then lay together on our sides, my manhood still inside her, as we fell asleep.

The next morning, over breakfast with our two wonderful children, I reflected on what a lucky man I was, how completely content and how beautiful my world. How there was truly nothing that I might desire outside what I already had.

"Father, what is a nigger?" my eldest daughter Elspeth asked suddenly.

My wife and I exchanged glances from either end of the table then I set down my half buttered toast and looked at my daughter. "Where did you hear that word?"

"I heard it from our teacher, Mr. Cummings. He says that the Americans will soon start fighting each other and that it is all the fault of the niggers," she said.

I said gently but firmly, "That is an ugly, ugly word that is applied to people of African decent by the uneducated and the misguided. Do not ever let me catch you using words like that again."

Elspeth looked down at her plate then looked up at me and my heart skipped a beat because her features were so like my dear Lavinia. "Forgive me father," she said quietly.

Lavinia spoke up then. "The papers are certainly saying that there is to be a war between the states." Throughout all this our youngest daughter Prudence had been eating her breakfast in silence, her big hazel eyes watchful.

"Will there be a war, Papa?" Prudence asked.

"I certainly hope not," I said emphatically, "and if there is, may The Lord in His infinite mercy make it a short one, and keep Great Britain out of it. Enough English blood has been shed because of the folly of overfed rich men of power whose false pride has led to the irrigation of European soil with the blood of countless young men who rallied to the colors. And what a bitter harvest we have reaped: My dear brother dead from a ball shot by a marine perched in the top gallant of a Russian frigate—Good Lord, on any other occasion they might have shared a flagon of wine; my father killed in battle with an American frigate." All the desperate feelings of despair and loneliness that were my sad birthright as a child rose within my aching breast then. I stared down at my plate with its scrambled eggs and bacon and hungered no more.

"Have a word with the Headmaster," I said to my wife. "Whatever Mr. Cumming's sympathies are, I do not want him uttering such words in the presence of our daughters."

"I agree completely. Whatever was that fool thinking?" Lavinia said, sipping her tea.

In the carriage I leaned forward to look out the window and wave farewell to my wife and children, not then knowing that it was for the last time, then pulled the cord for the coachman. "Drive on," I ordered, and we whirled down the long driveway with the coach's wheels clattering on the cobblestones then down the road that led to the city.

I settled back on my seat for the ride to work. Outside the glass window the countryside whirled by, bare limbed trees, houses of the wealthy set well back from the road. Clip clop clip clop. I loathed slowness. One day soon the inefficient horse would be replaced with an engine that would drive a carriage's wheel, I thought. Not electric but perhaps a smaller version of the steam engines that propelled locomotives along iron tracks from town to town. The horse would be a thing of the past like chariots and men in armor. Clip clop clip clop. Outside the carriage window the sky was gray and lowering. I drifted away into a fantasy world where machines eased men's lives, and cities were no longer places of filth and want and disease but clean—with air free of coal smoke and wide boulevards of smooth pavement free of garbage where men dwelled in harmony with one another. My work with the Admiralty over the years had sown the seeds of an inner conflict in my breast. Did I not engineer the vile tools of war used by men to slay and maim other men? I sighed heavily. Why couldn't I be like other men, untroubled by such dark ruminations? Perhaps it was the loss of my father and brother, seeing close at hand the anguish on my poor late mother's face. I confess that even as a child I was unlike other boys. I cared not for competitive games—I much preferred building very detailed models of sailing ships, and spending hours reading books. As I constructed my ship models, I at first strove to make them as true to life as possible and then I began to look for ways that a particular ship could be improved. Moving a mast back a bit, narrowing a hull here and eliminating a deck there. That was the genesis of my passion for naval design. It began to rain. Then we were slowing down. I poked my head out the window. A tree lay across the road and a band of black-clad men stood in the road with drawn pistols.

```
(Lacuna Begins)
Note: The text here is very
fragmentary due to much water
damage.
(Lacuna ends)
```

The room was as barren as a poor country parson's rectory. Indeed, more so, as there were but two small chairs and a plain table. Only one candle lit the room. The only natural light, cold and watery, came from a slit of a window set high on the wall. The door opened and my eyes went to it at once. Harrison came in and I felt an immediate rush of relief. "Thank God, Harrison. I am so glad to see you." He took a seat on the other side of the table and fixed his gaze on me, saying nothing for interminable moments.

I stared back at my best friend, silent and pensive, my mind racing. Questions, insecurities, and suspicions were replacing the intimate trust I had always felt for my friend, but the realization had come too late. His face was hard to read. He leaned forward and crossed his arms on the table. "Do you know why we are here, Jonathan?" he asked in a cold voice.

Although I was beginning to suspect, I said, "Of course I do not, Harrison. What is going on here? Why have I, a loyal subject, been treated so unjustly?"

His eyes bore into mine. "You have something Her Majesty's navy could use to great effect, and you are not being forthcoming with it."

"You are serious in this matter?" I said in tones of wonder. I could scarcely credit that a careless comment could be the instigation of Harrison's misguided behavior.

He leaned forward, one jabbing finger lending weight to every word. "I want the plans to that undersea boat."

"The stars will fall from heaven before I'll give them to you or any man," I said with a tremor of rage in my voice.

Harrison straightened then and looked down at me. "You always were a stubborn customer, Jonathan. Let's see if I can't change your mind."

He left me still. He left me silent and cold with a nameless dread. Long minutes passed in utter silence except for the steady ticking of a clock somewhere in the corridor. The door opened again and black clad brutes rushed in and roughly hauled me to my feet and tightly twisted my arms behind my back and bound my wrists with iron handcuffs. I scarcely recall what happened after the first blow came, followed by another and another—by kicks and gauges, my cries of pain ringing in my ears. Then I passed out.

The door opened and I lifted my bruised head. Lavinia came into the room with her flaming locks tied high and concealed by a bonnet, her hazel eyes downcast, with misery written on her features and hanging on her like a garment. I struggled to pick myself up from my dejected position on the floor so my beloved would not see me so compromised, but I could scarcely move for the pain in my limbs.

She kept her eyes averted from my piteous form, I thought at the time to spare my manly pride as I struggled to join her at the table where she now sat silently. "Jonathan, Darling," she pleaded with me, "why won't you give them what they want and end this infamous treatment of you and our family?" Her voice was full of pain and desolation, but behind that I heard doubt and, I thought, a twinge of anger.

I was a little startled by her tone, and was still trying to understand her position and gather my words when her eyes glistened as she drew them up from staring into her hands clasped tightly on her lap to look into my battered and bruised face. "Won't you give Barrington the plans to the undersea boat?"

I looked up with one eye swollen shut, my face a pulpy quivering mass of pain. "You understand little of these things, My Love. Such an invention would unleash untold terrors onto the world from which I fear we may never be able to return. I am not willing to be the man responsible for such a calamity. Surely you, my wife, understand and support me?"

"But I do not understand!" she stood up suddenly, raising her voice to me for the first time in her life, shocking me into silence. "You are bringing disgrace upon us! Do you know what will become of me and our daughters should you continue to follow this course? Surely that must measure in your thoughts somewhere," she said, accusing me with her stance, her words, and her look.

"But Darling, you must understand…"

I did not get a chance to finish for the door opened again and Barrington came in. He stood behind Lavinia, looking at me over her shoulder. To my shock and dismay, Lavinia turned away from me to face my once best friend and began to sob into his shoulder as his arms wrapped gently around her waist, a fiendish smile on his lips as he looked down at me and soothed my troubled wife.

I surged from my chair. "Lavinia, you can not believe what this man says. You can not allow him to poison your thoughts of me!" I was begging her, but she did not turn toward me. As she heard my voice and began to show weakness and may have softened and turned toward me, Barrington moved between the two of us, folded his strong arm around her fragile form, his hand resting on her waist, and lead her from the room.

"Do not be so troubled, my dear," I heard him saying to her as he lead her away. I could hear no more for I was calling, screaming for her, but she did not come back.

```
(Lacuna begins)
Note: Text destroyed by moisture
here.
(Lacuna ends)
```

"This is madness," I stammered to the hooded figures sitting high up behind the long desk. Where was the jury, my lawyer, my rights—the right of the accused to face his accuser? This sham court was no place of justice. I confess that I was overwhelmed by the rapidity and harshness of the day's events. "I am a loyal subject of Her Majesty. No dishonorable words or deeds can be appended to my name," I cried.

A man in a crimson robe and the white powdered wig of a barrister stepped from the shadows. He pointed at me like a prosecutor in a law court, but this was no law court that I had ever heard of. "Jonathan de Chevalier Mason, being a person owing allegiance to Our Majesty the Queen, did traitorously withhold from Her Majesty the concept and design of an underwater engine of war. Jonathan de Chevalier Mason, being a person owing allegiance to Her Majesty, adhered to the queen's enemies by withholding said naval vessel, an undersea boat of superior qualities and capabilities to all other vessels of war deployed by her Majesty's foes, and potential foes for his own selfish reasons. Jonathan de Chevalier Mason, being a person owing allegiance to Her Majesty the Queen, did turn deaf ears to the reasonable entreaties of the First Naval Lord of our Majesty the Queen to the prejudice of Great Britain and Her Majesty's navy."

I stared at this bewigged jackanape with my mouth hanging open in utter shock, and my eyes goggling. Surely, this could not be happening in my lifetime, a modern time far removed from the barbarities of the middle ages.

I shook off the hands holding my arms and surged from my chair. "By what right do you dare to try me, a loyal subject of Her Majesty's realm?" I cried.

High up on the dais behind the tribunal the three hooded figures, their countenances well-hidden by the shadows of their deep hoods turned to one another, nodding, then turned toward me. A voice, deep and rumbling like the sea on a beach during a winter storm, said, "Jonathan de Chevalier Mason, as you have just heard, you stand accused of High Treason against Her Majesty, thus consigning you to the ranks of traitors and knaves."

There was a long heavy pause during which I stood grasping the edge of the table, my eyes goggling and mouth agape in shock. One of the hooded figures broke the heavy silence with words so heavy and unbelievable that each syllable sounded with the finality of a death knell.

"How do you plead to these charges, Jonathan de Chevalier Mason?" His stentorian voice echoed in the wood paneled chamber that I noted was shaped like a star.

"Not guilty, of course," I replied, my mind in a whirl, going round and round.

```
(Lacuna begins)
Note: The text here was hope-
lessly smudged and rendered unin-
telligible by exposure to
moisture.
(Lacuna ends)
```

I woke the next day and I wished I had not, for the nightmare had bled into morning. I was in the crowded hold of a ship chained to the deck with heavy iron manacles bound for I knew not where. The night before, after the sham trial in what I later learned was the Star Chamber, a secret tribunal for hearing cases against noblemen and government officials and ministers accused of a crime, I was driven in a Black Maria, a carriage with iron bars on the windows, to a dock on the Thames where a paddlewheel steamer waited off shore. I rode with men jammed on either side of me, chained together with leg irons, as we jounced along. Even with air coming in through the barred windows, the inside of the carriage was thick with the foul reek of unwashed bodies. I sat in silence, my mind numb and my heart aching. I was awash in disbelief and misery and still in denial at my fate, thinking that at any moment someone would come to rectify this horrible mistake. When we got to the dock the carriage doors were thrown open and the guards shouted villainously at us to exit the carriage, a difficult maneuver as we attempted to work around our tight leg irons.

I stumbled at the bottom of the carriage steps pulling two men in line behind me down to the ground. Nightsticks and curses rained down on us three poor souls as we lay on the ground. With difficulty we regained our feet and then we shuffled across the dock to slippery stone steps and descended them to a waiting cutter. Then I sat hollow eyed as we were rowed across the black water toward the vessel that would bear me away from all that I had known and loved. I wept piteously and silently.

CHAPTER 3

Belial Island

And then there was Colonel Merrick. The sun beat down from a sky of blue steel. We stood in the infernal heat, with tattered scraps of clothing hanging from our stick-thin limbs, hollowed eyes peering from thickly bearded faces wraith pale from eighty four days in the dark cramped cages in the ship's hold. As I write about this a sharp rush of fear and rage passes through my frame making it tremble like an autumn leaf in a gale. Even now, I can scarcely fathom that such a hellish place could exist on God's earth. And the worst of it, even after the crocodiles, pestilence, sharks and buggery by the guards, was Colonel Stanley Merrick, veteran of the Indian Rebellion of eighteen and fifty-seven, where he lost his arm at the battle of the Basmiri Gate in Delhi.

The colonel stood on an ammunition box on the parade ground in his starched dun-colored uniform, close cropped head, flinty eyes, and sandy mustache shaded by his pith helmet, reading the ship's convict manifest. His mustache twitched in that way to be seen in captive hares as they nibble at the castaway greens of a turnip as he perused the document, oblivious to our suffering while we stood on wobbly stick legs, bound to one another by heavy iron chains. I had never before been in such heat and after a voyage of seven weeks in the cramped fetid depths of the convict ship, day in and day out hearing the groans of the sick and the sharp rasping sobs of the terrified, my body was as weak as my spirit.

Such heat I had never before experienced. My tongue felt like a thick piece of tanned leather in my mouth. Everything swam before my eyes. I tried with all my might to maintain my dignity, but my weakened state and the harshness of the climate defeated me. I collapsed in a heap. In an instant, Gurkha and English soldiers pounced on me with their cudgels in full swing. Worse still, they beat the two men standing on either side of me. That, as I later learned, was Merrick's rule. It was a simple rule that every one on the island understood. During assembly, if a man fainted or broke ranks, the men on either side of him were also beaten half senseless.

So while we new arrivals waited in the withering sunlight, Colonel Merrick studied the list, mustache twitching, and the cudgels rose and fell. Someone hauled me to my feet and I stood swaying with the men on either side of me murmuring curses and threats in my ears that I only dimly heard through a swirling haze of pain and shame. I was becoming used to the piling up of injustices during my captivity after the sham trial in the Star

Chamber. This was merely the logical extrapolation of something that weeks before would have been unthinkable—now I knew better.

Colonel Merrick read on and on while we broiled in the unrelenting heat. Then, ever so slowly, and quite deliberately, he folded the paper and slid it into his breast pocket. He looked down at us and the disgust was plain in his eyes. "I see that there are some among you who may think you are special, gentlemen born and bred. Well let me tell you this and you better mark it well: There are no well-born gentlemen on Belial Island. You are all dirt. Less than dirt. At least dirt has its uses. Not so, you men."

A thousand questions occurred to me but of course I kept silent. Colonel Merrick went on in the crisp tones of a military man. "I direct your attention to the jungle to your left." All our heads turned to stare at the impenetrable green wall. Merrick went on, "It is a swamp filled with crocodiles and poisonous snakes and insects. There is quick sand and tempting looking fruit that if eaten will cause your face to turn blue black and your eyes and ears to bleed before you die screaming for your mother. Now, direct your attention to the right at the lagoon."

We dutifully did as he commanded.

Merrick said, almost reverently, "It is beautiful is it not? Who wouldn't want to go for a dip in such an inviting lagoon, so blue and refreshingly cool?" Then his sharp gaze flicked back to us. "But I would advise against trying to escape that way. It is filled day and night with sharks. Do not take my word for it. Bring the prisoner forth!" Two sentries came from a low stone blockhouse dragging a whimpering man toward the jetty beyond which, standing a few cables off, was the paddlewheel steamer that had conveyed us here. When they got onto the jetty the man began to wail piteously. He was so thin, a bag of bones in dirty white rags, that it was no trouble for the guards to simply pick him up and throw him from the end of the jetty into the water, which they did with the casualness of one disposing of the household refuse.

He landed with a small splash and we could all see his head, his sparse hair plastered down over his scared face. I blinked. He was suddenly gone. Then the water began to boil into white and red froth. We stared in mute horror.

(Lacuna begins)
Note: Several pages torn from diary.
(Lacuna ends)

Our days were filled with harvesting timber in the jungle. Chained to each other, a long file of us prisoners trudged in to the steaming jungles escorted by armed guards. Not to protect us, of course, but to beat those who slacked off and to shoot anyone foolish enough to attempt to escape. Someone nearly always died. Snakebite, scorpion sting, or from sheer exhaustion a person would just drop dead. Then the guards would remove his manacles and the corpse would be thrown into a nearby small river where piranhas would strip the flesh from the skeleton in the length of time it has taken me to pen this sentence.

I was part of a two man saw team. It was our job to cut one cubit meter of merbau wood every day. We worked in the broiling sun, tormented by the clouds of mosquitoes that swarmed around us turning every minute of the day into pure Hell. The men in my team changed nearly every day as someone was overtaken by sickness, felled by snakebite, or perhaps just to keep us from forming any type of camaraderie. One day I noticed that this unspoken rule was not applied to one particular string, as the chained files of men were called. It was headed by an old man with a long beard and bare pate that reminded me of sculptures of ancient Greek philosophers I had seen in museums. He and the men in his string never spoke. Perhaps the stranger was a priest. Yes, I thought at the time, as I plied my saw, he is a catholic priest. They have a certain air about them.

Several times as I worked my end of the band saw, I caught the old man looking at me quizzically, but he always looked away quickly. I pulled and pushed the saw, the palms of my hands covered with blisters and calluses. Thinking about the fine English spring weather back home, I wondered if Lavinia and my daughters missed me. I despaired of ever seeing them again. My eyes stung then, whether from bitter tears or perspiration, I could not say. I yearned for them desperately.

But it wasn't just my love for them that kept me alive. It was Harrison Randolph Barrington that had sent me here. It was my best friend who had coveted my family and my best friend who was now, I was sure, attempting to step into the shoes of my life. And it was hunger for revenge growing in my belly every day that kept me alive.

At night we were locked in cells in a long brick building that wrapped around two sides of a large yard with a flagpole in the center from which the Union Jack fluttered. Next to the flag pole was a brass cannon with a small pile of cannon balls. Across from us stood the colonel's white plantation house with its enclosed veranda and staff of Indian servants. One night, on the way back from the timber camp, a guard came up to the officer of the guards escorting us. There was a brief spate of talking and head nodding. I saw the officer point in my direction. The guard came up to me and stood watch while another unfastened my shackles. Was I to be freed? Had the infamous lies been rectified and my name cleared?

"What is happening?" I asked in a feeble voice.

"Colonel Merrick wants to see you." That and a shove in the direction of the colonel's fine white house was all the answer I got.

"Come in!" An orderly opened the door and nodded me in. Merrick sat behind his desk smoking a straight-stemmed pipe. I briefly wondered how he was able to pack and light it with only one arm. He glowered at me from under his terrifying brows for a long time. "Ordinarily, Mason, prisoners are not permitted to receive letters but as this was sent by Admiral Barrington with express orders to see that it reached you, I had no choice. Frankly, I do not see the point as you are never getting off this island alive." He shrugged then slid a letter across his desk toward me. I picked it up with twitching fingers and read it. The letter was not from Barrington but from my love, my wife, Lavinia.

"Dear Jonathan,
    In the months you have been ab-
sent from us, Admiral Harrison

Randolph Barrington has comforted
me in my time of sorrow, and he
has also been most attentive to
our daughters. We have grown
close and have fallen in love. I
thought it right and proper that
you should know that the court,
in light of your crimes against
our country, has granted me a
bill of divorce. Admiral Barrington and I are to be wed in
June. He has won the hearts of
Prudence and Elspeth and will
make a fine father. Please understand that I had no choice. You
are a convict with no prospects
for the future. I am lucky that
he is kind enough to overlook
your notoriety and I hope that
you are thankful that your friend
is willing to raise and love your
family when you can not. I have
to look out for the interests of
the girls whom you have left with
no prospects and nothing but
scandal to follow them throughout
their days. I beg of you to understand and to bless our happy
union.
Lavinia."

I stared at the letter as if it were my death warrant.

Colonel Merrick stared hard at me through a cloud of pipe smoke. "Actually, you are lucky Mason. I didn't hear that my wife had died until I returned from India," he said with a thin bitterness that hardened his face. "So not only did I not have an arm when I returned to England but I found that I had lost my wife to illness as well. I can tell you that it was quite a shock to my system. Count yourself fortunate that you know the true state of affairs back home."

I began to shake my head, over and over. I was in a bad dream and trying desperately to wake up to find myself lying nestled like soup spoons beside my Lavinia, smelling her rich womanly smells, hearing her precious little breaths, gazing lovingly at the line of her jaw and her mass of red hair. I took in the letter in my hand blindly, unwilling to believe what I had read. *No, no, no...*

"This cannot be happening!" I cried. "I am an innocent man. I do not deserve any of this! Why is this happening to me?" I surged to my feet and put my head back and howled like a mad man all the while tearing at my now long unkempt hair. The door to the office banged open and many prison guards rushed in. They seemed to fill the room. A rain of clubs descended on me, and I fell to the floor senseless.

I came to consciousness in my little barren cell and lay a long while rereading the letter in my mind and then I began to sob piteously, my entire frame quaking as if I had an ague. I heard a thin clink of metal against stone. I stopped crying and lay in my cot listening. Clink, clink, clink. I swung off the bed and crawled on hands and knees to the rough stone wall, my frame still shaking from the depth of my tears. I saw a small hole in the mortar used to join the rough hewn stones.

A thin French voice issued from it in a whisper. "You are the man I saw today?"

"I do not know, Sir," I answered truthfully.

"The Englishman, no?"

"Yes, I am English." I then divined that I was speaking with none other than the old man I had exchanged glances with earlier that day. "You are a priest?"

"That is so," he admitted in the hollow voice of a man who has seen too much.

"I am a marine engineer."

"Ah, an educated man."

My ear was still pressed to the small hole in the wall. There was a silence that lasted so long I began to wonder if my mysterious interlocutor was still there, when he said, "I am Father Jacque Blondeau."

"I used to be Jonathan Mason," I replied flatly.

A low laugh came from the way. "We meet under less than ideal circumstances, eh, young Mason?"

A bitter laugh escaped my dried lips. "There is no denying that, Father."

"You were weeping just now."

I must be honest here. Sitting there in the dark, my face damp and heart shattered, I poured my heart out to this total stranger. He listened without comment or question as I related the Job-like tale of my sorry end.

"Sometimes an end is really a new beginning," he said when I was done.

"Not for me," I replied with a voice laden with a great weight of bitterness. "It is my sad fate to die here."

"You are giving up then?"

"Yes."

More silence, then, "You were right to withhold such a fiendish engine of war from them. No country should have such a vessel at their disposal."

"It cost me everything."

"Except your convictions."

I recall that I moved my head from the wall and stared at the cell's small iron-bound door. My mind didn't drift off anywhere; no fine English landscapes meandered across the insides of my eyelids, no images of my dear Lavinia, her legs high and wide as I thrust into her with all my passion. Not a single thought entered my head as I sat there.

Father Jacques spoke again. "It is rare to meet a man who will sacrifice so much for his beliefs, especially in such a place as this."

"I do not know what to say," I replied hesitantly.

"Some things require no comment."

Then we were silent. After awhile, I asked, "How long have you been here?"

"I was a young priest on Elba and aide to Bishop Daubusin who ministered to Bonaparte during his captivity. One day the Bishop, God bless his soul, summoned me and sent me to the emperor's estate. He handed me a note and asked me to take it to Monsieur Montserrat who was in charge of his finances." Father Blondeau fell silent.

"Did you meet Napoleon himself?" I asked

"Oh yes," Father Blondeau replied softly. "I was with him

when he left Elba, I almost ended up with him in Helena. For awhile I wished I had; things might have turned out differently for both of us. But I have made peace with how things turned out."

"How could you have?"

"Through faith in Our Lord. Have you no faith?"

"I believe in neither man nor god," I replied in a much harder voice than I intended.

"It is too early for you to give up on God and mankind," Father Blondeau replied. We spoke for many hours until the light coming from the small window near the high ceiling turned pearly gray. It was nearly time for us to be released from our cells for breakfast and the daily trek to the work camp in the jungle.

One night I heard a strange sound like stone grinding against stone. Suddenly a pale gray square appeared in the cell's stone wall. I sat up in my cot and stared in wonder.

A bony arm beckoned to me. "Does monsieur care to visit me in my chateau?"

I slid from my cot and crawled through the opening with the bitter thought that before arriving at the penal colony, I would have been too large to pass through.

The old priest greeted me warmly. I looked around Father Blondeau's cell. By the standards I was now accustomed to, it was furnished opulently with several piles of books standing against a wall; there was a low stool, and even a candle jutting from a bottle on the floor beside his low cot. My host bade me to sit on the stool, and he sat on the edge of his bed. A small framed picture of Bonaparte hung on one wall behind him.

Beside the books were several shells arranged from largest to smallest. I picked up a Chambered Nautilus, a large cephalopod whose bony body structure was extruded as a shell. Internally the shell was divided into several chambers. As the creature matured it created newer larger sections arranged in a logarithmic whirl. It was thought that with such a strong shell the mollusk could dive to one thousand meters. As an engineer I could see how this could be, and I further noted that the Nautilus had the further advantage of being able to withdraw into its shell for protection from predators. The creature was able to adjust its buoyancy by admitting water into special sacs. I had kept an especially fine specimen of the creature's shell on my desk at home. I put the shell back with the others and smiled at the elderly priest. "All the comforts of home…"

Father Blondeau said, "When I first came here, there was a different man in charge of the penal colony and he permitted me a few small comforts."

"May I look at your books?" I asked.

"But of course." He lit the taper and set it on the ground near the books. I was thrilled to see that among the many titles was Homer's Odyssey, which I had often carried around and enjoyed reading in the original Greek. I picked up the volume and opened it with reverential fingers, as I had thought I would never see a real book again.

"Ah, you read Koine Greek." Father Blondeau said. It was not a question.

"And Latin," I replied in French.

Blondeau chuckled. "Your French is very good, Monsieur." He nodded toward the volume in my hand. "You may have it." It turned out that Father Blondeau was a man of many interests including a well-developed appreciation for the natural sciences. For hours we engaged in learned discourse about the ocean and the mysteries it contained. He opined that an undersea passage existed between the Mediterranean and the Red Sea, as he had noticed that the same type of fish were to be found in both bodies of water. He mentioned that he had read a young professor's book on the natural wonders of the sea, a man named Arronax. He could not remember the scientist's Christian name.

"Monsieur Pierre Arronax is now a famous scientist and has penned many books about the world's oceans and seas," I replied, warming to the subject. "Of course, there are better ways to study the sea than a diving suit or dredging the bottom."

"Direct observation," Father Blondeau replied smiling.

We were talking one night, in low whispers so as not to draw the attention of the guards on patrol. "If you could do anything with your life, Monsieur Mason, what would you do?" The question was posed mildly, but the priest's gaze on my face was shrewd.

I looked down at the floor. "I would build my undersea ship and never step foot on solid land ever again."

"That is not all you would do though, is it?" he pressed.

I looked away to avoid the piercing stare fixed on my face. "I would find the man who robbed me of my life and make him pay for his crimes with his life."

"I can't say that I blame you."

I looked at the priest in surprise. He gave a careless shrug. "Vengeance is not always the Lord's sole prerogative. We here on earth must take into account the simple fact that we dwell closer to Hell than Heaven."

It was then that Father Jacque Blondeau gave my life back to me. He had been modest when he had at first told me that he was a courier between the late French emperor and the man who controlled his finances. Just before the battle of Waterloo, the young priest had been entrusted by the emperor with the task of taking the bulk of his vast treasure, loading it onto a ship in great secrecy and bearing it away to a place of safety.

"It is how I ended up here. They wanted to know where I had hidden it. I was flogged countless times, hung by my thumbs day after day, but I did not tell them. Finally, me and the young acolytes of my order, some boys not yet in their teens, were sent here. After a few years the English forgot about me. So you see Monsieur, I possess the means to make your dreams become reality."

I shook my head partly in warning and partly in disbelief. "My dreams are dark."

"I know about your dreams."

"Even if I had the treasure, I could not build the ship without help, and what men would want to consign themselves to a monastic life under the sea?"

Father Blondeau nodded. "My flock and I would be your helpers and your crew. Some of them have been with me since they were children, and others that have come here over the years have joined my order of Saint Mary that I have informally set up. We have vowed before Our Lord to stay together for all time in captivity or as free men."

I blinked several times. "You are serious then?"

"As a loaded pistol." His eyes went to the picture of Napoleon Bonaparte on the wall. "He would want me to do this thing. Now tell me about this ship of yours."

I took a terrible chance then. Trusting people had so far gotten me nowhere. But as I searched the priest's face, I could see no hint of treachery. My gut told me that I could trust this kindly old man with my very life. Maybe even in Hell one can sometimes find an angel. And I really wanted to slay Harrison Randolph Barrington. I told the priest about my proposed design.

It was easy to do. My engineering designs were always fully worked out in my head long before pencil ever touched paper. Over a period of several nights, I explained the principles behind my design. It seemed to me in those days that I was coming up for air from a still, deep pool of despair. "The secret lies in the dynamic force of electricity and the use of floodable tanks to adjust buoyancy. The pumps I propose to use are so powerful that not only will they rapidly fill and empty the buoyancy tanks, but they will fill my ship's oxygen tanks with enough air under great pressure for us to cruise in comfort underwater without surfacing for two or three days."

He stared at me with an expression I confess I could not altogether read. I cast around and my eye fell on the Nautilus shell lying with the others on the floor. I picked it up and held it out to him. "The creature that inhabited this shell has traveled like this since before we were around. But instead of using puffs of water for propulsion I will use a special screw propeller with four adjustable blades to drive the ship through the water at a speed at least three times faster than anything else afloat."

Father Blondeau raised a hand. "But what about the exhalations of the crew, will this not in time poison the atmosphere of your ship?"

"You are speaking of carbon dioxide," I answered. "I have devised a method for removing it with special canisters filled with an easily obtained chemical compound that will ensure healthful air for the crew."

Father Blondeau nodded in the dark. "I see. Pray continue."

"To submerge deeply with great rapidity, my design will utilize a scheme whereby horizontal planes that rotate along their long axis are placed amidships and can be adjusted…that is to say, rotated from within the hull. I call it hydroplaning."

As I spoke, Father Blondeau's eyes gleamed with admiration. I forged ahead with the description of my undersea boat. The hull was to be cigar shaped with an outer shell covering an inner hull joined by beams. The ship would be propelled at great speed by an electric motor that would turn a drive shaft via a series of gears and levers many thousands of revolutions a minute.

"But from where will you get the electricity to drive your boat?"

"I will use sodium mercury batteries with the sodium extracted from the sea," I replied. He did not enquire about the actual method to accomplish this and I did not volunteer the information. I thought that I should keep some facts to myself.

Father Blondeau's brows knitted together. "How will you be able to see to navigate while you are sailing under the water?"

He listened avidly while I told him about the great lighting apparatus that would make it possible to see where I was going while submerged beneath the waves.

"But you and your crew will need to eat," he pointed out. "How will you obtain food and clothing without putting in to some port and risking detection?"

"Nothing could be simpler. We will live off the sea. The world's vast oceans, unspoiled by men, will provide us with our sustenance and clothing for our bodies."

He closed his eyes. "Such brilliance...." They flicked open. "I am convinced of the validity of your plan. Now I will present my part for your consideration." He leaned close to me, so close that his face loomed large in my vision. I could see every careworn line in his bearded face. His eyes, as blue as mine were black, gleamed in the dark. "The treasure is located in an extinct volcano on a small island in the South Pacific Sea." He then gave me its exact coordinates. "It is located inside the volcano itself in an underwater cave beneath a rocky ledge. There is a geyser of steam that rises from one side of the lagoon inside the volcano so that from a distance it appears to still be active. Moreover, it is surrounded by a reef with only one way in, and one would have to know what landmark to steer by to approach the island without having the hull ripped open."

He did not volunteer the identity of the landmark and I did not ask for it. When I asked how he knew to take it to that island he shrugged and said nothing. I knew from his expression that he would say no more of it and I dropped the subject.

He fixed his gaze on me then. "So tell me, Jonathan de Chevalier Mason, if I give you this treasure, will you use it to build your boat and shepherd me and my monks from this place, and keep us safe from those who would treat us like beasts to be caged?"

I looked him in the eye and said, "As God is my witness, I will build this boat and we will call no man master, and all who try to come for us will find a watery grave."

"We will be able to defend ourselves if we have to?" Father Blondeau asked.

"My vessel's design incorporates a special steel ram that will make it an engine of great destructive power should that be required, and utterly immune to terrestrial weapons. We will be as safe from our enemies as if we were living on the moon."

The old priest bowed his head and spoke so quietly that I had to strain my ears to hear him. "Ever since the day I got here I have prayed to Our Lord for deliverance from this island for me and my followers. I knew that He in His infinite mercy would not let me die here."

I insisted that we do nothing, lay no plans, for a month. I needed time to observe our captor's movements. He readily agreed, and not a day passed that I did not make a point of noting every small detail about the penal colony's routine.

In the days that followed I asked myself, again and again, if I could trust the Frenchman. What if he was merely a crazy old man, or merely spinning a yarn to get me to come up with a means for him and his monks to escape? An even darker thought occurred to me. What if he had been recruited by my foes to extract from me the principles behind my undersea vessel? I thrust away such thoughts as unworthy. I knew I could trust him with my secret. My instinct told me he was not lying about the treasure.

And I had not told him about the heart of my vessel—the special substance that would generate unlimited electricity for its powerful engine and pumps. I told him nearly everything about my undersea vessel, but I said not a word about Atlantium.

One night we were sitting in his cell devouring a coconut that one of his monks had slipped him already nicely cut in half. "Have you thought of a name for your boat?"

I picked up the chambered seashell. "She will be the Nautilus," I said darkly.

CHAPTER 4

The Sons of Belial

It sometimes happened, as it did one day, that the bugle was blown. And we prisoners were lined up in rows and columns until the entire open vast space was packed with sweltering men under a punishing pre-monsoon sun. A Gurkha soldier placed an empty ammunition box on the ground. Colonel Merrick strode forward, his boots crunching on the rocky ground, and mounted the box. He stood ramrod straight staring out at us from under his white pith helmet as if we had just crawled out of a latrine. Behind him, guards went from cell to cell looking for contraband, particularly the cells of the Irish nationalist or the English revolutionary. Here would be found the jar of marmalade they sought, as had been found a month ago—the precious commodity that had been discovered missing from the prison kitchen.

The colonel moved not at all as he stood there in his scarlet tunic and black trousers seemingly impervious to the broiling sun. But the guards suffered as the convicts in the parade ground suffered, so the search was done half-heartedly. My stomach growled like a ravenous beast. There never seemed to be enough food even on the best of days. My ribs seemed to stand out more with each passing day on Belial Island. When after three hours the sergeant reported that the purloined marmalade had not been found, Colonel Merrick cursed him for his incompetence with such eloquent profanity as would make a hardened old tar weep. He had one of those voices that could fill as much space as it had to. Was no other contraband found then? The sergeant called out a command and a guard ran forward with an armload of books and a small painting. The colonel commanded him to drop it on the ground, which was done at once.

"What's this, then?" Colonel Merrick got down from the ammunition box and picked a book up and read its title aloud, "The Writings of Marcus Tullius Cicero? I see we have a man with academic pretensions among us, do we?" His face, already red, took on a purple hue when his gaze fell on the painting of Napoleon. "Whose cell did you find these things in?" he asked the sergeant. The man pointed at Father Blondeau.

Colonel Merrick barked an order and Father Blondeau was shoved forward. The colonel pointed at the pile of books. "What were these doing in your cell?"

Father Blondeau answered but I could not hear from where I stood near the back because the priest spoke with the quavering voice of a very old man. We could hear Merrick though as he

berated Father Blondeau. We sweated and cursed under our
breaths. Some of the convicts, overcome with dysentery, voided
their bowels where they stood. The rest of us did not notice the
smell for we all smelled of defecation and urine and perspiration
and festering sores. Clouds of mosquitoes swirled around us like
hungry Furies. A few men succumbed to the heat and fainted.
They and the men closest to them were beaten while the
Colonel fired more questions at the priest. Was he still an admirer of Bonee? How did he come to have these books? Merrick's mustache twitched as he glared down at the Frenchman.

"Right! Twenty-five lashes for you, then!" Merrick said.

My head jerked up in outrage. That would kill the old man.

"No!" I cried, unable to stop myself.

"Who said that?" the Colonel cried, his sharp eyes flicking
over us.

My hand went up. "That will kill him!" Believe me when I tell
you that, although I fought to maintain an even tone, my insides
were twisting into knot upon knot.

The Colonel nodded to a guard. "Bring that impertinent swine
to me."

In the span of a heartbeat, I at once found myself on my knees
before Merrick.

"Who gave you permission to speak?" he demanded sharply.

"No one. Let me take the old man's place," I replied baldly.

Merrick's hard eyes bore down into mine. "You fancy yourself
a hero, Mason? Willing to take a flogging for this Frog Papist?
Very well, but you will get an extra twenty five good ones for daring to speak without being asked to speak."

And moments later my stay in Hell went from bad to worse.
I was dragged to a wooden pole set in the ground, stripped, my

wrists tied to an iron ring. Merrick was addressing the other convicts but I could not hear him over the thud of my heart. The
wait seemed forever. Over the crack of the whip I heard shrieking and realized that it was my own voice I was hearing. The
whip seared my back as if with Hell's flames. Before each swing
the guard shouted out the stroke. I think I fainted after the twen-
tieth.

I woke in my cell some time during the next day with Father
Blondeau squatting on the ground beside my bed, a look of concern on his kindly old face. I was lying on my stomach. I tried to
move but my body was a mass of searing pain. A cry escaped my
lips before I could stifle it. "Do not move, my son." The priest
dipped a rag in a cup. I cried out at the fresh pain. "The vinegar
will keep your wounds from being infected. The colonel ordered
his sergeant to give me a cup of water and vinegar and to see to
you."

I lay there in silence as the old priest tended to my wounds.
"I owe you thanks, and more than thanks, for what you did for
me." He went on. "The colonel destroyed my painting, but he
merely contented himself with confiscating my books, so at least
they were not destroyed. Perhaps he will read them and acquire
some humanity."

I twisted round to look at him and my voice was a hoarse rasp.
"Did you speak the truth when you told me of the treasure?"

He smiled down at me. "As the good Lord is my witness, I
have not deceived you Jonathan. I am counting on you to deliver
me and my flock from this hellish place."

"You did not mention my undersea craft." Even though the
words left my cracked lips, I did not know whether it was a question or a statement of fact.

The corners of Blondeau's eyes crinkled merrily as he smiled. "And you did not betray the secret of my stewardship of the Emperor's treasure. Can we not put distrust behind us, my son? We are looking to you to deliver us from here and provide us with a refuge from man's tyranny over man. Only your fabulous underwater craft can do that."

I turned my head on the straw filled mattress to look at him and said, "I believe you, Father." Then I fell asleep again. When I woke it was dark and the priest was gone.

(Lacuna begins)
Note: text smudged here for three pages.
(Lacuna ends)

Monsoon season was almost upon us, and not too soon, as the days were growing even hotter. But I was counting on it for more than relief from the unrelenting sun. I would use the monsoon to our advantage. My plan was simple enough, with the kind of simplicity that often succeeds, and it was helped by the routine our captors maintained, of having the prisoners unload the supplies from the small packet steamer that came to Belial Island every four months. On the day the ship arrived, the most fit of the convicts would be selected to play the part of stevedores and unload the cargo from the ship. This operation was typically completed by noon. The line reversed course the balance of the day as we convicts hauled sacks of coal onboard the ship. For, with typical British efficiency, a coal dump was maintained so the ships could be refueled for the return voyage to

Liverpool. They were fully stocked with supplies for a round trip journey. Another fact that would ensure our success. It would stay moored overnight to the end of the jetty while the officers enjoyed a convivial dinner with the Colonel in his fine house.

As I healed slowly, Father Blondeau and I laid our plans each night in his cell, talking in whispers. After obtaining arms from the small blockhouse that contained the prison colony's small armory, we would seize the steamer and make good our escape. He had already spoken to his men and every one of them gladly agreed to join us. My good fortune also lay in this simple fact. Many of the monks had been fishermen so were not strangers to the seafaring trade. I could teach them all they needed to know about steam engines, which, as they were primitive machines, were quite simple to operate.

In a very short while, we would be leaving Belial Island.

While I waited for the packet ship to arrive, the sky grew darker day after day, the clouds piling up on one another in great soggy heaps. Then the rain began to fall. First it came down in fat pellets that left craters in the soil then the fat drops turned to long glassy grey green rods of water that the soil could not absorb and the earth turned to ankle deep mud as we labored in the jungle cutting down trees. And not a one of us, convict or guard, failed to turn his face up to this refreshing gift from the Heavens. Throughout the camp there were loud whoops of joy. Men happily splashed muddy water at each other, the harshness of their incarceration lightened for the moment.

The days slid by while I waited for our main chance. Meanwhile, I seized every opportunity to study the movement of the guards, with equal parts great interest and discretion, as I did not want the bastards to guess at my intentions. As our island was bounded on one side by inhospitable jungle and encompassed by shark infested waters, the guards were neither punctilious nor overly motivated about the performance of their duties. Why did they have to be when there was nowhere to go? At night they ...

```
(Lacuna begins)
Note: Text heavily damaged by
water for six pages
(Lacuna ends)
```

It was night. I stood waiting in a corner of Father Blondeau's room with the sharpened wooden stake I had fashioned over the last week while working in the jungle. Every night the sergeant made the rounds checking every cell door to make sure it was locked, peering through the small barred window in the door. I looked at the priest. Could the man act his part? Would he be able to hold up under the pressure? If we failed, we were all dead men. "Are you ready, Father?" My question was rhetorical. Tonight I would die or regain my liberty. We waited in silence. Without the benefit of watches or clocks, we could only guess at the time of his arrival. What seemed hours later, there was the telltale rattling of the door lock and a murmured, 'goodnight Father' from the English guard. Father Blondeau called out. "Help! Help me...please!"

A face appeared in the door's opening to my right. My heart was in my throat as I stood there rigid, my breath slow and even, the sharpened stake clenched in my fist.

"What's wrong?" asked the guard.

"Help...help....oh God...help...."

I heard the jangle of keys, then a key sliding into the lock and the door opened.

Father Blondeau turned on his bed and moaned loudly. The guard filled the doorway, unaware that he stood on the verge of life and death. All the roiling fury over the many injustices that had been visited upon me drove away any lingering compassion for my fellow man. I felt a blackness rise within me then. The stick became an extension of me and I do not think I breathed a breath as I stood there tense as a ship's newly laid-on standing rigging.

"What's the matter with you?"

"I am sick...dying....this is it."

"The infirmary opens in the morning," he said with the casual cruelty of one whom lords it over someone in an utterly helpless position.

Then the old priest did something that at once impressed and frightened me.

"I won't make it...." Father Blondeau coughed violently, his body contorting on the bed. "I need to tell someone about where I hid it before I die...."

"Hid what?"

"Napoleon's treasure.... I need to confess my sins to spare my immortal soul..."

That brought the guard into the room.

In one motion I kicked the door closed, clamped my hand over his mouth and drove my stake into his neck with such force that its bloody point emerged from the other side. I will not deceive you. It was done with unabashed savagery. The man was dead before he hit the floor. I stood there for a moment holding the bloodied instrument, eyes wild as a rabid dog with my entire frame vibrating. It was then that I realized that I was forever done with all the conventionalities that were the hallmark of a civilized man. I had resolved to quit that hellish place and, in time, to have the means to enter into a voluntary exile from the so-called civilization that had founded it. I loathed mankind. Father Blondeau marked the change in me. He looked up at me with the eyes of one who has seen a fine thing go away for evermore. Although I held him in high esteem and thought him a friend, I could not have cared less what he thought of the matter.

I bent over and took the heavy brass key ring from the still warm hand, and removed the revolver from its holster and tucked it in my waistband. We put the guard in the bed covering him with the thin threadbare coverlet that was the sorry comfort of the convict on cold nights. The priest was kneeling beside him murmuring.

"We have to go," I hissed. It began to rain hard outside.

Father Blondeau rose and we crept from the cell like mice entering a pantry guarded by cats. I led the way unerringly. In my mind, I had made the trip many times before. As an engineer it had taken little effort to note the layout of the prison and estimate the distances involved from one objective to another—and it had taken even less effort to commit it to memory. I crept along with the old priest behind me, every sense alert. There was one guard to pass. He had no set route, just a wandering patrol, but I knew that during the monsoon season the guards often huddled somewhere out of the rain. It was no different tonight. It began to rain harder by the minute. But it could cease as suddenly as it started and we needed it to conceal our movements.

After an anxious time, a time when every twig or sloshing seemed to shout our passing and every errant shadow seemed to want to hold us back, we reached the other wing of the prison block. Now the rain was coming down in sheets and there was the sententious rumble of thunder somewhere out over the sea.

We got to the first door. I looked at Father Blondeau and he nodded. I unlocked the door and a wraith of a man emerged. The three of us moved onwards in silence going down two more doors. I looked at the priest again and he nodded. I unlocked that door and out came another man looking spectral in his white rags. We went from door to door until all the monks had been released. There were soon thirty of us and I do not doubt that but for the hard driving rain and the thunder we would have been discovered.

We entered the jungle behind the prison cell block and began to circle round toward the armory. The rain was pelting the heavy ceiling of foliage above us and the mud was halfway up our calves. With the priest and his followers walking behind me in single file, we headed in the direction of the blockhouse. I used hand signals to indicate where we were going. At a fork in the track, I pointed to the right to show that we had to pass the rear of the colonel's residence to reach the armory which was beside the storeroom and the barracks.

I led the priest and his men toward our objective. We stayed within the verge of the jungle, dropping to the muddy ground and flattening ourselves when a guard came walking toward us along the path that wound round the perimeter of the prison. I slowly cocked the pistol. We lay in the mud with the rain pelting down around us until he had rounded the corner. I rose, motioned the others to follow, and we moved onwards slowly. The colonel's house was brightly lit and I could see him with the officers from the ship on the veranda. Laughter and cigar smoke wafted our way. How I wanted to go and shoot that one armed bastard, but I stuck to my larger purpose.

I studied the barrack from a screen of dripping ferns. Every window was dark with the only light coming from a lantern over a doorway. My gaze flicked to the kitchen. Its windows were also dark. But it was the little stone blockhouse that held my utmost attention—the place where the tools that were the *sine non qua* of our liberty were stored.

Father Blondeau was lying beside me staring at our objective. I turned to him and whispered. "I will go first to make sure it is safe. When I signal, send your men." Then I rose and bounded along at a crouch to the blockhouse and flattened myself against its side. I peeked around the corner and looked into the prison yard. The rain was coming down so hard I could scarcely see the buildings on the other side. It then occurred to me that there was every possibility that my companions would not see my signal. I swung around the corner and unlocked the door, then shimmied back to the corner and waved.

The priest and his men came running toward me and I ushered them inside the building. Inside were racks of gleaming muskets and pistols with boxes of ammunition. We seized what we needed, loading our weapons in the dark and I was surprised at how ably and quickly the peaceful monks were able to accomplish this feat, even though Father Blondeau had informed me, somewhat mysteriously, that they would be able to do just that. I poked my head out the door just in time to see a solitary figure emerge from the heavy curtain of rain. With my heart hammer-

ing in my chest I counted to three hundred then eased the door
open.

The doorknob was yanked from my hand with such a violent
force that it very nearly pulled me forward off my feet.

"What's this then?" asked the guard who had apparently
sought shelter under the blockhouse eaves. I pulled him inside
by his tunic and got him in a headlock, cursing when his teeth
clamped down on my arm. I stabbed him with the stake again
and again until he was dead and on the ground. I felt the stares
of the others on me as I rose.

Father Blondeau surprised me, though, by reaching out and
touching my arm. "God bless your immortal soul. You did what
you had to do," he whispered, then nodded toward the door. "Do
you think we are discovered, my son?"

My grin was savage. "Even if we are, now that we are armed
we still have a chance. But no, Father, I do not believe our absence has been discovered."

I cracked the door open and looked outside. The rain was de-
creasing by the moment. "Let's go," I said, and we exited the
building and melded back into the jungle.

The last leg of the track led toward the strand, bone white
when dry, black as Hades' marrow now that it was wet. I could
hear the waves surging against the shore.

We gained the strand and I cast a hungry look toward the
moored vessel. A guard tower stood between where we crouched
and our objective. I studied it carefully. The lone guard seemed
to be asleep at his post. So it was under such slack measures, I
thought, that we poor souls had allowed ourselves to be held
captive for so long. But I knew that this was deceptive. The
guards were lax in their duties because of the very obvious fact

that there was no refuge for the fugitive on the island, and who would ever dare to conceive of as bold a plan as mine? I watched the tower for a long time. The rain was now coming down in a fine drizzle.

More ill-fortune!

But I was undeterred.

God himself rot in Hell, I was getting off that island or dying in the attempt.


```
(Lacuna begins)
Note: Text severely water dam-
aged.
(Lacuna ends)
```

Had someone not discharged his Navy revolver into the belly of a midshipman we might have gotten away without further incident. That shot, echoing like Zeus' thunderbolt, brought the colonel and his guests out onto the veranda of the official residence. Naval officers and guards came running toward us shouting. I won't conceal the fact that we had already slain most of the crew after taking the ship by stealth. There is no point in describing the scene act by act—our actions were those of men who know they have only one chance to reclaim that which God bestows upon every man upon his nativity. It is only through the actions of men of ill-will that any hindrance of liberty is ever imposed upon other men. There was no doubt in my mind that ship would be haunted by the shades of the poor souls we had killed. I did allow the few remaining alive to depart the ship. Not from any misguided sense of compassion but to provide a screen between us and our attackers. They scurried along the jetty with cries of 'cease fire!' while we exchanged musket-fire with the Gurkha soldiers and British prison guards.

A random musket ball smashed through the wooden railing of the bridge where I knelt with my musket, just missed my face, and buried itself in the housing of the starboard paddlewheel housing behind me. The air was filled with the crack of musket fire and the sharp bark of pistols. Musket balls rained down on us as our foes advanced along the jetty toward us. Below me I could hear the men firing the boiler. It would take an hour for the water to be hot enough. I would have cut the lines and hoisted sails but the wind was blowing hard against us, and there were too many musket balls in the air to send men aloft. No one would have lasted long up there.

To make matters worse, I observed soldiers wheeling the small brass cannon to the mouth of the jetty. I cursed the lack of rain that might have been our salvation.

It seemed to happen so slowly: The men training the artillery piece on us, the colonel shrieking orders like a banshee and waving his one arm like an inmate of Bedlam, a soldier pulling the lanyard. A tongue of orange and yellow flame stabbed toward us.

My heart was thundering in my chest. One shot to the boiler or the engine or the paddlewheels and we would be lost. Lost… The shot whistled overhead harmlessly.

I shouted to the men to direct some of their fire at the artillerymen. Then I heard the chuffing of steam and the walking beam just forward of the funnel began to seesaw on its pivot. Clouds of dark smoke were beginning to pour out of the smokestack.

"Keep the men shooting," I cried to Father Blondeau. I crawled for the stairs and dropped down to the deck and bounded toward the helm, shouting for the lines to be cut.

Another stab of flame from the cannon and the gunwale railing just below the bridge exploded into a deadly cloud of flying splinters. The paddlewheels began to rotate.

I took the helm and gave it a turn and we moved away from the jetty. More gunfire and then **The Lord** in his mercy opened the Heavens again and the shore was obscured from view. I guided us out to sea. Through the heavy curtain of rain we saw shadowy figures on the strand and long thin spears of yellow red light.

A musket ball slammed into my arm passing through the muscle—I am sure I cried out—but my grip on the helm never faltered. My feet were planted wide apart on the deck as I guided us all to freedom. Now the rain was coming down hard and the seas were dark and heavy and running hard abeam so that I had to bear down on the wheel. I reckoned our speed at about four knots, as fast as we could go under the circumstances.

(Lacuna begins)
Note: more water damage.
(Lacuna ends)

Father Blondeau's face, weathered by many years of sorrow and a million disastrous broken dreams, crumpled in utter joy even as he lay dying in my arms. He had been lying on the bridge when the hull below it was struck by the cannon ball.

"You will look after my flock, won't you Jonathan?"

"They are my family," I replied truthfully, "and you have been a teacher and a friend. I will care for them as you would." Tears ran down my face, for I had developed a real fondness for the old priest.

Father Blondeau stared wide eyed at the dawn. "See? He is calling for me."

I was silent, frozen, still cradling him in my arms. I did not know what to say. Finally, I spoke, my voice cracking, "Father, I am so sorry I failed you." My heart ached for the loss of my dear friend, my confidante, the man who had made our escape worthwhile.

He reached up and clutched my arm. "Because of you, I will die a free man. I am well pleased with our escape, and I go happily into the arms of my Lord." Just then the sun rose, sending vermillion light skipping across the sea below the clouds.

He clutched my arm. "Look for the eagle. Steer straight on…" A death rattle issued from his throat and he went limp in my arms.

For a few moments, no one spoke. All was silent except for the heavy sound of the wind through the rigging and the deep sorrow that enveloped us all.

I was still holding Father Blondeau up to face the sunrise and looking toward her myself when a big man, even in his state of emaciation, stepped forward from the group of monks who stood round us. "We owe our allegiance to you now. Father Blondeau told us that if something happened to him we were to obey you in all things."

I looked up at him, all too conscious of the many eyes on me.

The man said, "You are in charge now."

"What is your name?" I asked.

"Jacob."

I nodded. "You will be my second in command."

"I still can't believe it," Jacob said. "We are away from Belial Island and we have more food than I have seen in years. Real food!"

"You know how to get there?" Jacob asked, around a mouthful of food.

I nodded. "I am well acquainted with the tools of navigation." It was true, and I could read a nautical chart with the same fluency as a page of Latin or Greek text.

I rose from the wardroom table. "I am going topsides to make sure everything is all right." The men nodded as they ate and I left, pulling my newly acquired officer's coat on. It had been hours since we cast off from the island. Once we were well out to sea, I had ordered the fires banked to conserve fuel and the sails set. We were running with a stiff wind coming in from our stern quarter under easy sail. The masts and standing rigging looked sound but I was not taking any chances.

When I got to the bridge I swept the horizon with my glass. I blinked into the eyecup. At first there was just a fleck of dirty white on the horizon. And then I saw the thin line of black smoke followed shortly by a long black hull. It was a steam sloop of war. She wore ship to intercept us with a bone in her teeth. I could see from her build and rig that she was of American design.

Whirling around I shouted at Jacob who had followed me topsides. "Stoke the fires and engage the engines!" Then it was a race, our paddle wheeler against the screw driven warship. Even with all the sail I dared lay on, they were gaining on us.

The hours wore on. With my well-honed engineer's ear, I could hear the engine straining. My eyes went to the walking beam just forward of the bridge. It was flying up and down on the crankshaft and the paddlewheels were slapping the water into foam.

The American vessel was now only three cable lengths away. I raised my glass and saw several officers in the unmistakable blue tunics of American naval officers. Several of them were studying us through their glasses.

The American overhauled us then drew abeam and hailed us. "What ship is that?"

I raised my speaking trumpet and cried, "Her Britannic Majesty's packet ship Swift! What ship are you?" I ordered the Union Jack hoisted.

"The United States sloop of war Kearsarge! If you please, I am sending a boat over with an officer to board you." Her guns were run out and she had beaten to quarters. She could outrun us and we were unarmed. I had no choice. I raised the speaking trumpet. "We would be delighted to have you as our guests!" I called across to the warship.

But I found myself standing before a desk in the commander's cabin on the American warship. I had introduced myself by the name of the commander, whom was no doubt still on Belial Island cursing his ill fortune, Charles Ryder. I could see that Captain John A. Winslow was a solid courageous officer of the type to be found in the American Navy.

"You are sailing for New Zealand?" he asked, reading my ship's papers.

"Yes," I answered.

A naval chronometer ticked on the wall to his left, and I thought of my chance meeting with Captain Maury on the occasion of the celebratory dinner in honor of the launch of the HMS Warrior—had that been a different lifetime? It seemed so as I stood there in a uniform to which I was not at all entitled in this lifetime, but which would have been below my rank in the other.

"I see you put in to Belial Island."

"To land supplies."

Captain Winslow frowned down at the papers, scratching his mutton chop sideburns as he went over them. I felt the stares of his officers ranged behind him. "Your country has not exactly been an ardent supporter of the Union." He looked up at me.

I inclined my head, conceding the point. "That is true Captain, but not all Englishmen are supporters of the Confederacy, either." I caught his eye roving over my ill-fitting uniform and I added, "Between you and I, Sir, many Englishmen would prefer to help the Union, but we are all bound to observe the Neutrality Act."

"Yet, your government has sold warships to the South."

"An act I heartily disagree with."

Captain Winslow's startling blue eyes narrowed in his tan face, as he took my measure. Then he gathered my papers up from his desk and handed them to me. He said, "I am convinced you are not a Confederate pirate. You can go on your way, whatever you are, with my compliments. Have a good voyage, Captain Ryder."

Note:
Mason apparently did not see fit
to chronicle the balance of the

voyage to his destination, a mysterious island that exploded suddenly in 1883, sending a plume of
volcanic ash into the sky that
circled the entire globe. Only
Krakatoa, a few years later, was
more powerful.

With ocean temperatures that rarely descend below twenty degrees Celsius, and never rise above seventy degrees Celsius, the South Pacific is home to many Coral reefs.

I looked astern where the wake ran crisply in the calm sea. Ahead lay a volcanic island. Coral heads shown brown above the creamy water and beyond them the water was dark blue. We executed a neat starboard turn and circumnavigated the island slowly under steam, as I studied the flanks of the volcano. If I failed to find the correct spot to enter we would tear our bottom out and end our days as castaways.

The island was kidney shaped and cliff bound with a fringe of palms on a small beach at the base of the volcano. I studied the island closely. No sign of habitation presented itself to me, and no sign of an eagle, either.

Jacob standing beside me at the rail stiffened. "Sir! Look at that rock!"

I raised my glass and studied the landmark. There on the side of the volcano was a rocky outcropping that nature had fashioned into the glorious shape of an eagle in flight. And directly in front of it was the narrow channel through the reef.

"It is the eagle!" Jacob said in hushed tones.

I shook my head. "For us, my friend, that is a phoenix."

CHAPTER 5

Puzzle Pieces

July of Our Lord – as a matter of fact, I say to Hell with the Lord!
Any God that would allow the world to become what it has is
no Lord of mine. The year – eighteen hundred and sixty three
was an emotionally tumultuous month for me as that was when
I began in earnest to obtain the components to build the ship
that would allow me to live apart from this infernal world forever.
I had arrived in New York from Argentina with a stop in Panama
City on the Pacific coast where I had purchased a warehouse on
the waterfront with funds drawn from my bank account with
Banco de Plata SA in Buenos Aires. Thanks to Bonaparte's treasure, I was now an immensely wealthy man. I could have defrayed
the operating cost of the French government for three years and

still had money left over. Father Jacques Blondeau had come through—I was committed to building my undersea haven for myself and the loyal companions I had inherited from my friend. It was a matter of some internal angst that I had never reconciled myself with the God whom he so revered, but that I believed to be either non existent or disinterested in mortal affairs, but my heart and my resolve had hardened and I could not look or go back.

The slaughter taking place in America was the latest proof of the absence of any compassionate Divine Being in my mind. My men, also hardened by life's circumstances, still believed in some higher power of mysterious intentions, but seemed content with the notion of leaving the world behind, which made us ideal companions.

I had purchased a large villa in Panama City for my men. Jacob, as my second in command, was to oversee that the components were complete, as ordered, and properly stored in the warehouse as they arrived. We were operating as an international mining company so the arrival of machinery, heavy lifting cranes, explosives, and supplies of all kinds would not be suspect in the eyes of the casual observer—or the spy. Moreover, with the newly laid rail line running from the Caribbean to the Pacific, it would be easy to freight the pieces overland since that entailed only a journey of forty seven miles.

This plan was not, however, free of danger. Panama was a hotbed of Union and Confederate spies, each vying for intelligence that would give their side an advantage over the other. I was anxious to avoid the notice of Union agents or their belligerent Southern counterparts—both of whom would have coveted my ship, as my own country and best friend had done. Permitting anyone to know of my ability to build such a ship would again land me, and all of us, in prison with the gallows sure to follow soon after. I was, of course, eager to avoid this, but was also beginning to form an intense hatred and need for revenge upon the country and man who had brought me to such ruin.

I was gambling everything on this intricate scheme. My plan was to order what I needed from different places under different aliases, and then have the finished modular components shipped to me in a condition whereby I only needed to assemble them the way a child assembles a model boat. It had to work. If that failed for whatever reason, I failed. I would not allow that to happen. The world of so-called civilized men, and especially Harrison Randolph Barrington, would soon know my wrath.

New York was in those years filled with soldiers and sailors of every stamp, for America was in the grip of a bitter Civil War over the issue of that hateful institution, slavery. Yet, it was a thing of surpassing strangeness to me that the Negro was often reviled and the victim of violent actions in that most Northern of American cities, which had been famous for its abolitionist leanings for many years in all the capitols of Europe.

From my room in the opulent Fifth Avenue Hotel, I had looked on as great amorphous crowds of Irish immigrants and other Anglo-Saxons surged along the streets. Any Negro they encountered, whether man or woman or child, young or old, could be set upon with clubs, sticks, or lynched from street lamps without provocation. Soldiers were employed to put down these riots. Then the staccato crack of musket fire and the fireworks smell of burnt black powder would fill the air. This hardened my resolve to forever have done with what is loosely termed civilized

society, and a desire to mete out some sort of justice upon it grew
stronger in my dark heart.

I strove at first to overcome this new tendency toward hatred
and the ever mounting desire for revenge, but I could see daily
before my eyes the evidence of man's evil. His predilection for
violence and oppression of his fellow man sickened me. Each
morning I rose and meditated, without prayer, in the way that
my friend had taught me. I believe this to be only thing that held
me together. Only after this daily attempt to overcome my rage
was I able to operate in a world I loathed more with each passing
day.

Hart Brother's of New York was the first stop on my odyssey to
obtain the parts for my ship. Under my pillow were two things
hidden which I kept on or near my person at all times: an 1851
Colt revolver and a small flat leather satchel containing multiple
engineering drawings. Knowing now, as I had not truly understood before, the cupidity of men, it would have been altogether
foolish to give drawings of my undersea boat to manufacturers
of hull plating and naval machinery. So I had taken the precaution of drawing up a set of dummy blueprints: The spindle
shaped bow and stern were disguised as church steeples that
would stand 'a thousand years'—the keel that was the backbone
of my ship was the central truss for an iron bridge over a deep
but narrow gorge in Columbia. The driveshaft was for a shallow
draft steamship that would convey miners to the goldfields of
California from Argentina. The hull was to be made by four different manufacturers: two for the bottom of my Nautilus and

two for the top, but each blueprint would be for a single ship's hull. I had a plausible cover story for each piece.

So I was fully prepared when I stepped through the doorway of Hart Brothers Instruments. Junius Hart came out of his office with a smile on his face after his bandy-legged secretary announced my arrival. "Welcome, Sir. Welcome! We've been expecting you. I trust your voyage was pleasant." It was both a question and a statement of hope.

"It was...uneventful," I replied evenly. With every contact I had with another human being, it required more effort to observe the outward niceties of civilized intercourse—and to forget about the treachery I knew dwelled within the hearts of all men. This kindly looking fellow would have betrayed me in no time had he known the true purpose of the instruments I intended to order from him. Deep, calming breaths and meditative techniques helped to keep me centered on my goal.

Junius Hart nodded. "Given that so many ships are being captured and burned by Confederate pirates, an uneventful trip is a good thing." He was a short rotund man with a florid face and cottony white side whiskers. I noticed that he constantly fiddled with his watch fob as he studied the drawings I laid out on the table. "Hmm...this looks like a ship's telegraph. Why not go to Chadburns in London?" He looked up from the drawings.

"I am sympathetic to the Union cause, to which England is not, and would prefer to support American businesses, especially as this is for an Argentinean steam ship and they are not overly fond of the Confederacy," I said easily, playing a game of manipulation with this man. Other than a few odd words spelled out on the dial, the device looked like any other telegraph found on a ship's bridge.

Speaking of which… Junius Hart nodded toward my drawing. "The commands on the dial are rather odd. What do you mean by *crash dive?*"

I had anticipated this question and had an answer ready for him. "This device is to go into a new type of steamship that will ply the Pacific to Australia. In order to save money the ship's owners plan to use steam winches to work the sails. Crash dive is an emergency term for furl *all sail straightaway.* It is in English because the bridge crew is likely to be mostly British or American. I suggested Spanish wording but they said they wanted English, and as they are the clients…." I gave a shrug as if to say '*what can one do in the face of such reasoning?*' I was gaining confidence as my acting ability grew.

Mr. Hart rolled his eyes in commiseration with my difficult situation. "The customer is always right—even when he is wrong."

That won a restrained chuckle from me. "You see my position then?"

"Perfectly," he replied. "Where do you want the instruments shipped?"

I gave him the address of a freight forwarder (a company recently purchased by me) in Aspinwall Panama on the Caribbean side of the isthmus. He said, "They will be ready in six months. Sorry for the delay but we are deluged with Navy orders." I thanked him then left. The next day I was on a British steamer bound for England.

I both dreaded and anticipated my return to the land of my nativity. I almost hoped that the ship would not arrive, that it would founder in a gale or that somehow everything that had happened to me these past two years had been but a nightmare—and there would be a great crowd of cheering admirers with my Lavinia at their head to welcome me home. Yes, that is what beset my days and nights, what haunted my dreams for the few moments that I managed to sleep during that heartrending trip. It seemed that the closer we drew toward England the more violent these thoughts and emotions became. To hate her would have been to cauterize a deep wound, but I could not bring myself to steer for that compass heading, salubrious as it might have been. Perhaps she hadn't been given a choice in the matter. Perhaps she was a victim, not an accomplice in the outrages that had been inflicted upon me. For how could I have ever loved a woman who was capable of such evil? I didn't want to think thus, for my cool engineer's mind knew that it would only lead to more heartbreak, but my heart would not be stilled.

As our ship approached the place of my greatest joy and my greatest pain – the place of my betrayal and headlong tumble from the pinnacle of society, from the life as I knew it, my inner turmoil rose to a nearly unbearable pitch. I was coming home to a home that was no longer mine, and mounting rage tinged with a desperate denial of the plain facts was my daily companion. I struggled mightily to not give in to my volcanic emotions, but strove to draw power from them. It was a moment-by-moment struggle.

I stepped off the ship with my head in a whirl, fear of discovery, emotional pain, and remembrances of a life that was no longer mine haunted my every move. I scarcely recall passing through customs and hailing a carriage for hire to convey me to my hotel. Somehow, in the fog of my fevered mind, I found my way to my hotel then to Birkenhead Ironworks. I wanted to get my business finished then leave this accursed land as soon as possible. I didn't know how long I could keep from killing the man who had stolen my life. It would have been a simple matter to walk up and shoot him, but that would have resulted in me being hunted down like an animal. And I wanted to survive—not just for the sake of mere animalistic survival: my companions were counting on me to follow through with my scheme, and because I didn't just want to slay Harrison Randolph Barrington.

I wanted to destroy him utterly.

But I could not get my wife and my daughters out of my mind. Yes, I still regarded them as mine and I could not convince myself otherwise. I had to see for myself what had become of my family. If they were in trouble, it was my duty to rescue them and bring them with me to safety or to arrange for their safe harbour. Oh, the foolish thoughts of a man wracked by unbelievable pain, and filled with a fool's hope! I can only justify my folly by adding that if I found that my Lavinia's crime was as it seemed, then I wanted my inconstant wife to pay as well, for her sin was then the greater in my eyes.

It was with a head full of conflicting thoughts that I went to see John Laird of Birkenhead Ironworks first. Shipbuilding was then the foremost of England's many industries because goods for export had to be shipped. **Her Majesty's** empire encircled the globe, which meant providing enough ships to carry the steady stream of men (and their families) that went out to India or Australia or Canada to administer the colonies. And there were the goods from such far flung places as India,

Africa, and the Orient that had to be carried back to England—those required ships too, a good many of them.

Thanks in part to my efforts during my prior life, England was then the foremost builder of iron ships, a complicated endeavor under the best of circumstances. A ship's iron hull, funnel, furnaces, propeller shaft, boilers and engines would be fabricated at the shipyard. That meant that a shipyard was a small city unto itself with foundries, machine shops, and offices where the ships were designed. I was sharply reminded of this when I arrived at Birkenhead on the bank of the Mersey River across from Liverpool. A thick pall of soot hung in the air. I had been away for so long I had forgotten about the forest of blast furnace chimneys that belched smoke all day, and turned the sky crimson at night; how everything and everyone soon acquired a coat of soot. The air was filled with the rhythmic sharp bang of steam hammers, and the shrill of steam whistles.

John Laird studied my drawing through his lorgnette spectacles. Before him was the bottom of the middle section of the inner and outer hull each joined by I-shaped iron beams. It soon became apparent to me that he thought me an agent of the Confederate States of America. I swallowed my distaste and let him think what he wanted.

"It is imperative that the tolerances be adhered to," I said evenly.

He nodded. "That shouldn't be a problem."

"Plus or minus two millimeters is not beyond your capability then?"

"The advantage of working with steel is that it is more precise than wood, and the Bessemer process we use will result in an extremely strong hull." He looked up at me then. "No projectile currently used by the Union will be able to penetrate it."

I let this pass without comment. "How soon can you have it ready to ship?"

"Two months from the start date."

"Very well, let us draw up the paper work," I said.

"I will have my secretary draw up the contract." Laird waved the man over and gave him instructions. When the man had scurried back to his desk, John Laird fixed his blue eyes on my face. "What about the bow and stern?"

I met his gaze with eyes black as a prophet's. "We have those already, but need this section to be particularly strong." My answer seemed to confirm his suspicion that I was an agent for the Confederacy that this ship was clearly destined for.

He started to ask another question but seemed to think better of it.

"I require this work to be done in the strictest confidence," I said baldly.

Laird dropped his voice to a conspiratorial whisper that was entirely unnecessary as we were alone in his office. "We have built two state-of-the-art cruisers for our friends in the Confederacy, The CSS Alabama and the CSS Florida—all done in secret, of course. The Yankees are making much of it now that they are out on the high seas doing good work for The Cause, but as we sold the vessels to a neutral third party, we are not responsible for what they choose to do with their ships. Once a ship leaves our hands, the customer can sell or give them to whomever they choose. If you ask me, the Yankees need to be knocked down a rung or two." He gave me a smug smile.

It required a mountain of self-control to conceal my distaste as we signed the contract. Then I bid him a good day and left.

> (Lacuna begins)
> **Note:** more water damage here.
> Jonathan Mason apparently took a train from Liverpool to London where his small house once stood. The current site is now an office park attached to a shopping mall and automobile dealership.
> (Lacuna ends. Text begins)

The carriage came to a halt just a few blocks from my home. The coachman got down and opened the door and I stepped down, ordered him to wait there, and strode up the street toward my former residence. When I got there, I stood perfectly still, looking across the street. I knew I looked different: the smooth faced young man with the pale complexion and slender frame was now swarthy with a full salt and pepper beard. Moreover, I was powerfully built, used as I now was to hard manual labor, I bore no resemblance to my former self. I stood there a long time watching the strangers that now dwelled in my former residence. I thought I knew where I could find my family.

The moments between standing in front of my old home and coming to the spot where my family now lived I no longer remember and is now unimportant. On that bitter sweet summer morning I cast eyes on my Lavinia and my daughters for the first time in two years from the shadowed confines of my carriage. I watched Harrison leave his fine townhouse followed by my wife and daughters. Harrison and Lavinia were all smiles, hands clasped in the way of loving couples, their eyes bright. He looked resplendent in his fine blue Admiral's uniform with its gold braid. Perhaps it was simply the passage of time, but my daughters seemed to have grown much since I had last seen them and I ached to hold them in my arms. Every smile or laugh exchanged between my wife and daughters and my former friend was a dagger thrust to my heart, but then my eyes flicked to my wife's figure. It was easy to see her swollen belly as she turned to throw her arms adoringly around my former best friend's neck and whisper something gently into his ear. Their mutual love and companionship was evident in their every move and look. I thought my heart would surely give out from the pain of watching the scene in front of me and I could take no more.

"Drive on!" I said hoarsely, and pulled the cord for the coachman. He jumped at my signal, and the horses leaped in the harness to sweep me away from the scene of my broken dreams. It was then that I realized that to them I was already dead, a ghost—I was no one. I let murderous rage envelope me as that accursed place was left behind, for it was the only way to keep from being overcome with despair. I heard and saw nothing as we whirled along the streets that would convey me back to my hotel. With each mile away from that hateful scene, I felt the last vestiges of my humanity being ripped away from me, and I knew then that Jonathan de Chevalier Mason was no more.

From now on, borrowing from the *Odyssey,* and transposing the Greek to Latin, I would be known to myself and my companions as Nemo—No One.

Over the next two months, I traveled to various ironworks and steel companies placing orders for the other hull components, throwing myself violently into the immediate work of building my ship and the delayed workings of revenge. The spindle shaped bow and stern was ordered from The Glasgow Iron and Steel Company in Scotland. Oh how I smiled with assumed piety, as I described to Mr. Thomas Morton that the strange design was for a church with twin steeples in California that 'would stand for a thousand years' upon their Italian marble bell towers. The pious Scotsman seemed ready to canonize me as I spoke about the church that would rise on a bluff overlooking San Francisco bay. Naturally they had to be made of the finest steel and constructed to the closest tolerances, as spelled out in my drawings that showed the bow and stern rising like two steel spires from a church.

At Patterson and Mercer at Bristol, I met with the chief engineer and drew up a contract for the top portion of the hull. "Oh yes, we have been using steel for some years now. It will not foul as badly as iron. What type of vessel is this, Captain Nemo?"

(Lacuna begins)
Note: the next page is missing.
(Lacuna ends)

The train came to a stop with a loud huff of steam at the station in Essen. Before leaving Paris, I had telegraphed ahead and a carriage was waiting for me. We clattered along the cobblestone streets past crowded sidewalks with market stalls where one could buy fresh produce or meat or bread. Crowds of men and women and children thronged the markets. And being Prussia, everywhere I looked there were stern faced military men.

The city of Essen was home to Krupps Steelworks, a company famous for their engineering and manufacturing prowess of sophisticated armor and industrial machines. Prussian navy officers in sea blue tunics with silver epaulettes and civilians in black frock coats streamed in and out of Krupp's building, as if the place was a bee hive. As my carriage pulled up in front of the building I stepped out and strode up the steps with the air of a man on a mission. I paused in the foyer to let my eyes adjust to the dimmer interior light. Rich dark wood paneling, statues, framed drawings of steel breech loading cannons adorned the wall, as well as paintings of Krupp built iron and steel warships.

Alfred Krupp's smile was as cold as an ice berg. "We could of course furnish this machine to you. I cannot help asking, if you will pardon this forwardness, how you intend to power it? There is no source of electricity I can think of that could drive this engine." He stroked his long full white beard thoughtfully, as he stared down at the drawing of the engine that I had casually mentioned was for a new high speed mining drill.

My German was imperfect but we were able to communicate adequately, and engineers from different nations can converse with ease in the lingua franca of mathematics. His round thick spectacles gave him the air of a watchful owl.

"I have solved that problem," I said, giving him no more than that.

The glasses with their bottle green reflectance shone in the office's dim light. "Ah, I would like to know about this source of electricity."

I blinked once or twice. "That is none of your concern, Sir. If you do not wish to obtain this contract then tell me straightaway and I shall take my business elsewhere." It was a bluff—I thought no one else on the continent more capable than Krupp's. There were English firms that could turn out such a machine but that entailed too much risk. And I was cautious, for I had developed a strong feeling that something was wrong, that trouble (worse trouble, I amended to myself—just being an escaped convict with a no doubt heavy price on his head for stealing a British navy ship was a surfeit of trouble), would overtake me if I did not exercise all due caution. I had felt the curious eyes of strangers on me as I journeyed from one British or European city to another. I had learned not to ignore those feelings—doing so had landed me in the Star Chamber. I was still alive and in possession of my liberty, so I suppose that my instincts had so far served me well. I had developed the habit of changing trains and carriages frequently, registering at hotels under different aliases, and never engaging in idle conversation with strangers.

Alfred Krupp's pale blue eyes met and held my black ones, as he took my measure. "Naturally, Herr Welles, I will respect your wish for discretion."

I swept his words away with an impatient gesture. "I expect no less."

He sniffed. "How soon do you need this machinery, Herr Welles?"

"As soon as you can fabricate it," I replied at once.

"We could have it ready in six months. Our capability to generate electricity in sufficient quantity to test it is quite limited."

I dismissed this out of hand; I was relying on my perfect understanding of the principles of Ohm's law and Maxwell's equations, and I was an avid student of William Sturgeon's work with direct current commutator motors. But my design for an electric motor was to his, as a limelight lamp is to a tallow candle. Not only would my engine work but it would be the most powerful electric motor devised by man. According to my calculations, which I knew to be correct in every detail, the engine on the blueprint lying on the table before his eyes would drive my undersea ship through the waters at fifty knots.

The secretary came forward with the contract which would bring this all about.

It said in German that herein was a contract for Krupp Ironworks and Thaddeus Welles for the fabrication of a dynamic electric motor to be delivered, as per specifications, in six months time. Holding it in my hard callused hands, I sniffed at the smell of the wax seal and felt the texture of the rich vellum as I scanned the document.

The next two months were a whirl. In France, I placed an order for the zinc lined steel reservoirs that would hold the air, and other reservoirs that would hold the water that would permit me to adjust my ship's buoyancy. The powerful centrifugal pumps and water distillation equipment, also of my design, came from Sander'sche Maschinenfabrik in Augsburg in Bavaria. So the puzzle pieces were being cut and would soon be gathered together in my warehouse. I took the precaution of ordering spare parts for everything. The diving suits were ordered from the Belgium agent for Roxbury Rubber of Woburn Massachusetts. I ordered thirty cut in various sizes with brass wrist and neck rings that would mate with the brass helmets that I had ordered from Seibe Gorman & Company of London, also ordered by the Belgium agent so as to prevent arousing any suspicion.

At Calais the train wheezed to a halt. Among the swirling crowd of people greeting new arrivals and seeing off loved ones was a portly man in a claw hammer coat. He pushed his way through the crowd. "Cecil Petit at your service, Captain Nemo." At first I was surprised that he knew me on sight, then I recalled that in my telegram I had told him I would be wearing a black and gold waistcoat under my black frock coat.

I extended my hand and said in nearly perfect French, "Delighted to meet you, Monsieur Petit." I smiled then because the man standing before me and sweating in the summer heat was anything but small. The silver buttons on his waist coat looked as if they were going to fly off at any moment, and when he spoke his fleshy jowls wobbled.

When the formalities were complete, Petit said, "I have my carriage here. May I drive you to the hotel? I have made arrangements for you at the Hotel du Pompadour, the finest establishment in Calais. I am certain you will be well satisfied with the accommodations, Captain Nemo."

I inclined my head. "I have no doubt you have done everything necessary to ensure my comfort. Your letter said that you had found three ships?"

"Yes, three first rate seagoing vessels. You will be pleased when you see them."

A porter carried my bags to the carriage. My leather portfolio with the disguised drawings and specifications for my boat was tucked, as always, under my arm. I gave the porter a silver franc. "Merci beaucoup."

The man touched his peaked cap. "Di rien, monsieur."

"Tell me of these ships," I said, after we had settled into Monsieur Petit's carriage. Again, that feeling that curious eyes were observing my movements sent a frisson of unease racing through me. I was all the more glad when the carriage sped off.

"All three are steamers, very large as you specified." He told me about them as we jounced along. The first two at 900 tons would not suit my purposes. My ears perked up at the last name. I knew the ship well, having been a passenger on her. The Great Western at seventeen hundred tons would be perfect. I looked at Petit. "How much?"

"She is listed for twenty thousand francs," Petit replied, consulting his notebook.

"I will want to inspect her as soon as possible."

We pulled up in front of the Hotel du Pompadour. Porters in elegant uniforms swarmed down the broad stone steps to take charge of my luggage.

I stepped down from the carriage. "You are no doubt weary after your long train trip, so I shall take my leave," Petit said. "I shall return tomorrow and take you to the harbor so we can tour the ship."

I inclined my head. "You are most kind, Monsieur. That will be most satisfactory. I will expect to see you at seven o'clock, if that is not too early for you?" From the look on his face I guessed that it was. I added in a casual tone. "Of course, we must have breakfast first, hence, my desire to start so early."

Monsieur Petit's face brightened then. "Seven o'clock will be fine." His eyes went to the hotel behind me. "The restaurant in this establishment makes a fine breakfast." The carriage whirled away and I went up the steps into the hotel. From the corner of

my eye, I saw a small black closed carriage parked down the
street, its window curtains drawn, with the coachman's face hidden under a wide brimmed hat. I turned and hurried inside, and
heard the carriage rolling slowly by.

Another frisson of unease seized me then...

> (Lacuna begins)
> **Note:** More water damage for a
> page and a half. Fortunately, we
> were able to recover most of the
> remaining text for this chapter.
> (Lacuna ends)

With Monsieur Petit huffing and puffing behind me, I examined every part of the steamer. Her hull was still sound and the
engines in passable condition. In my pocket was the ship survey
Mr. Petit had thoughtfully furnished me with. The Great Western's best years were clearly behind her but she would serve my
purposes well—with a few very necessary modifications.

I turned to Monsieur Petit. "I want the passenger cabins and
the forward mast removed, and the hull painted medium blue.
Can you oversee this work?"

"But, of course, captain. She is your ship. You may do with
her as you please, and I shall be honored to act as your representative."

I liked the Frenchman. He did not attempt to pry into my affairs, and was very knowledgeable, unlike some of the ship bro-
kers I had corresponded with. I made arrangements for a small
crew to take her around the horn and thence up to Panama City

where they would be paid off. My men and I would crew the ship ourselves when we took the components to the island. We were standing on the ship's bridge. My eyes drifted to the road running along the pier and I stiffened. There was the same carriage I had seen outside my hotel. A mad surge of apprehension raced through my chest, but my face betrayed nothing of this, of course. My manly pride would not permit it.

Behind me, Monsieur Petit, asked, "Will you want to retain her name?" He had his leather bound notebook out, and had been writing down my instructions.

"No. I want her renamed. She is to be the PS Sea Phoenix."

"I will see to it."

We returned to the hotel where a telegram was waiting for me. Father Blondeau had developed a language, not unlike Esperanto, so that he and his men could communicate in private. Jacob had written to me in this language which I had learned from the priest, so I had no difficulty reading what would have looked to anyone else like a madman's gibberish. It was a short message: "Come at once. There is trouble."

CHAPTER 6

Devil in a Red Hoop Dress

The day I heard the name Naomi Woods was a black day indeed. Naomi Woods. Even now as I pen this memoir, the name rolls across my tongue with a certain piquancy and there is an involuntary quenching—a spasm if you will—of my stomach. This creature was that bad. If the Devil had breasts and a cunt, he would look like Naomi Woods with her raven tresses, alabaster complexion, and eyes the color of cabochon amethysts. Behind the serene face of an angel lurked the devil's own hellhound.

She was a Union spy, and utterly ruthless in the pursuit of her ambitions.

So believe me when I say that she was in equal parts agreeably stimulating and terrifying; as relentless as a hangman on execution day, and as beguiling as a siren… and she had turned the cold steel of her attention toward the Mason Mining Company. To say that we were buggered was to say that a rattlesnake bite was a bad thing. Attention from Union or Confederate spies was the thing I had wanted to avoid at all costs.

I stood in the warehouse with a Havana cigar clinched in my teeth listening while Jacob recounted the events that had transpired in my absence. And so I will share it with you so you may judge for yourselves the gravity of our situation. To begin with, set apart any group of men, bind them by the most potent oaths, place them in what they regard as paradise on earth—and there will inevitably be one man who is dissatisfied and yearns for more. That is the plain and simple truth. How easy things would have been had this phenomenon not overtaken our little band of brothers.

Picking his words with care, Jacob told me, "I've always had doubts about Brother Claude, but Father Blondeau said we ought to give him a chance, and that heaven smiled down on both noble and knave," Jacob recounted while smoking his pipe. Unlike many of his comrades, Jacob was a Greek nobleman from Cyprus, although he had been sent to school in England at a young age and had all the mannerisms of an English gentleman. He was a swarthy man, squarish in build, thick shoulders and arms—and utterly devoted to me, as the successor of the pious man he revered. My regard for Jacob was high and I trusted him with all my secrets—he was that type of companion one meets only once in life.

He went on, "Claude has never been strong, but Father Blondeau loved him like a son."

"As he loved all of us." I then looked to my left. A gangly young man named Philippe had spoken out from the ring of silent men that surrounded us. I nodded to let him know that I had heard him, but all my attention was directed toward the broad honest face of my dear Jacob—my right hand and second set of eyes.

"So what happened?" I asked, prompting him, as I could sense his reluctance to speak of something he considered unfortunate at best and disastrous for us all at worst. I think Jacob was also a little embarrassed that a member of his order had shown himself to be cut from such inferior moral fabric—a straw man in an iron and steel world. So I let Jacob proceed at his own pace, conscious of the stares of the others as we spoke.

"I should have known this was going to happen," he said, shaking his head. "Before we escaped, Brother Claude had spoken out against your scheme to live forevermore beneath the waves. We were working in the forest hewing those accursed trees while Father Blondeau spoke to us in artlang about your ship. Claude alone had voted against it, saying that he wanted to live in a regular monastery and would miss the smell of flowers in the spring, and the sound of rain pattering on the paving stones of a rectory's courtyard. He did agree that whatever the Father wished and we all voted for would be his destiny also, but I doubted him even then.

"About a month ago, just after the heavy lifting crane arrived from Holland and it was safely stored, a black haired woman appeared in the doorway of the warehouse. She was accompanied by a giant Indian wearing a stove pipe hat with a big knife tucked into his belt. The Indian didn't utter a word. But it was Naomi

Woods that was truly frightening to behold, even though she was blessed with the form and face of one of God's angels."

"What are you gentleman doing here?" she had called out. At first we all ignored her, but then she stepped over the verge of the doorway so that she stood foursquare in the center of the warehouse with the big red man in his blue frock coat and buckskin breeches. "I know something *interesting* is going on here." Her voice was lilting, and I could hear her hoop skirts rustling as she turned around to look at the stacks of wooden crates, and the steam tractors all gleaming with the newness of unused machines. I had just finished stacking crates of nitroglycerin in the loft when I heard this she-devil's voice echoing in that vast space. I dropped down a ladder and hurried toward her.

"'Ah, you must be the man in charge here', Miss Woods had said, flicking her fan open. She was smiling but her eyes were as cold as an eagle eyeing a mouse. I asked her what she wanted, and she gave a laugh that sounded like a many stringed instrument—it almost disarmed me too, Sir, but I remembered my larger purpose. She wanted to know what we were doing and how was it that a group of men living in an expensive villa never sought the company of women of ill-repute or visited one of the city's many saloons. She asked, 'What miners anywhere on earth ever lived like monastic hermits when so much liquor and pretty Latin senoritas for hire were to be had in that fine seaside town?'"

Jacob fell silent a moment. "I should have handled it better than I did," he said. "I ordered her off the property and told her to never come back. She laughed and said she would go but she paused at the doorway and called out to the men that had dropped what they were doing to see who the stranger was. She told us she was staying at the Excelsior Hotel and would give a bag of gold coins to the fellow who could entertain her with a good story about our true aims; she was a representative of the Union and had authority to grant pardons or inflict punishment unto death on rebel trash. She dropped a handful of her calling cards on the floor then left," Jacob said, handing them to me.

Jacob looked at me then with eyes full of wonder. "I have never heard a well-born lady speak that way. What should I have done?" I told him that he had handled the situation well and to pray continue. He got right to the point. It happened that Brother Claude was responsible for going into Panama City and purchasing victuals and supplies.

That was our first mistake, I thought.

"I know now that I should have been more suspicious, more wary. Even after all I have been through, I thought I could place my trust in at least our own men's innate goodness, as I learned to do from Father Blondeau—God rest his soul. It never occurred to me that one of us would turn traitor. I won't make that mistake again."

He looked away from me and I felt sorry for him. Jacob was a trusting soul who could never imagine a comrade intentionally steering a wrong-headed course.

"We have all made mistakes," I said reassuringly, "do not assume blame for the shortcomings of others. Continue with your story."

He ducked his head and went on. "As I said, Brother Claude went into the city, as he always did on Market day, but this time he was several hours late. I became suspicious of his absence. At first I thought to myself, 'Well, he has to make stops at several merchants, then I put it out of my mind, as we were very busy that day with a shipment of mining equipment that had just come in. By nightfall, I was just contemplating what should be done, for I feared by this time that he may have succumbed to temptation and gone to that evil woman's hotel, when there was a loud crash against the door. When Brother Constantine went to investigate, he discovered Brother Claude lying on the ground having been dumped like a heap of rubbish with his face and body a mass of pulpy, bloody tissue, and his breath coming in short rasping gasps."

Jacob looked at me, saw my black eyes darken and mistook my anger for fear. He said, "Brother Claude swore that he had not intended to betray us. When he went to Miss Wood's hotel the only thing in his mind, he said, was a desire to return to a peaceful life in some French monastery. He thought he could tell her just enough to satisfy her infernal curiosity without compromising our position, but enough to gain passage on a ship for France. Miss Woods was not at all happy with his half truths and, being convinced that we are working somehow for the Confederacy, she insisted on knowing the whole truth behind our actions. When Brother Claude demurred, she set her Red Indian on him."

I let out a long shuddering breath. What secrets had that weak fool revealed to save his cowardly skin? But Jacob moved quickly to assuage my fear. "Brother Claude did not disclose anything, Sir, so we are still undiscovered."

"How do you know that?" I asked more sharply then I intended.

"I took his confession before administering last rites," Jacob replied solemnly. "But Miss Woods sent a message through him. He was to tell us that we would all suffer a like fate if she isn't informed about the exact nature of our enterprise, but that any man who goes to her with the truth will be given amnesty. No other terms are possible."

As Jacob finished his story, my resolve hardened. I would have to deal with this harridan at once, but with great stealth to prevent any retribution from her masters in the United States Government. But how does one deal with such a creature? That question tolled through my head over and over. "Where is Brother Claude?" I asked.

"I slew him," Jacob said. He looked down again.

I reached out and clapped a hand on his broad shoulder. "You did what had to be done." Looking at the others, I said, "Let this unfortunate incident serve as a lesson to us all. We are only as strong as the weakest amongst us. Understand this, all of you. None of you is a prisoner. If any of you wish to depart, speak up now and I will provide you with ample funds to start a new life of your choosing." I looked at the men standing around Jacob and me.

The youth Phillipe spoke up again. "We are all with you, Sir."

"Very well, then. Let us be on our guard and prepare for the happy day when we will once and for all quit terra firma and be forevermore our own masters," I said, with a curt nod. Tomorrow I would seek Naomi Woods out and attempt to deflect her curiosity from our private venture—or I would do away with her.

That night I dreamed, as I always did, of my undersea ship. I saw her long spindle shaped hull, her bulkheads with their watertight doors, her gleaming electric motor and the banks of batteries, her glass view ports in the salon, felt the warm teak wood helm trembling in my hand. And there were the equations that always flowed across the inside of my eyelids as I lay there in my small plain room—with the ship's plans and revolver beneath my pillow. Then I sank into the deeper realms of Hypnos and knew no more.

The next day, I dined at the Hotel Excelsior, Panama City's most elegant hotel surrounded by rich wood paneling, delicate curlicues of gilt wood, heavy crimson and emerald green draperies, and large feathery potted ferns. This was the nexus of the social political hub of Panama City's elite society. Hanging from the coffered ceiling were rows of ceiling fans connected by leather belts, providing a welcome relief from the heat.

I sat in my chair studying the men in their fine frockcoats and brocaded vests and the women in their elegant hoop skirts and arm length gloves. I looked up from my coffee just as a ravishing woman descended the wide staircase at the other end of the dining room. In my gut I knew it was Naomi Woods. She moved with her head high, and the easy gracefulness of royalty, as though she were conferring a great boon on the dining room by deigning to enter it. She was in a crimson dress and her hair was parted in the center, tied into a heavy chignon that hung low on her slender neck, with bunches of raven ringlets framing a classically beautiful high cheek-boned face. She smiled at the headwaiter and asked him a question. He gave a deferential smile then gestured in my direction. She turned her full attention toward me, then headed for my table with her hips swaying and her eyes locked on me like a sharp-eyed bird of prey. The Red Indian that had followed her downstairs remained at the foot of the stairs, his dark gaze fixed on me. Indians and Negroes not in the employ of the hotel were not allowed in the dining room.

I rose from my seat and felt my chest constrict so that I could not breathe.

"Captain Teague, I presume?" Miss Woods asked in a lilting voice, even as her shokingly vibrant eyes pierced me to the marrow of my bones.

I bowed low. "I am at your service, Miss Woods." Then I held her chair for her as she took her seat. My first instinct as I settled into my own chair was one of extreme irritation that this meddlesome creature had seen fit to intrude into my life. As she sat across from me smiling, though, I felt my heart racing like a steam engine's flywheel. I could not stop myself from devouring her with my gaze.

A waiter came and I ordered sherry and a plate of teacakes and biscuits.

"Would Señor like the Oloroso sherry?"

"No. The Palo Cortado, if you have it."

"Si, Señor." He returned with a silver platter holding two wineglasses filled with a tawny liquid and a plate of teacakes and biscuits. She took up her glass with a delicately boned gloved hand and sipped her drink. "This is very good sherry."

"I am very glad to hear that you like it, Miss Woods" I replied courteously. "It is a rare variety aged much like an amontillado but over time it develops a character more refined than even Oloroso sherry." I sipped my sherry too and the tawny liquid was sweet on my tongue and warm in my belly. For long minutes Miss Woods and I sat looking at each other in silence, a contest of wills of sorts. From within the deepest reserves of my inner strength I summoned my commonsense back to its proper place: Firmly in command of the helm of my cool engineer's mind.

I withdrew a small stack of calling cards from my waistcoat

pocket, set them on the table then slid them toward her. "We have no need for these," I said evenly.

She did not touch them. "You speak for all your men?"

"Yes," I replied firmly.

That brought her up short, then her lips, pink as a rose petal and full as a topgallant sail in a strong breeze, curled up into a smile. She had beautiful even white teeth. "I can think of one man that didn't hold true for."

"And thanks to you he is dead," I said, scanning her face for a reaction.

She shrugged negligently. "When I left him he was but a little bruised."

I was shocked by her utter heartlessness, but somehow this only added to her appeal. "Shouldn't you be at home taking care of your husband and children?" I asked boldly. Miss Woods was nibbling daintily on a frosted teacake.

She gave me an impudent smile. "My doctor back in Boston said I must maintain my health with plenty of good food and high adventure so here I am in Panama City, doing just as he advised—and as my government has seen fit to instruct. I am sure you can see where a husband and children would be a hindrance to such a strict regimen."

So that is how it is, I thought frankly, a wealthy adventuress with a singular aversion to boredom. Of course she would find the life of a government spy alluring.

"I expect you are right," I replied, amused despite myself. "What do you want?"

"To know what you are really up to," she replied sweetly.

"I am not accustomed to discussing my private affairs with

strangers," I said, as politely as I could. Her violet eyes looked
into mine, frankly appraising me.

Miss Woods' dress, cut low in the Parisian fashion, revealed
the swell of her bosom. As she leaned forward I saw the inviting
hollow between her pale breasts. "Then let us get to know one
another better so we will no longer be strangers. My suite has a
lovely sitting room." Her eyes flicked to the broad stairs at the
other end of the room.

As if pulled by two invisible wires, my eyes were dragged toward the wide carpeted stairs. The Red Indian was now nowhere
in sight. How easy it would be to accompany this beguiling creature to her suite, I thought. How long had it been since I had
lain with a woman? The answer came to me, then, hot and hard:
two years and six months. My member in my trousers was as
stiff as an oar handle. I could smell Miss Wood's perfume, rose
and lavender. And in my fevered state I imagined I could smell
her womanly scents, her hair black as a raven's and as soft as
silk, her warm flesh, and the rich tide pool smells of her sex. In
my mind's eye, we were in her suite, standing by her bed, locked
in a fierce embrace, broken only long enough for me to slowly
disrobe her.

But the vision was a brief one.

Her voice broke through my reverie like a wave on a shore.
"My dear Captain Teague, I harbor no ill-will toward you. I am
but a young woman in a foreign land, with a gentleman she finds
herself quite unexpectedly taken with. Forgive me for being so
forward, but my passions sometimes conspire to rob me of my
commonsense. In these Latin climes, as I am sure you are aware,
men and women are not constrained by the tired dictates of our

polite societies in America and England, and I think they are much happier for it," she added with a meaningful dip of her long eyelashes.

Two years and six months without the touch of a woman was a long time for a man in his prime, I thought again.

My eyes returned to Naomi Woods' face. "That is a tempting offer, Miss Woods."

"And not made lightly, Mon Capitaine," she said in a low voice that was a caress. She leaned closer toward me, her eyes half shut, as if in expectation of my kiss, an outrageous act between two strangers in a public place. But one I was sorely tempted to commit against all common sense and propriety.

The world was spinning around me.

I was frozen in my chair, teetering between two worlds, a life as my own master beneath the seas, or as sojourner in the lush paradise offered by Miss Naomi Woods.

In my fevered mind I cast about for a lifeboat with which to make my escape and Father Blondeau's old careworn face suddenly flashed into my mind, his dying eyes and withered voice pleading with me to look after his beloved flock.

A shaft of fear struck me like an arrow. I knew then that this woman would stop at nothing to meet her objectives, and that I and my men were locked firmly in her sights. She was a threat to all of our plans. She could bring down all of us and I would never see the Nautilus built. A woman I had loved had been my demise once, but never again.

I hardly knew the sound of my own voice; it was so filled with the barely controlled roiling anger that suddenly came to my rescue. "Pay very close attention to what I am about to say, Miss Woods." At the change in my voice, she sat back in her chair and her startled eyes flew to my face. "I'm sure you think you have a job to do for your country, but it does not involve me, my mining company, or my men. You will stay away from us or suffer the consequences." Never had I imagined a time when I would speak to a woman in such a manner, but I was finding it harder to be a gentleman everyday. Nothing would cause me to desert my comrades or my undersea ship.

Jacob had not exaggerated. Naomi Wood's voice was like a many stringed instrument—I am sure that like the fabled queen Cleopatra, she had often used it and her other charms to lead men astray. "That is no way for a gentleman to address a lady."

"Do—not—doubt—me," I said, spacing out each word for emphasis, leaning toward her and placing both hands on the table as she pulled away from me, "when I tell you that I am no gentleman. And you will *not* be treated as a lady if you persist in meddling in *this* man's affairs."

A startling change came over Miss Wood's face. The soft an-gelic face of a young woman yearning for her lover's caress was replaced in an instant with a Gorgon's mask: teeth bared sav-agely, and her eyes blazing like two hellish bonfires. "You will rue the day you spurned me like some slattern," she hissed. She took another drink of her sherry but without taking her eyes off me.

"You have nothing I want," I replied, almost truthfully.

"I can see that I was wrong about you." Miss Woods set her empty glass down then rose from her chair in a whisper of silk and leaned over to caress the side of my face with a gloved hand. My flesh prickled, as if I was being touched by the hand of Death. "Until we meet again, Captain Teague…. Or whatever your real name is."

The cold hand of fear gripped my gut. *Or whatever your real name is....* I watched her retreat across the dining room with her head erect and shoulders squared. I let out a long ragged breath. The sooner we were out of Panama City and on our little island hideaway the better. My soul slipped deeper into darkness, as I contemplated the strong possibility that I might have to kill this woman, and very soon.

I heard a voice behind me say, "Quite a woman, isn't she?" The speaker came and stood at my elbow and watched Naomi Wood until she had ascended the stairs. "She comes from a very wealthy old Bostonian family, was educated at Mount Holyoke, and she is as lethal as a cornered cottonmouth." The stranger looked down at me, smiled, and extended his hand. "I am Patrick Bullard of the Special and Secret Service Bureau…"

"Of the Confederate States of America," I finished for him.

He bowed. "At your service, Captain Teague."

"What do you want?" I asked baldly.

"Oh, the same thing she does—information," he replied easily. "May I join you?"

I nodded and he sat. A waiter came up at once. "Whisky," I said, holding up two fingers. He returned a moment later with a silver tray and two shot glasses filled with amber liquid. The man sitting across from me was about thirty, of medium height and athletic build, brown-haired and green-eyed, with a neatly trimmed mustache. He was attired fashionably in a suit similar to mine, an off-white linen frock coat vest and trousers, and wore a straw planter's hat. He had the slow easy drawl of an educated southerner. Another time, we might have been friends. Now, he was just another nuisance.

My chuckle had a bitter edge to it. "It would appear that a

man cannot go about his own business in Panama City without being meddled with. Why are your governments so bloody interested in my mining company?" A direct question that deserved a direct answer. I was curious to see if I would get one from the southern spy.

"With a war on, we have to pursue anything that might give us an advantage."

"You say that so coolly, as if it explained everything," I replied, "but as I am not a citizen of either the North or the South, your war concerns me not at all."

"You have no leanings then?"

"No."

Bullard put his head back and laughed, then held up his shot glass. "Then let us drink a toast to the sacred institution of neutrality."

I raised my shot glass and said, "To neutrality then, and the right to pursue one's private business unmolested," and knocked back the shot. The whiskey burned its way down my throat, and filled my gut with a warm feeling that all-too-quickly faded away.

Bullard set his empty shot glass down on the table, leaned back in his chair, and gave me a speculative look. "Still, I do wonder if you are indeed what you claim to be."

"A mining company…"

"Where will you be setting up? Panama has no mineral wealth to speak of."

"That is true," I replied, choosing my words with care. "We are just assembling the equipment here for our venture but will be setting off for our destination soon enough. You will understand that it would be against my interests to trumpet the ultimate location of my mine. Suffice it to say that it is nowhere on the North American continent."

He smiled. "I can see that you are a plain spoken man, Captain, but…" He nodded toward the staircase. "…when Miss Woods evinces an interest in something, in anything, then it is incumbent upon me in my official capacity to poke my nose into the same places she does. You can no doubt understand that."

I said nothing to this. There were a number of places, I thought, that Patrick Bullard and Naomi Woods could go and stick their noses into—none of them pleasant.

"Not that I owe any man on God's green earth an explanation of what I am doing, but you have my oath that we are not in any way involved in the war between the states."

And then Patrick Bullard of the Confederate Secret Service surprised me, as few men have. He looked boldly into my eyes, as if testing my words for their truth then said, "I believe you, Sir. Let us speak no more of this matter then. I will say this though: you will have a far more difficult time convincing Miss Woods."

I rose from the table. "Good day to you, Sir."

Patrick Bullard smiled. "Watch out for her, Captain Teague. Naomi Woods is a ruthless woman." I nodded, donned my straw hat, and left without another word. And from that day, I maintained a round the clock armed guard over the warehouse.

(Lacuna begins)
Note: the following two pages are missing.
(Lacuna ends)

The PS Sea Phoenix arrived on a warm September day and tied up to the wharf fronting our warehouse. The British Packet ship I had made off with was there too—much altered by me in Argentina and repainted, for it would require two vessels to convey the sections of the undersea ship, and all the construction equipment and supplies.

I inspected the Sea Phoenix carefully straightaway, and soon discovered that my confidence in Monsieur Petit had not been misplaced. The huge paddlewheeler had been modified as per my instructions, and now sported a gleaming coat of blue paint that would make her harder to see from a distance. I then moved my men from the villa to the two ships and saw that watches were maintained around the clock to prevent sabotage, as I would not have put anything beyond that horrible woman Naomi Woods.

With a squeal of brakes and a huff of steam the train rumbled to a stop before the yawning door of my warehouse. I had chosen that warehouse because on its landward side ran a spur of railroad tracks that made it possible to offload shipments from boxcars or flatcars and convey them directly to the warehouse with little or no difficulty, which would also afford little opportunity for prying eyes. Sitting on a flat bed truck wrapped in canvas sheets was the bottom of the mid section of the Nautilus' hull, compliments of Birkenhead Iron works in Liverpool. The hull piece was lifted by crane from the flatcar and transferred to the warehouse where I had prepared a special cradle that rested on railroad trucks, a chassis with train wheels that in turn rode on a spider web of tracks in the warehouse. Once it was resting safely in its cradle, I ordered my men to remove the protective tarp. Imagine my ineffable joy as I beheld that first manifestation of my dreams! The first of the puzzle pieces was in my hand.

Ah, Nautilus, Nautilus, sacred undersea home and refuge from tyranny—

I gazed with loving eyes at my handiwork. Each steel plate was flush with its neighbor, rivets evenly spaced; the long half cylinder terminating at either end in a truncated taper where bow and stern sections would go. There was the main deck and the lower deck, the watertight bulkheads. It would have been a sublime moment if it hadn't been spoilt by that insufferable woman.

"That doesn't look like mining equipment."

I spun around. Miss Naomi Woods was standing there with her Red Indian smiling at me. "I thought I told you to stay away from my company?"

"What mining company requires an armored boat?" she persisted.

"Get out, and stay away or I'll lodge a complaint with your secretary of state."

"Oh, Bill Seward is a very dear friend of mine," she replied with a ripple of laughter. "Give your letter of complaint to me and I will see that it goes right to him."

"I have had my fill of your meddling, Madame." I moved toward her and the bodyguard in the stovepipe surged forward and swung at me. I ducked and came up swinging, quick jabs with the power of years of hard labor behind them. I hit him in the mouth with a left and his mouth started to bleed. He swung again and I hooked him hard to the left eye twice. He grabbed hold of the lapels of my waistcoat and it tore when I slammed my fist into his belly with my left and then pushed him away.

The bodyguard swung again at me weakly, I grabbed him hard, pulled him forward, and boxed his ears. That brought the Red Indian up short. His hat had long since flown off his head. His face was bruised and bloody. I saw his hand fall to the knife in his belt. I slammed my fist into the side of his head and yanked the knife from his belt as he crumpled to the floor. I stood over him breathing fast, prepared to finish the job if he did not yield to common sense. "Touch one of my men again and I'll kill you," I warned.

Miss Woods was looking down at her bodyguard with a peculiarly dispassionate expression. "Go to the carriage," she said flatly. Dazed and reeling, the Red Indian rose very slowly, picked up his hat, and stumbled from the warehouse. Miss Woods turned and looked at me. "Well, that didn't turn out as I'd expected."

"Nor will the rest of your game if you insist on following it to it's conclusion," I seethed. "Now get out of here before I snap your neck like a chicken, you evil bitch!"

Her eyes widened and she inclined her head. "As you wish, Captain Teague," and there was ice in her voice, "but I see that you are neither as controlled as you seem to be nor is your company as straightforward as you present it to be. I *will* find you out." Her eyes flew to the hull resting in its cradle one more time, as if she was committing its shape to memory and she left the warehouse. When she was gone and I had seen her carriage roll away, I turned and was greeted by the approving, if somewhat shocked, stares of my comrades. Starting with Jacob, they began to clap slowly, then a chorus of cheers rose from twenty nine throats.

Over the next several weeks, more hull components arrived. It started as a trickle then rose to a stream of hull plates, the bow and stern sections, the two great oblong slabs of thick glass for the salon. From Ticknor and Fields Publishers came twelve thousand volumes of books on various subjects, all bound in fine brown leather. The binnacle and the ship's engine room telegraph, the teak and brass wheel for the helm. The air reservoirs and the water ballast tanks. To be sure, I didn't pass my time merely waiting for shipments. I had designed special air guns that would fire a small hollow glass projectile that would discharge a powerful charge of electricity strong enough to bring down a bear. I worked in my machine shop fashioning the rifles and the machine for making the pellets.

We were still waiting for the electric motor when we began to load the Nautilus' pieces onto the Sea Phoenix, a dangerous and laborious process, even with the use of a heavy lifting steam crane and steam tractors. The huge steamer sank low into the water with each piece added until her plimsoll mark almost vanished.

I was not uneasy about the electric motor arriving in a timely fashion. I had received a telegram from my freight forwarder in Aspinwall advising that he had received a shipment from Krupps of Prussia and loaded the crates onto a train. If the Atlantium was the heart of my Nautilus, then the motor was its muscles—an electric motor unlike any that had come before it—with its high rate of revolutions, and the mechanical power transmitting apparatus with its levers for switching gears, which would permit a transfer of force between the motor and the propeller with the concomitant changes of torque and speed. My engine would have accomplished this alone by varying the amount of electricity fed to it, but the mechanical transmitting apparatus would yield even higher speeds— that and the adjustable pitched four-bladed propeller (now safely stowed onboard the PS Sea Phoenix).

(Lacuna begins)

Note: water damage for one page. Text is completely obliterated. Apparently Captain Nemo had renamed the British steamer Odysseus in addition to changing her outward appearance, an easy enough task with his naval engineering background and great wealth. Although he does not mention it in the surviving text, the electric motor and what we moderns would call a transmission must have arrived because he is at this point preparing to leave Panama City.

(Lacuna ends)

"Hear me, all of you," I said. We were sitting at the great table in the Sea Phoenix's mess room. "Tomorrow we will load the rest of the supplies onto the Odysseus and sail with the evening tide. The fewer eyes that see us depart the better. As the Sea Phoenix is so heavily laden with the Nautilus' components, she will require towing until she is well underway."

Jacob raised his hand and I nodded at him to speak. "I think we should sail toward the north then change course once we are out of sight of land."

"That is good idea," I replied.

A short man named Constantine suddenly asked, "Does anyone else smell that?"

He was right. There was the faint but unmistakable aroma of burning wood.

Just then there were sharp cries coming from the men standing watch. I surged from my seat and pounded up the gangway to the main deck. The air was heavy with the acrid smell of burning wood. I looked aft where the other ship was moored behind us.

"No!" The low moan fell from my mouth before I could check myself. From the hull to the mast peaks the Odysseus was aflame. I whirled round to Jacob. "We have to move this ship before she catches fire!"

He spread his hands helplessly. "But how, Captain? It will take an hour to fire up the engines."

"Lower a cutter and run the kedge anchor out into the harbor and we'll warp her out of harms way!" I cried.

"It shall be done, Captain!" He ran off shouting orders.

Moments later, the cutter, manned by half a dozen of my able companions, had taken one of the kedge anchors out. I called out orders for the mooring lines to be cut. Then my men and I raced to the capstan in the bow where the foremast had once stood.

Slowly we pushed against the capstan bars and the cable's slack was taken in then we came to a stop. Behind us, flames from the Odysseus stretched fiery fingers toward the night sky. A crowd had gathered on the wharf to see the spectacle. My one comfort was that none of the Nautilus' pieces were onboard the Odysseus as a precaution since that was where we had stored the nitroglycerin, and the warehouse, except for perishables, was nearly empty.

Naomi Woods had done this.

Naomi Woods had committed this crime. It was she who had

launched this filthy unprovoked attack—this dark evil act of arson. In the midst of the conflagration, I found my mind clearing and sharpening to a dagger point of raging hatred. Naomi Woods would pay. No one could do what she had done to me and hope to escape unscathed. If I could have had the vile woman arrested and horsewhipped, I would have done so. But as she was an agent of the United States, I knew that her influence would shield her.

The wind changed direction and small orange embers began to rain down on us.

Men were aloft pouring buckets of water on the furled sails, but that would not keep the ship from burning. I stared in impotent horror as the flames from the ship behind us grew taller and taller. Her rigging was red with fire. A mast toppled over the side and crashed with a splash and loud hiss into the water. More fountains of flame geysered from the ship. I felt the heat from the burning ship though she was a hundred feet behind us, a heat almost as hot as that of my hatred for Naomi Woods.

I cried to the other men working the capstan. "Lay into her or we are doomed! One two three…push! One two three…push!" Slowly, so slowly the movement was at first imperceptible, the capstan began to turn—and the ship's bow inched away from the wharf. We pushed against the bars and the capstan turned and we crawled ever so slowly toward the anchor. We were a cable's length away from the Odysseus when a deafening explosion that lit up the sky. The shockwave raced across the water and actually pushed us in the direction we wished to go. ()We glided toward the kedge anchor and out of harm's way.

My Nautilus was safe, but I slept very badly that night.

CHAPTER 7

The Box

The following morning I paced back and forth along the wharf. It could have been worse. The Sea Phoenix could have been the ship the She Devil had set on fire; the Nautilus could have even now been lying on the bottom of the harbor in pieces.

But the situation was bad enough.

Jacob and some of the men had come ashore with me. They stood at the edge of the wharf looking at what remained of the steamer. Jagged pieces of charred wood and metal thrusting from the black oily water were all that remained of the paddle wheeler. The fire had been so intense the paint on the warehouse had blistered. Fortunately for us the warehouses on the waterfront in Panama City were made of brick with corrugated metal roofs. We were fortunate in another way. The harbor was filled with ships hiding from the Confederate commerce raiders scouring the seas for American merchantmen.

I gathered the men around me. "Comrades," I began. "This event is but a setback. We have been through worse, and believe me when I say that this incident could have been much worse than it was. Basically, we lost an empty ship."

"Empty except for nitroglycerin," the lone Chinese man in our group pointed out.

"Even that was a blessing in disguise," I countered mildly. "The shockwave from the blast shoved us away from the fire. There is plenty of nitroglycerin to be had in Panama City since the miners on their way to California and Nevada stop here for supplies." Wisps of smoke still rose from the part of the charred wreck above the water. That bitch will pay for this, I thought, and that became my mantra over the next few days as I sought to remedy our unfortunate situation.

"What do we do now, Captain?" Jacob asked me.

"We look for another ship," I replied. "Meanwhile, we must keep close watch to ensure that another event like this is not visited upon us. We'll keep the Sea Phoenix anchored out in the bay with round the clock armed watches. If any boats approach unbidden they are to be hailed and ordered to halt; if they don't, shoot to kill."

Jacob gestured toward the building behind us. "What about the warehouse?"

"Don't worry. I'll take care of that." And I was as good as my word, for I hired guards to patrol the perimeter of the building and also gave them orders to shoot to kill.

Fortune smiled on us in our time of need. Three wharves down from ours was a large screw driven steamer that had not left her berth in a year. She was a fine ship with steeply raked masts and bright paintwork and taught iron standing rigging.

I turned to Jacob. "Find out who owns that ship," I said pointing to the steamer. "I am going to go have a word with that Woods woman."

(Lacuna begins)
Note: Severe water damage to next four pages.
(Lacuna ends)

"She'll cost you fifty thousand dollars, and she's worth every penny of it." I liked Mr. McAdoo on sight. He was punctual and did not mince words. He was a slight man, a lifelong seafarer to be sure, but attired like a successful townsman with well-cut clothes, snowy linen like mine, and boot tops as bright as an admiral's. He knew and I knew that there were more ships for sale than buyers for them—American shipping had been much affected by the depredations of the Confederate commerce raiders. Insurers were refusing to issue policies to them and many just remained in port rotting at their moorings.

The ship in question, the SS Samson, was a large screw-driven steam ship, bark rigged—another thing in her favor as it would require less manpower to work her sails. I examined the ship from stem to stern, crawled down into the bilges, and closely inspected the engines and boilers. She was American built by the William H. Webb Company of New York. At three hundred feet she was larger than the Odysseus, another factor in her favor.

We were seated at the big oak desk in the captain's quarters—
me behind the desk in a green leather chair, and he on the other
side on a plain wood chair. I thought the ship would be more
than adequate, but fifty thousand dollars was out of the question.
I was immensely wealthy, but I was no fool.

"I will give you twenty thousand dollars," I said firmly.

Mr. McAdoo cocked a black eyebrow at me. "She is only three
years old, Sir, and in fine condition. No Sir. I cannot accept such
a paltry offer."

"She has sat for a year," I pointed out. "Without any chance
of receiving cargo or passengers to carry anytime soon, this ship
is costing you money every day."

"My price is my price," he replied obdurately.

"Indeed?"

"Have I not said so, Captain Teague?"

I let out a long breath. "You have spoken plainly, Sir. I will do
no less. There are plenty of other ships for sale. I will continue
my search. Good day to you." I rose from my seat and headed
for the door. It was not a bluff. There were plenty of other ships
to be had and although I was partial to this one, I was fully prepared to look elsewhere.

Mr. McAdoo called after me. "Haul your wind, Captain
Teague. Perhaps we can work something out, after all."

I hesitated at the doorway. "Aye," I said dryly, "I am listening."

"Can you do thirty thousand?" he asked, watching me closely.

I came back into the captain's cabin then pulled out a notepad
of paper and a small silver pencil from my inside coat pocket
and scrawled a figure on it then handed it to him. "Here is my
offer, Sir. I will not haggle with you," I said smoothly. "If you ac-

cept my offer, I can have the funds in your hands by tomorrow morning."

He nodded and frowned down at my paper. It was clearly less than he had hoped for at twenty five thousand but still generous considering the going rate for commercial ships. In truth it was twice what he could have gotten from anyone else and he knew it.

He could not refuse me even if he had wanted to. "That blasted war is ruining everything," he said bitterly.

"Yes," I said neutrally.

He let out a long sigh of resignation and gave me his hand. "I accept your offer, Captain Teague."

"Good," I said, "but I want her taken to a dockyard and all her passenger cabins removed and the holds enlarged."

His head jerked up in outrage at that. "That wasn't part of the deal!"

"Of course not," I said easily. "I will cover the expense." I rose from the table and we shook hands again and I left the ship. SS Samson was a good strong name—and she would have to be a good strong ship for she would be loaded to bursting at the seams with heavy equipment and supplies, and would tow the Sea Phoenix out to sea until the paddlewheeler gathered enough momentum to maintain her speed under her own power.

The shipyards in Panama City were not run with the efficiency of their British counterparts. The workers were mainly South Americans, Mexicans, Indians, and free Caribbean Negroes and Chinese—and they were lazy and sullen. A task like the removal of cabin doors that would have taken at most an hour or two at

Birkenhead, required an entire morning. The removal of cabins walls—not the bulkheads mind you—dragged on.

The boilers had acquired a thick crust of salt in them that needed to be removed. This ought to have been the work of a single shift but was still not completed three days later.

Given the sorry state of affairs, I decided to supervise the work myself. It was unseasonably warm for a fall day, as if the gods wished to add to our misery. The sky over the harbor was like an oven and the air was thick with an oppressive humidity.

But I was used to much worse.

So I harried the dockyard workers. I was the first one at the dockyard every morning and the last to leave every night. I rode them mercilessly, and they would have lashed out if they dared. But they could not—not if they wanted to get paid. Whenever they halted to wipe their heads or to rub the stinging sweat from their eyes they would hear me or Jacob shout. "Get moving!" And there would be much cursing in Spanish, or French, Chinese or Indian. I cared not. I wanted to be quit of Panama City as soon as possible. My undersea ship stored in pieces on the steamer was vulnerable, as the explosion of the Odysseus had illustrated all too clearly. Day in and day out, the air in the dockyard was filled with the sound of timber being sawed, the hammering of nails being driven home and the fowl language of dockyard workers being worked hard.

She was ready in two weeks time. Each day we loaded cargo into her yawning holds and at nightfall the steam tugs I had hired towed her out into the harbor where she was anchored within rifle shot of the Sea Phoenix. I had divided my men and placed them onboard supplemented with private gunmen I had hired to maintain watch. But not a moment went by that I did not think about Miss Naomi Woods and consider my options.

To slay her outright would have brought the awesome might of the United States government down on our heads, so I soon dismissed that, once my anger subsided, as a bad idea to be shunned. But I could not let what she had done pass. Under my watchful gaze, the giant steam derrick was loaded on board in pieces beside the steam tractors and the floating bucket dredge. And I had recently acquired a new type of explosive that would make my excavation on the island a lot easier—dynamite, a dozen crates of it.

But Miss Woods cast a long shadow over my days, and my nights were filled with bad dreams about our undertaking being discovered or the Nautilus being destroyed.

Sometimes as we worked to load the ship, I would see her carriage roll by slowly with the Red Indian perched on the back, his dark brooding eyes locked onto me. Behind the carriage's closed curtains I felt another gaze on me too, curious and focused, like a pinprick of light from a magnifying glass held up to the sun.

One day, as we were loading the last of the supplies onboard the ships—mainly food stuffs and spirits, and clothing I had ordered from a tailor in Venice, I heard a southern voice hailing me from the wharf. I was at my customary place on the bridge overseeing the lashing of the hatch covers over the forward cargo holds.

"Captain Teague, permission to come aboard?" Patrick Bullard called again.

I went over to the rail. "What do you want?" I asked baldly.

"To speak to you, Sir," he replied.

"Permission granted but mind where you step, Mr. Bullard. The deck is still cluttered." He took the steps of the gangplank two at a time and once again, I found mΩyself liking the Southern secret agent despite myself—very strange as I loathed deeply the government he represented and the cause it was fighting for.

When he came up on the bridge, we shook hands. He looked around, said, "It appears as if you are about ready to depart."

I said nothing to this.

He ambled over toward the starboard rail and I followed him. He was leaning against the rail staring out at the sea beyond the harbor. "I have not met many mining engineers that seem to know as much about ships as you do. Were I Miss Woods I, too, would suspect you of being an agent of the Confederate States of America. But you are not one of our agents—," here he gave an ironic smile, "—and obviously I would know." Then he turned and looked at me. "What are you then, Captain Teague?"

"I thought you agreed to stay out of my affairs?"

"And so I have."

"Then why are we having this conversation?"

Patrick Bullard frowned into the bright Panamanian day. "Well, I wonder what it is about you that has gotten Miss Woods all fired up, no pun intended, Sir—I heard about the ship fire. She has exchanged a bushel of telegrams about you with her masters in Washington. They seem to think you up to no good—on our behalf. As I just said, I know better, of course, but it is all rather mysterious and I am not sure what to think."

I battened down my anger and said tightly. "You are entitled to think what you want, Mr. Bullard."

He nodded. "Well, Sir. It was not my intention to make a nuisance of myself. I find you an interesting, if somewhat confounding man, and I came because I was sure you would want to know that the interest in your activities seems to go to the very highest echelons of the Federal government, which I find very curious."

I must admit I softened my countenance then. Mr. Bullard was evidently trying to do me a good turn. I held out my hand and he took it. "I appreciate your warning."

"Have a good voyage, Captain," Patrick Bullard said, shaking my extended hand.

"Thank you," I replied, and he left my ship without another word. Toward the end of the day, I summoned my carriage. There was one important task I had to perform before we weighed anchor and sailed in the morning.

"Right this way Captain Teague." I followed the banker into the vault. The bank was all dark wood, tall feathery ferns, half shadowed in that way of churches and temples, which is, if you think about it, what a bank really is to some men.

Inside the vault the banker withdrew a key from his waistcoat, as did I. We inserted them in the two locks, turned them, and swung the door open.

He said, "I shall be outside if you require anything, Sir."

"Thank you."

I reached within the vault and removed a small brass bound wooden casket, closed the door and exited the vault quickly. I wanted to be back on my ship straightaway as we were to sail with the morning tide which was two hours before sunrise.

"Will you require anything else, Sir?" the banker asked.

"No, thank you." I headed through the door with my precious

cargo tucked under my arm, thankful for the revolver in its holster beneath my coat. My carriage was waiting outside and as it was late in the day, the shadows were long and the daylight sepia toned.

The last thing I remember was heading for my carriage parked across the street.

When I woke my head was throbbing, and I was stripped to my shirt sleeves and trousers, bound to a wooden chair in a dark room. The only light came from an oil lamp on a table. My head whipped wildly back and forth. I felt the penetrating gaze of someone watching me from the shadows. I did not unman myself by shouting for help. Clearly that would have availed me of nothing but humiliation in any case.

Then I heard the staccato click of heels on a concrete floor and she emerged from the shadows. I gazed at her, open mouthed and utterly dumfounded.

Her black hair was arranged in ringlets high on her head and although her glossy red lips were curled up into a smile, her piercing eyes were as warm as two chunks of ice. And this was not even the most singular aspect of this situation, dire as it was. For Miss Woods was clad in only a scarlet whalebone corset, black stockings, and ladies short lace-up boots. A black ribbon choker with an obsidian cameo of the Furies pinned to it was tied to her slender neck. She wore no pantallettes or bloomers. Indeed, beneath her corset which ended at the swell of her hips, she was nude.

Her pubic hair was black as ink against her pale, pale skin.

My eyes were drawn to the sight as iron to a lodestone. She smiled when she saw this—but her smile held no warmth. Then I saw what she held. And the world came crashing down all around me. In her hands was the little brass bound casket I had retrieved from my safety deposit box—it contained the sine non qua of the Nautilus.

Atlantium....

I could hardly suppress a cry of bitter surprise. My mind lurched. I could suddenly hear the jeers of the crowd as the thick rope was slipped 'round my neck as I stood at the gallows; see Harrison Barrington smiling up at me, with my wife and children at his side.

"So, here we are, Captain Teague," she said. "Oh, pardon me. I meant to say Jonathan de Chevalier Mason, formerly chief naval engineer of Her Britannic Majesty's admiralty, fugitive from Belial penal Island, pirate, and murderer."

I sat frozen as if her words had turned me to stone.

No…! No….! No…! This can't be happening…!

She wagged a finger at me. "You have been a very naughty boy, Johnny."

The long breath I let out sounded like a dying man's groan as she held up this ghastly mirror to my life. My heart thundered in my ears, and I felt icy rivers of sweat pouring down my face and trickling down my chest. We were doomed, even before we started. All our hard work had been for naught. It was over for us, my comrades and I. Worse still was the looming fate of my beloved Nautilus. Sent to the United States or Britain to be studied and copied, and, ultimately, turned into a weapon of war. Harrison Barrington would have at last won—my wife and family, my life, and my undersea boat.

And it was all the fault of the half naked bitch standing in front of me.

Her eyes were bright and very sharp on my face. "Well, come

on," she said teasingly. "Tell me about yourself. I am all ears. Regale me with tales of your daring escape. Of course I want to know all about this," she added, holding out the box.

I said nothing, nothing at all.

"This…thing…whatever it is…is most curious, is it not?" She unlatched it and swung the lid open. A silvery light bathed her face. "Just extraordinary," she breathed, "it's so lovely." Then she closed the lid and set the box down on the table very carefully.

Then she came over to me and grabbed my chin and turned my face up. "I know all about you, Mason. Where you came from; where you have been. What I don't know, and what you will tell me before the night is over, is where you are going and what you are planning to do." Quick as a snake her hand darted down and she seized my scrotum through my linen trousers and gave them an impossibly hard squeeze.

A jagged bolt of pain shot from my crotch to my torso.

"Do I make myself clear?" Her eyes were hard but her face remained serene.

I understood what would take place. And I did not try to talk her out of it. Everywhere I looked, were shadows. The place had a vast echoing hollowness to it.

"Where are we?" I asked, choking on my pain and coiling rage.

She bent down so close her beautiful face was only inches from mine. Her breath smelled of mint and she wore her customary rose and lilac perfume. "Why, we are in your warehouse. Who would look askance at an obviously inebriated man being helped into his place of business by two solicitous chums? You helped things immensely by dismissing the guards. And those monks of yours are all on your ships waiting for you to come back—to read them sermons no doubt," she added with a gurgle of laughter.

"Witch!" I hissed at her. "You should be burned at the stake!"

Miss Woods pulled a mock hurt face. "Oh dear me, now you have hurt my little ole feelings." She reached down between her shapely thighs, inserted a finger inside her sex then slowly, teasingly, wiped it on my lips. She straightened and said, "I will be right back." She turned and walked away quickly, her bare hips swaying, then returned a moment later with a rather large flat wooden box. She set it down on the table and swung the lid open with reverential fingers. A set of steel medical tools gleamed in the box's red velvet interior. She selected a scalpel. "Some old friends of yours are arriving soon and....," she dropped her voice to a conspiratorial whisper, "....they don't care how alive you are, as long as you can talk. Have I mentioned that my papa is a prominent surgeon?" She fingered the edge of the scalpel lovingly. "Honestly, Jonathan, I am rather sorry it has come to this pass. You see, I had hoped that you and I could be friends."

"If you were the last woman on earth, Madame, I would still have nothing to do with you. You disgust me!" I said, speaking the truth that leaped unstoppably to my lips.

"I do so wish you would stop saying such unkind things to me, Jonathan."

"Cunt...!"

"Yes, as you can see and even just now tasted, I do have a quim—a very nice one if I don't say so myself—and if you hadn't been so priggish you might have had access to it, and it would have cost you nothing but a little information."

I looked away from her. "I have nothing more to say to you."

"We'll see about that!" She took three quick steps up to me

and stabbed the scalpel down into the top of my hand which was tied at the wrist to the armrest.

I screamed and screamed and screamed, as she twisted the blade in my flesh.

Her eyes suddenly went all hazy with the lust of one who enjoys inflicting pain.

"Tell me what that thing is in the box, Mason!"

"No," I said through gritted teeth. "I will not tell you or anyone what it is."

A strange, a very strange, thing happened then. As she twisted the scalpel in my hand, her face turned red and her breath came out in sharp gasps. Her mouth fell open, as she cried out in a low half moan, "oh, oh, oh my....oh god...!" Then as suddenly as her orgasm had started, it stopped. She pulled the scalpel out of my hand then stood staring at me, her nostrils flaring, but her eyes on me were as inscrutable as a cobra's.

"I am not done with you." She turned away from me and went over to her surgeon's kit. As she bent over to examine its contents I saw that the back of her thighs glistened with womanly juices. She turned toward me and held up a tool that looked like steel pliers. "You won't like what happens next, Mason," she said, with the smooth voice of one who knows she has the upper hand. "Are you sure you don't want to talk?"

"Go bugger yourself!" I cried, the pain from my hand rocketing up my arm.

She gave a careless shrug. "Suit yourself...."

A thunderous roar filled the room. Miss Woods' head whipped to one side as brains and bone jetted from the side of her head. She toppled over and lay dead on her side with her legs and arms akimbo. A thick cloud of acrid smoke filled the air.

Patrick Bullard stepped from the shadows, the long barrel of his Spiller and Burr revolver still smoking. He pulled a bowie knife from his boot top and cut my bonds. Then he straightened and looked down at Miss Woods' corpse, a spreading stain of blood formed a halo around her angelic face that in death held a shocked expression.

"I really hated having to do that," he said evenly.

I looked at Bullard and could only say one word. "Why?"

He sat down on the chair I had just vacated with his revolver dangling between his knees, and his face suddenly looked haunted. "I have been asking myself some hard questions lately, Mr. Mason—yes, I heard everything she said. The news coming from the states is not good. Disaster after disaster has overtaken the South. Might it not be, that, after all our trials and sacrifices, the cause for which we are struggling is lost? More to the point, could it be that our Just Cause was not such a Just Cause after all?"

I said nothing to this. Their war had nothing to do with me.

Bullard went on. "It might surprise you to know that although I come from a wealthy plantation family in North Carolina, I do not personally own slaves nor do I believe in the institution of slavery, which as you can probably imagine did not sit well with my father." The whole time he spoke he was staring down at the floor.

I sought a reply and found none. Perhaps I was overwhelmed by events.

He looked up. "I care not who you are or what you are up to." He nodded toward the door. "Go in peace. Your secrets are safe with me, but our friend here summoned three Federal warships—

two steam sloops of war and one steam frigate. I believe they intend to seize your vessels. They are racing down here even as we speak."

I had started toward him with my hand extended in a handshake and a thank you on my lips when a bloody knife point appeared in the center of his chest. He was lifted from the chair by the knife, his hands grabbing at the bloody blade, gurgling sounds coming from his mouth. Then he was flung away like an unwanted rag doll. The Red Indian surged into the lamplight, the big knife swinging in a red and silver arc.

I sidestepped him and swung a fist at his head. He jerked to one side and spun around and lunged at me with the knife. I got hold of his arm and tried to twist it but my injured hand could not close properly. He flung me off and I went flying back. I landed with the wind knocked out from me. From the corner of my eye I saw Bullard's revolver lying on the floor nearby. The Indian rushed at me just as my hand closed around its handle. I swung the heavy revolver just as his massive figure blocked my view, his knife poised for the death stroke. In one fluid movement I cocked the hammer then squeezed the trigger. The pistol bucked in my hand. The blast hurled him back, arms and legs flung wide.

He was dead before he hit the floor.

I got to my feet and cast around for my coat but could not find it. I removed one of Miss Woods' short boots, rolled her stocking down then wrapped it round my bloody hand. Then I snatched up the brass bound casket and raced for the door.

Note:

Mason does not speak of his ac-

tual departure from Panama City's
harbor. This may be because the
actual towing of one ship by another out of a harbor, even when
both were under steam, was considered routine. Of course this
is mere conjecture at best.

It was that quality of blackness one sees between midnight and three am, and the Samson was three hundred yards ahead towing us out of the harbor. A thick cable ran tautly from her main mast through a freshly cut port in her transom to the main-mast of the Sea Phoenix. It would have been good if we could have run out with the tide but in view of our situation, I had thought it wise to weigh anchor and get underway at once. I was on the bridge half listening to the rhythmic huff and chuff of the engine, and the paddlewheels on either side of us slapping the black water into a white froth. It was as dark and dirty a night as I had ever seen with an on-shore wind filling our sails.

I consulted my Waltham pocket watch. It was one twenty in the morning. We were preceeding the outgoing tide by three hours.

Jacob was in command of the Samson. I was easy in my mind regarding his competence. I knew that he was equal to the task, and so he proved to be, as later events would demonstrate. I was in a dark and thoughtful mood. How much had we been compromised? I wondered. When I had gone to Belial Island, Great Britain was just a hair's breadth away from declaring full support for the Confederacy. Now, they were apparently in league with the Union to the extent that they were sharing information about me. Had they tracked my pilgrims' progress trek across Great Britain and Europe, noting the acquisition of the components I would need to assemble my Nautilus? Perhaps it had been the eyes of American agents I had felt on me in Europe.

The balance between triumph and ruin now rested with our ability to be gone before the Union warships arrived. Laden as heavily as we were there was no question of outrunning them. My heart was not light—it was an anchor in my chest, and I despaired of ever feeling it lift with joy at simply being alive and free. But my cool engineer's mind was calm—it took refuge in infallible equations and the precise diagrams of my undersea craft; and the certain knowledge that once she was built and launched, we would be liberated forevermore from oppression. I would no longer fear my fellow man and the harm he could inflict upon me. He would fear me.

So I stood on the bridge with my legs braced wide, gripping the railing and staring ahead into the blackness, watching the cable, a grayish line in the dark and taut as a fiddle's string, running from the Samson to my ship and I felt...exhilarated. My hand was now wrapped in a proper bandage but it ached mightily. Jacob had suggested a dose of laudanum and rest: he would oversee our departure. But of course, I could not permit that.

In view of the fact that Union warships were racing from the north to entrap us in the harbor, I had discarded the earlier idea of sailing north than cutting southwest once out of sight of land. Instead, we were heading southwest without any running lights, but our ships' funnels threw up fountains of orange embers that would certainly be noticed by any pursuing ships. I watched the low dark mass of the coastline recede from view.

The rhythmic slap of the paddles in the water was almost hypnotic.

One hour passed, then two. I called out, "Heave the log," to determine our speed. Just then a lookout perched in the bow shouted, "Ship dead ahead!" My guts seized up in me. In the black heart of night, our larger ship, having gained momentum and the paddlewheels now biting deeply into the water, was rapidly overhauling the Samson.

The now slack towline was completely submerged. With my heart thundering in my ears, I whirled around and shouted through my speaking horn to the helmsman, "Helm, hard right rudder!" Then I called to the men in the bow. "Cut the cable!"

The acknowledgment came back "Hard right rudder!" but I barely noticed it. My eyes were locked on the vessel ahead of us. Ever so slowly our bow swung ponderously to starboard. We surged past the Samson's stern so close I could have leaped onto it from my ship—and, as we were in a sharp turn and nearly pivoting around our center of gravity, our stern was swinging toward the stern of the steamer ahead of us.

"Ease up on the rudder twenty degrees!" I cried to the helmsman. The turn slowed, then we straightened and were running close alongside the Samson. Very close.

I looked over at the other steamer's bridge and saw Jacob's round face, pale with fear looking at me. Raising my speaking horn I called to him, "Be of good cheer, Number Two. A near miss is as good as a mile."

Jacob grinned and raised his speaking horn, "Aye, but I still almost shit myself!"

Dawn on the morning of the next day broke clear with a fresh wind and the sea glassy as a mill-pond. We were running with sails set and steam laid on to make good time. I was not worried as both ships' coal bunkers had been enlarged. We could have run non-stop on steam alone all the way to our destination if we had to.

About midday, the lookout in the top high above us called, "sail, ho!"

"How many?" I cried.

"Three!"

In a very short while I saw the telltale smoke from the warships' funnels even before their hulls rose above the horizon. They were making for us with all sails set and a full head of steam. I raised my glass and studied them, two steam sloops and a steam frigate. I dropped down from the bridge and bounded along the deck and clambered up the mizzen backstays, and watched them as they ran toward us. I cursed our misfortune bitterly. Heavily laden as we were there was no way to outrun them. As I was counting on stealth, there was no thought of sailing swiftly, an impossible task given the weight of the cargo we were carrying. At best, we would be lumbering along. Now here were three swift Union warships bearing down on us with their cannon run out and all canvass set. It was irksome to be caught in the middle of a foreign country's war.

Then fate intervened in our favor.

Or at least so I thought at first...

Even though I knew we could not outrun them, we were desperately trying to get as much speed as we could from the two ships' engines when a thick wall of fog appeared suddenly ahead, as if it was a gift from Poseidon himself. We sailed into it gratefully. The fog deepened as we sailed onwards, then the sea became choppy and a light rain began to fall. Then it came down in marble sized raindrops then in great glassy gray green rods. We tightly reefed the sails and steered a southeasterly course. At four in the afternoon the wind veered around to the southwest, pushing us further leeward of the Yankee's warships. Then the gale hit us full force and the pursuing warships became the least of our problems. The wind roared through the rigging, and the bow of the great steamer rose as we climbed up the face of a gray green mountain in a heavy, confused sea. The rain grew heavier and heavier, as we crested wave after wave, then bow plunged into the sea all the way to the catheads. The falling rain and sea became one roiling mass of water, and where one began the other ended.

In the afternoon the gale increased, tossing the big steamer like a wine bottle cork in a mill race, throwing everything not tied down about with terrible violence. I heard the Nautilus's heavy steel components groaning against the heavy iron chains securing them. I dashed below and, taking up a lantern, peered into the vast cargo hold where the Nautilus' main hull sections were stored. With every pitch or yaw of the ship, the great steel pieces clanged like Hell's dinner bell, and the iron chains holding them in place looked as if they would snap at any moment. I gave an involuntary shudder. If one of the heavy pieces broke free it would make the deeply laden ship unmanageable, or it would burst through the wooden hull and we would find ourselves dining at Davy Jones' table.

There was nothing I could do. The chains would either hold or they would not. Even before night fell, we soon lost sight of our sister ship, as well as our pursuers. We could not see ten yards in any direction because of the spray and heaving seas.

The next day the gale increased to a full-blown hurricane with winds veering sharply south west to south then south east. Mountain after mountain of water rose before us. Over the demonic shriek of the wind I heard the engines straining to drive us forward. Time after time, my eyes went to the great walking beam seesawing on the axle that drove the great paddlewheels in the paddlewheel boxes. We plunged into a cavernous trough. The force of the waves broke along our foredeck, carrying away the forward boats.

There were sections of the Nautilus lashed to the main deck where the foremast had once stood. A chain parted and the Nautilus' forward upper hull pivoted to one side crashing through the gunwale. While the ship pitched and rolled, we used block and tackle and the capstan to winch it back in place, working with the water sometimes up to our waists, and then we lashed it to the deck with many cables and fervent prayers.

At times the seas rose high above the mast peaks. I confess that I began to despair of us every reaching our destination. And what of my other ship the SS Samson? Had she been captured by our pursuers or foundered in this hellish storm? Without the equipment she carried in her wooden belly we would not be able to assemble the Nautilus.

In the middle of the night we shipped a sea that carried away great jagged sections of the port paddle box and a water closet. Then our rudder was ripped away and we would have been doomed had we not acted decisively. While we were lying in a trough another wave carried away the jib boom. The hurricane had moderated its force a little but we were still in grave danger. The continued good operation of the engine was all that kept us from wallowing helplessly while we rigged a relieving tackle to work a temporary tiller and rudder. The force of the waves pounding the ship had opened some of her seams and we were beginning to take on water. The donkey pumps were employed to pump the water and pillows and blankets were stuffed into the leaky seams. Never has a group of men worked so desperately to stay alive. Just before dawn a massive wave carried the bridge away. I was in the stern working the jury-rigged tiller with two of the men when it was smashed into kindling.

For two days we battled the elements arrayed against us. And in that time I became even more convinced that only in an undersea boat could one traverse the ocean in complete safety and comfort, down deep free from the vagaries of wind and wave.

On the third night the storm died, and when Hesperus ripped away the night's black shroud with her rosy fingers, the day dawned bright on a calm sea. I swept the sea with my glass. Four miles away to port was the SS Samson. Much beaten up to be sure, but sailing proudly. And not a Yankee warship was anywhere in sight. My guess was that their commanders had wisely run for the nearest port to escape the wrath of the hurricane.

A week later we reached the island of our hopes and dreams.

CHAPTER 8

The Hidden Lagoon

The volcano rose from the sea as we drew near. All my attention was on the island and the reefs surrounding it—the big greenish coral heads rising like teeth from the blue green water. "Steady as she goes. Slow to one quarter," I called out from my perch in the mizzen shrouds. Then the helmsman sang out, "Steady as she goes, slowing to one quarter!" The helmsman hit the engine telegraph handle and my well practiced ears heard the engine revolutions drop. I looked over my shoulder where the wake ran crisp and white and blue in a long curve. The Samson was following us smartly. I'd ordered all sails furled as I doubted our ability to navigate such a narrow channel under *sail and steam* and decided that we would power through, carefully and watchfully.

I turned my head and studied the island. Beyond the reefs and the pale green water(), there was a long black beach. Further along, to the north east, was a dense mangrove swamp. The swamp concealed a large deep lagoon where I intended to anchor my ships. Rising above it all was the volcano. Father Jacque Blondeau was so constantly on my mind at this time that his presence was almost palpable, and I smiled into the rising sun. Had it not been for the kindly old priest and his utter faith in me, my dream would be as far away as the solar orb. I had the knowledge, I had the Atlantium, but I did not have the will to go on or the funds necessary to build my undersea ship. Then I thought, correction: *Our undersea ship.* My eyes swept the deck and the tops where my comrades were stationed. The Nautilus was just as much theirs as it was mine. I would not lord it over my comrades. To be sure I would be the captain(), but the Nautilus was our refuge from tyranny, our home, and our means of swift and terrible retribution should anyone attempt to rob us of our liberty. There would be no tyranny on our undersea refuge.

But there was one exception. The Nautilus would also be the means to Harrison Randolph Barrington's utter destruction. That would be my one selfish act, and I had been candid about this with my comrades from the very beginning—it was only fair.

We eased our way through the gap in the reef steering straight on for the eagle outcropping on the volcano's flank, the paddle wheels slapping the water with lazy strokes. The reefs on either side came perilously close to the paddle wheels; they were brown and jagged and so close I could see the waving fingers of purple and yellow anemones and the light brown starfish lying in the shallow hollows of the reef heads. Once we were through we steered straight for the beach. Then came the tricky part, for we had to execute a sharp turn to port, pivoting on our center of gravity. With thankful hearts, we glided into the lagoon on October thirteenth, eighteen hundred and sixty five. We dropped anchor with the Samson beside us. I raised my face to the sky, relishing the sunlight that felt so good on my face, and finally exhaling all the fear and worry that we may not have ever reached our destination. We were so well hidden from view that a ship could sail right along the reef and not see us – we were finally safe. Across a wide strip of black sand at the base of a steep cliff was a lava vent, big enough to admit a railway car with room to spare. A small channel of water ran through the center of it and cut a shallow creek to the lagoon. I would set up my shop inside the same extinct volcano where Father Blondeau had secreted Napoleon's treasure.

(Lacuna begins)
Note: water damage for next three pages.
(Lacuna ends)

We had done a lot in two months. Ordinarily pitch black except for the small round opening a thousand meters above us, the interior of the volcano, our dockyard, was now brightly lit. I had set up arc lamps that flooded the interior with bright light powered by an electric generator I had designed and constructed in my warehouse in Panama City, based on the work of my celebrated countryman Michael Faraday.

At the far end of the chamber was a fissure from which a geyser of steam periodically erupted sending a tall plume of steam up the cone which was sucked up and out the volcano's crater, as was the smoke from our fires.

Resting in her cradle on a basalt ledge beside the subterranean lagoon was the lower hull of my Nautilus riveted to its long steel keel. Towering over her was the steam derrick from which even now a steel reservoir was suspended in chains. The fuel to power the derrick's hungry furnace came from the massive Sea Phoenix's wooden hull. By day, clouds of smoke and steam issued from the volcano and at night its summit glowed with our artificial light, all of which made a landing by seafarers highly unlikely since they gave the appearance of an active volcano. To transport the Nautilus' parts into the volcano, we had poured a concrete slab from the beach to the lava vent, lay railroad track on it, then loaded them onto wagons pulled by the steam tractors. After the track was laid, it had taken but a week to haul everything inside the mountain's cavern.

Brother Michael Moreau was at the controls in the derrick's iron cage. This self-contained lad of twenty handled the machine with the precision of a surgeon. I watched the crane's boom swing toward the hull and the winch slowly lowered the reservoir into the hull, followed shortly by the staccato hammering of rivets being driven home. Then my gaze shifted to the far end of the cavern to a spur of rock where I had set up my machine shops. There, gleaming in all its glory was the electric motor on a concrete pad and behind it the direct force transmitting device that would send power via a drive shaft to the adjustable pitch propeller. It was operated via a series of levers, with the largest attached to an iron disk coated like a locomotive brake that would temporarily disengage the engine so that different gear ratios could be selected by the engine room crew.

The plans were laid out on a long table. I straightened and rubbed the fatigue from my eyes and then stooped and rechecked the blue prints. Yes, that was the correct reservoir and it was going into exactly the right place in the bow. Although the building of an iron ship ordinarily requires many more men and facilities than I had at my disposal, only a few men and the barest facilities were necessary to build my ship, as she was largely prefabricated. It was just a matter of bolting and riveting large sections together. In this I was not an innovator, iron hulled steamships were often prefabricated and shipped in pieces to their overseas customers. It was simply more economical.

At nightfall when we ceased our labors for the day, we dined at a long table where I sat at the head, enjoying seafood which we harvested ourselves. And here we were, as in many instances, very fortunate, as we counted among our number a nobleman from the island of Japan. He was a small, lithe man with intelligent dark eyes, sparse chin whiskers, and a grave manner. Michi Shichirōma had been Daimyo – that is, a great lord of a powerful territory in Japan – but had been overthrown by a treacherous brother.

Lord Shichirōma had been on a visit to Great Britain to examine her shipyards when he was arrested by the British, who favored his younger sibling because of his pro-British sympathies. Great Britain was desperate to get a toe into the country that had recently been opened by the upstart Yankee navy. Michi Shichirōma had soon found himself on Belial Island toiling in the steaming jungle forest. He was a philosophical man, a gentleman in bearing and birth. He did not speak English or any other European language, but he was fluent in Artlang, and had been converted to Christianity by Father Blondeau. And he could do amazing things with seafood! Daily we dined on makazushi, delicately flavored rolls of rice and fish wrapped in pressed and dried seaweed and cut into bite sized slices, and tempting servings of sashimi, precisely sliced raw fish.

I delighted in watching his expert hands filet and cut the fish and then lovingly drape it over shaped mounds of rice. All of us grew stronger and healthier than most Europeans on his Japanese food, our brains and reflexes quicker.

And after dinner, the men gathered around to watch me indulge in one of the few luxuries I permitted myself, a special item I had purchased and stowed on board the SS Samson. I admit that it was a luxury that may well have been dispensed with, but it had been a lifelong passion of mine. While my comrades sat in a half circle at my back listening appreciatively, I played my pipe organ—and my men sat and listened with rapt attention as I filled the great echoing space of the volcano with Girolamo Frescobaldi's haunting Gregorian strains, sometimes an offertory such as *Dopo il Credo* or other pieces from his *Fiori Musicali,* musical flowers. But there was one piece I played for myself when the black dog had fastened his teeth upon my soul and I was raging inside my tortured being against the injustices that had been visited upon me, and the betrayal of my wife and best friend—Johann Sebastian Bach's *Taccatta and Fugue in D minor.* Then the men would melt away in some silent acknowledgment of my private pain and my need for solitude. For bright in my mind's eye was the memory of my eldest daughter when barely two years old toddling into our drawing room, big blue eyes bright, her hair a golden halo around her angelic little face, and her high little voice saying, 'Papa play. Play, play, play...' And I would laughingly throw up my hands in surrender and take my seat at our piano; then my fingers would fly up and down the keyboard, as she watched and danced with the innocence of children and the unspoiled savage (not a perjorative, by the by, in my lexicon).

One night, soon after we had set up our operation in the volcano, I gathered the men around then set up an easel and walked them through the Nautilus' plans to familiarize them with the ship. It was important that each man know his job.

"Here are the over all dimensions of our ship," I said, pointing to the drawing, "Eighty meters from stem to stern and nine meters at its maximum breadth, not including the diving planes. Notice that it is shaped like a cigar, a cylinder with conical ends. Can anyone tell me why I chose this shape?" I looked at my comrades. Several hands went up.

I nodded to one of the Frenchmen, an older man named Pierre Boulanger. "Like a fish, it will cut through the water with much ease."

"That is exactly so," I confirmed.

Jacob raised his hand, and asked a question that I am sure had been discussed among my comrades many times, well out of my hearing. "How do you know she just won't sink to the bottom of the ocean when you fill her tanks?"

"She is designed to do just that Number Two," I replied baldly, and then I elaborated. "When I designed the Nautilus, I intended that nine-tenths of her should always be submerged when she rides on the surface. Now, when I open the valves and fill the reservoirs with water equal to this one tenth, she will submerge until she is just level with the sea." I pointed at a drawing of the diving planes amidship. "These stubby looking wing-like structures are controlled by a lever on the bridge. I call them diving planes. If kept parallel with the hull's long axis, the Nautilus will move horizontally. If we slant the diving planes then our undersea ship will either sink or rise diagonally."

The man I had in my mind singled out to be chief engineer raised his hand. Ian MacKay was a young Scotsman, a former ship's engineer with a wide knowledge of steam engines; a devout Catholic, convicted for agitating for voting reform and an eight hour day for workers. He had lost everything, but in a manner even more brutal than my own loss, as he had been forced to watch as his wife and children were slain by British soldiers. "Filling 'er tanks and sinking underneath the waves be one thing, Captain Nemo. But I be sore pressed to see how we canna regain the surface with ease."

I suppressed a smile. Mister MacKay knew the answer perfectly well—we had spent hours pouring over the drawings and discussing the principles behind them—his question was for the benefit of his comrades. "When I wish to rise to sea level," I said evenly, "all I have to do is engage the pumps to empty the reservoirs. And gentlemen, these are the most powerful pumps ever devised by men. They use centrifugal force as opposed to mere piston action, and they are powered with electricity."

There was a pause as the men digested this.

Philippe asked, "But how can we see where we are going while underwater?"

"A good question, young man," I replied warmly. I pointed to the drawing of the structure at the front of the deck. "The helm is located in this box-like structure here on what I call the boat deck as that is where the cutter will be kept in a sealed recess— notice that there are round portholes located on all four sides. This glass is very thick and will withstand many pressures of atmosphere. All good enough, but the water the helmsman will be steering through may not always be clear, especially at lower depths," I said, warming to my theme, "so, gentlemen, kindly direct your attention to this other square structure located at the rear of the boat deck. In here is the powerful electric light that will illuminate our path beneath the seas. By my calculations the light emitted from this apparatus will illuminate the sea for half a mile around us."

"And we will be safe from our enemies?" asked another man. I nodded. "Oh yes, we will be as safe as if we were on the moon looking down at them. The steel hull will withstand any cannon shot or explosive round. We will move beneath the waves at more than three times the speed of the swiftest surface vessel. And this device here,"—I pointed at the drawing of the steel spur jutting from the bow—"will punch through even an armored iron hull. It is case hardened steel from Motala Metal Works of Sweden. Trust me when I tell you that we will live in a style that even the wealthiest men would envy, and in complete security. Danger is the constant companion of even a Cunard liner, subjected as they are to the wind and the currents and unreliable steam engines. We need not fear masts being carried away by storms or boilers exploding, or fires since our Nautilus is made of steel; no coal to run short of since she operates on electricity. And we need not fear collisions as we alone sail beneath the waves, and the tempest raging on the sea will have no effect on us, for we shall enjoy perfect tranquility far beneath the waves. There my comrades, is our new home; the perfect vessel! And if it is true that the engineer has more confidence in his creation than the builder, and the builder than the captain, you may all take heart, for I am all three!"

My comrades rose as one and clapped and cried out my name—

"—Nemo!

Capitaine!

Bravo!"

To be sure that was only one of many nights spent familiarizing my comrades with their new home. And by the time we launched, each man knew his part to perfection. Over a period of several months, I walked them through the various systems, the reservoirs, and the proper operation of the ....

(Lacuna begins)
Note: Six pages severely water damaged. The text is irretrievably lost.
When Nemo speaks of his 'mechanical force transmission device,' he is referring to what we moderns would call a transmission.
(Lacuna ends)

May I tell you candidly that, as I clicked the brass ring between my lead bottomed diving shoes and the India rubber suit,

I was more than a little apprehensive. Consider this: I was going to shut myself up in an airtight rubber suit, with lead boots, a round brass helmet with three thick glass portholes; strap on a tank of air based on the design of Rouquayrol-Denzyrouze then jump into a lagoon. Yes, I was relying on the Ruhmkorph apparatus to light my way, but this was then all new and untried technology. Who was to say that I wouldn't end up on the bottom in forty feet of water, gasping for air while flailing around in the dark until I suffocated?

"Are you sure you want to do this, Captain?" Jacob nodded toward the air tank, a steel sphere fastened to a leather harness, hanging from my back by an additional special harness. "I mean. What keeps all that air in the tank from just rushing pell-mell into your lungs and blowing you up like a puffer fish?"

I pointed to one of the two brass cylinders on the center of the tubing running from the spherical tank. "This tube contains several valves that regulate the amount of air, and…" I pointed to the other cylinder. "…this one absorbs carbon dioxide."

"Ah…I believe I see. Still, it is brave of you to do this, Sir. "

I gave a careless shrug. "I couldn't very well ask one of you to wear this diving suit without trying it out myself to ensure its safety, Number Two."

Jacob's honest face broke into a broad smile and his in his eyes I saw respect and honor. "Father Blondeau knew what he was doing when he put you in charge, God rest his soul."

"Only time will tell about that, Number Two. Now help me with the helmet."

He lowered the helmet onto my head, securing it to my suit's brass neck ring.

At first I could not make myself take that first step toward the ledge. Then I saw and felt the eyes of my comrades on me, penetrating the heavy brass helmet. They had left off their various tasks and had come over to watch me make the test dive.

We had set up a small pulley with block and tackle at the edge of the water with a windlass. I had a thick rope tied round my waist. Because of the sounding we had taken I knew that the sea floor was only forty feet below. When I wished to come to the surface I would give it three sharp tugs then Jacob and the men would haul me to the surface.

My purpose was not limited to the testing of the diving apparatus. The Nautilus would have to leave by the same opening she had come in, but as a completed ship, and she was much too large to do that. I had brought dynamite and steam tractors to dredge a channel but I had soon noticed that the water level inside the volcano rose and fell by as much as three feet twice a day, and it was good clean sea water and not merely seepage. All the evidence pointed to an underwater passageway of significant size.

I stepped off the ledge and went down feet first, feeling the coldness through the India rubber suit. Down and down I went until my feet touched the sandy bottom. I looked around. Flying buttresses of bright blue light surrounded me in the blue water. I was astonished at the water's clarity! It was as clear as Venetian crystal glass but wore away into darkness that makes one a little uneasy and wary.

Breathing underwater for the first time was awe inspiring, and a little frightening. After all, we humans are not intended to do that. As I let myself get used to the sensation and worked to slow my rapid breathing, I could hear the breathing apparatus working faintly, the regulating valves clicking open and shut rapidly like a Flamenco dancer's castanets, and the larger gurgling sound of the air bubbles rising from my gear. I let this steady working of the equipment, doing just as it should, comfort me. I could not resist a slight backward bend that allowed me to look up with wonder toward the surface high above me. What a miraculous sight!

Hundreds of silvery fish, most no larger than my thumb, flitted around me in an intricate sarabande. I stared in wonder at a guineafowl puffer fish swimming lazily by. A bright orange garibaldi fish swam up to my glass face port and gave me a fishy eyed stare before moving off. Several flame angelfish true to their name flitted by.

Then I turned my attention toward a dark void to my right. I nodded to myself. It was as I thought. There was indeed an undersea opening to our subterranean lagoon. I lifted a leaden foot and moved toward it. The bottom was sandy but I felt the crunch of sea shells under my heavy boots as I walked. I went from a cathedral of light into darkness. I reached down and thumbed a rubberized switch. The Ruhmkorph apparatus buzzed audibly then hummed and the light attached to my belt flickered on.

The underwater tunnel yawned open before me. Here the current was strong and even with my lead boots and lead weights at my belt, I felt it tugging at me. I went to one side of the tunnel and paced off my steps to the other side. Forty five feet—just barely wide enough to pass through safely, but the tunnel's ceiling was only about fifteen feet from the seafloor, not nearly enough. The lava vent was bifurcated by a tongue of basalt. I moved deeper into the passageway. It went down at an angle and grew wider and deeper. I did some quick calculations. At the mouth of the subterranean lagoon, the strip of volcanic stone separating the underwater passageway from the lava vent was only about fifteen feet. I had brought more than enough dynamite to remove this hindrance to our egress. My feet slipped suddenly on the mossy rock that had replaced the sand I had been walking on and I fell onto my back with a dull clang from the air tank hitting stone. I lay there a moment stunned frozen with fright that some catastrophic failure might be a result of the fall, but then turned on my side and pushed my self up to all fours when I realized this wasn't the case.

I had just gotten to my feet when there were three sharp tugs on the rope. As I was hauled up, I had not even had time to take off my helmet before I heard the ominous words, "We have a problem".

Hidden in the mangroves whose dark gnarled roots looked liked a gnome's legs, up to our waists in water, I studied the American sloop of war riding at anchor just beyond the reef. She was low slung and rake-masted, screw driven, with her sails furled neatly. I recognized her as one of our pursuers after we had slipped out of Panama City's Harbor. Had they somehow tracked us here? I wondered, or is this just good luck for them, and bad luck for us? The air over the mangrove swamp seemed to thicken.

I trained my telescope on the American warship. Her officers were gathered on the bridge forward of the smokestack. The stars and stripes fluttered aft and, although her engines were obviously disengaged, grayish puffs of cottony smoke issued from her buff-colored smoke stack and swung over her lee quarter.

"What do we do, Captain?" Jacob asked quietly.

"Eh?" I could think of nothing more to say as my unbelieving eyes stared at the ship and I inwardly cursed the stinking world that would not leave me alone.

"They will probably come ashore. What then?" One of the men asked, but I knew not who.

"Why would a ship put into a deserted island?" Jacob asked.

"They must be looking for water. They probably noted the island's lush vegetation and reasoned that there might be a freshwater spring. The Americans have eschewed the use of water distillation units on their ships as a waste of money," I said, my fury over this unwarranted intrusion on our island growing by the moment.

"The same holds true for the French navy," Jacob observed with a nod.

"But not the British, which is one of the reasons they rule the seas," one of my companions put in. A few of the men had come with us and were studying the sailors too.

"So you don't think they are here because of us?" asked someone from behind me.

"Note the closed gun ports." Although I wasn't paying enough attention to note who said it, I was proud of my men for their deductive capabilities under duress.

Jacob nodded. "Ah…that is so."

Then my stomach tensed with panic. A longboat was being lowered. I tasted the wind. There will be a storm in a few days, I thought absentmindedly, although the sky was as clear and blue as a robin's egg. We watched the longboat pull away from the warship and make for the beach. The lagoon where I had moored my ships was well back from the shore, but if they penetrated the swamp or went round the end of it….

I left the thought hanging, but a chill ran down my spine.

Then the longboat came over a saddle in the reef and the men jumped out and ran her up on the beach. Snatches of conversation were carried to us on the breeze.

"There be likely a stream somewhere's around here-un..."

"Mangroves...likely"

"Lookee forr fissures...like the Sand Witch Islands..."

"Or Krak ah toah island...there be fresh water here for sure..."

I felt my face hardening in the rosy afternoon light. "We will have to kill them."

Jacob looked at me full in the face. "Doesn't Our Lord teach mercy, Captain?"

"Aye, but we don't have that luxury, Number Two," I replied with finality. "Sparing them would mean sacrificing ourselves, and that I am not willing to do."

He said nothing and I added nothing. Our safety and security was paramount. Then the worst thing I could have imagined happened. The American tars waded through the mangrove swamp, calling loudly to each other. And then they found the Sea Phoenix, half consumed as we had made free use of her wooden hull. The Samsom was lying offshore submerged in twenty fathoms of water. A cloud of surprised cries and exclamations floated toward us on the warm island air, but a chill raced down my spine.

I watched intently as they scrambled over the disemboweled hulk, with a seed of icy fear growing within me. I turned to Jacob, "Assemble the men in the cavern."

It was well after sundown and the sea would have been black as India ink except for my light. I waded across the seafloor with the Ruhmkorph apparatus lighting my way. I strode on and on toward my objective.

"Let me come with you," Jacob had said.

And I had shaken my head. "No, it is too dangerous," I had replied. "If anything happens to me, you are in charge."

He shook his head. "I am not ready."

"No one in charge ever is."

"Who will guide us through the seas…?"

"You will. And Mister MacKay is completely familiar with the mechanical operation of the Nautilus."

Jacob had nodded his great head, and said, "God be with you, Captain."

And I replied, "God has nothing to do with what I am about to do."

It seemed like a lifetime as I made my way toward the Yankee warship. I had noted her position and was very certain of finding her where I expected her to be.

Sure enough, the long dark bulk of her hull loomed ahead. Without too much difficulty, I found the anchor cable and clasped my gloved hands around it and hauled myself up. When I broke the surface I discovered that I was a good sixty feet from the hull. The dynamite in its wooden case was hanging round my waist from a cloth belt. Here was the tricky part. I reached down and released the metal buckle holding the lead weights around my belt. To be sure, my lead-soled boots still kept me orientated feet downwards in the water but the helmet filled with air would not permit me to sink.

I let go of the anchor cable and used my arms to propel me toward the hull.

Something struck my helmet with a loud clang and my heart

leaped into my throat. Someone, perhaps a vigilant sailor on watch, had seen me and taken a shot with his musket at the strange brass orb moving across the water toward his ship. Another sharp clang on my helmet and my whole frame tensed in the diving suit. I swung my arms forward, my scissoring legs dangling below me.

Bang..!

Bang..! Bang..!

Someone was shooting at me. I propelled myself through the blackness, my breathing labored, then bumped against the hull. I unhooked the box from my belt, took up a hammer from the same belt and pounded the heavy nail already attached to a metal flange on the box through the thin copper plates of the hull.

Another bullet hit my helmet with a loud clang. Then I turned the knob on the box, one two three six.....thirteen clicks, and grabbed the tether then hauled myself down to the lead weights lying on the bottom. With no small amount of difficulty, exacerbated by anxiousness over the outcome of this endeavor, I pulled the weights from the seafloor and fastened them to my waist then set off for my island home.

I strode across the seafloor—it was sandy in most places but then I found myself walking across vast fields of crustaceans, and heard and felt through my suit the crunching of exoskeletons beneath my feet. On and on I strode, wading through the water with much difficulty, a bright oblong of greenish illumination before me.

I could hear my heart pounding in my ears, and my breathing was labored like an asthmatic vacationing in the Swiss Alps. I could not move fast enough, try as I might; the water impeded rapid movement. My breath came in short gasps, as I planted each foot down on the seabed firmly so as not to slip. Suddenly, I heard a dull roar somewhere behind me. A shockwave slammed into my back hurling me forward. I landed on my belly arms and legs akimbo. The lighting apparatus winked out. I waited a moment, gathering my strength. Slowly, so slowly, I got up on all fours then stood up. All around me was impenetrable blackness and the water was much agitated.

Not only was my heart thundering in my chest, but tears were starting in the corners of my eyes. The bald faced truth is that I was scared nearly out of my senses, as I turned around and tried to peer through the murky water. Nay, not murky but black as the Devil's blood—and me with no idea of what was north or south. I was as fucked as a bitch in heat in a dog pound. What direction should I go? There was no moon to light my way, and repeated thumbing of the button controlling the light failed to turn it on.

I fought a rising tide of panic.

Yes, yes I know that fool, the so-called professor Pierre Arronax, waxed poetic in his scurrilous memoir about my ability to remain underwater for hours on end and even take a nap (I really ought to have drowned his sorry ass like a plague-ridden rat)—but may I tell you that that was pure bilge water? We were limited as to the depth and the length of time we could safely dive. I had at best, according to my reckoning, two hours of air remaining in my tank. And there was no way of telling which direction I should go.

I drew a long calming breath, as I had learned from Father Blondeau. The worst that could happen was that I would suffocate on the seafloor, not that I regarded this as a small thing mind you; it was the acceptance of this worst case scenario that liberated me.

My nerves steadied, I peered through my thick glass view port at the swirling back waters before me. There was another loud explosion to my right. Ah, the ship's magazine must have blown. Now I thought I knew which direction to go and I set off for the island with a hopeful heart.

Note:
This explains the disappearance of the USS Dakota, a Mohican class sloop of war that vanished somewhere in the South Pacific in late December eighteen sixty four. It was assumed until now that she had either fallen prey to a typhoon or had suffered a mishap such as fire or an exploding magazine, or been sunk by a Confederate warship.

I scrambled over the reef then dropped down into the lagoon which was a good thirty feet deep. Gradually the seabed rose and I was soon wading ashore in long sluggish strides, as I was much wearied from my exertions. I emerged from the surf then sank to my knees on the beach, reached up and unfastened the helmet's neck clamp and drew a deep breath. It was night and there was a light breeze coming in from the sea bearing the acrid scent of gunpowder and burnt timber. The volcanic sand was even blacker at night and I heard the breaking roar of the sea coming over the reef. I turned and looked over my shoulder at the white line of breakers. Beyond the reefs, there was nothing left of the warship but a few burning timbers. I had placed the charge about where I thought her powder magazine to be, and my educated guess had been correct. It was hot and muggy and the rubber dive suit made it worse so I removed it, and wearing only my underwear, headed back to the cavern.

(Lacuna begins)
Note: Text water damaged for half a page.
(Lacuna ends)

"I'll see that you all swing from a yardarm!" said a lieutenant, "if someone doesn't start talking." He had my men lined up. His detachment of marines, ten of them, stood with their rifles trained on my comrades. The lieutenant was tall and thin and he had a sandy colored mustache and mutton chop sideburns and held his head very high.

I had come into the cavern through a small lava vent whose entrance was about halfway up the mountain concealed behind bushes. It descended at an angle to a ledge in the cavern. I crouched behind a rocky outcropping watching the scene below. Even from where I was, it was easy to see that the Americans were itching to start shooting.

"By what right are you detaining us?" Jacob asked.

The officer, a youth in his early twenties, drew himself up. "I am the senior American officer here now that you scum have somehow managed to destroy our ship." He pointed to the Nautilus, even though she was only half completed she dominated the cavern with her bulk, and demanded, "For what purpose are you building that ship?"

My comrades stiffened but not a one broke his silence.

"There is something going on here and I want to know what it is."

"Sir! Over here!" A marine was standing at the draughstman table where I kept the Nautilus drawings. The lieutenant turned to a sergeant and said, "If any of these bastards tries to make a run for it, shoot him down like a dog."

"With pleasure, Sir," he replied, his voice hard.

The lieutenant strode over to the table and looked down at the drawings, and his mouth gaped open in astonishment. "Good Lord, this is an undersea ship!"

CHAPTER 9

Egress

"They that go down to the sea in
ships;
That do business in great waters;
These see the works of the Lord,
And His wonders in the deep…."

"Whatever we are doing here is no concern of yours," Jacob said forthrightly. "Your civil war has nothing to do with us. We are not American subjects, and not subject to your laws."

The naval officer whirled around. "Citizens!" he spat out. "Americans are *citizens*, not goddamned subjects to some stinking queen or pox ridden emperor! Being a Frenchy you should know that. And the war of secession has been over for months, you fool. And as for this," he made a wide all encompassing gesture, "this must be some nefarious enterprise or why go through such effort to conceal it? Who is your commander? Why did you blow up our ship? Answer me, goddamn your eyes!"

Jacob clammed up tighter than a wife with a guilty conscious.

"I say we kill them and be done with it, Sir," said the sergeant of marines.

"Not before I get to the bottom of this, Sergeant!"

I had heard enough. These swine would know my wrath, the wrath of a man whose home has been unjustly invaded, and by God they would suffer for their insolence. When their ship went up, I was not at all sorry that it was by my hand. They were the spear point of civilization pointed right at our hearts, here in our own home. Everything we had worked for had been jeopardized by their coming here. Sometimes when everything is at stake, one has to risk everything to win through a difficult situation – and my comrades and I had already lost everything once. We would not do so again.

A narrow ledge, a foot or two wide at most, snaked down from my perch to the cavern floor. Sidestepping, with my back pressed against the rocky wall, I painstakingly inched my way down this treacherous path, my eyes darting between my carefully chosen steps and the intruders below. The ledge ended where wooden packing crates were stacked beside the two steam tractors – a perfect place from which to begin my attack.

As I inched my way toward my objective, several of my comrades cast surreptitious looks in my direction, but all were wise enough to ignore my approach and keep their eyes trained away from me. The lieutenant was still ranting at *my comrades*, his voice echoing in the cavern like a vengeful god pronouncing judgment, a vein on his forehead swelling into a purple snake.

"You goddamned swine are up to no good, and you have sunk a warship of The United States of America!" With each impudent word he spat out, my rage grew hotter and hotter inside of me, a fire stoked into an inferno. I vowed that this would be the last time that someone who thought himself in authority imposed himself upon us. This was our island and no one had rights here save us.

One of my men, a well-born French gentleman named Alain said, "How could we have done as you accuse us when we were here? You are mistaken, Lieutenant."

"Liar!" the lieutenant's voice rose to a shriek. He took half a dozen quick steps to the Frenchman and backhanded him. "You are all liars and pirates and scum. Tell me what is the purpose of this monstrous vessel? Ships of our valorous navy were sunk by infernal submarine boats. Only pirates and criminals would ever deploy such a vessel!"

Alain wiped the blood trickling from his mouth and clenched his fists.

Hold yourself in check, man, I thought.

Not yet…not yet….

Choosing wise action over a more satisfying one, Alain un-clenched his fists and held his tongue.

I was now at the cavern floor.

The lieutenant pulled his Navy Colt revolver and pointed it at Jacob's broad forehead. "By God man, tell me your purpose here or I shall shoot you dead!"

An aero rifle, its reservoir filled just that day, lay on the work bench where I had left it. Unlike muskets or muzzle loading rifles, it would fire a dozen times without needing to be reloaded and was silent, both of which I would use to my advantage. From my hiding place I had a clear view of the lieutenant and his marines. I thumbed the safety off near the butt stock, raised it, breathed out, and slid the trigger back on the exhale. There was a quiet phfsst sound as the glass ampoule streaked through the air.

The lieutenant contorted then collapsed like a rag doll, electricity crackling from his head to his feet. His men looked around, startled and uncertain.

I missed the second shot, but my third round caught the sergeant in the forehead when he spun around. He went down too, twitching as if struck by lightning. Instinct rather than military training, which I lacked in any case unless one counted my casual perusal of *Caesar's Commentaries,* induced me to move away from my hiding place. Scarcely had I vacated that position when a hail of bullets ripped into the packing cases, splinters flying everywhere. Ah, the Americans were using some type of repeating rifle.

Never had I felt so naked, the feeling compounded by being clad only in my underwear, as I hurtled across an open space to another stack of crates. The Americans were coming toward me, firing as they came, working a lever-like device on the bottom of their rifles. My comrades had scattered and were taking cover.

I heard a man scream bloodily. Looking toward the sound, I saw that Jacob had buried a big fisherman's knife into a marine's chest and was now using the dead man's rifle to shoot at our foes. The intruders scurried for cover.

A yelled, "Watch out Captain!" caused me to hurl myself aside. Thomas, one of my younger recruits, had dove at a marine who had his gun trained on me, and was grappling with him. Thanks to the worthy Thomas' heroics, the marine's shot missed my head by inches, smacking into the stone wall beside me. I couldn't fire for fear of hitting Thomas and, when more shots hit the stone beside me, I was forced to dive for cover. That second's delay cost Thomas dearly, for when I turned back to help him, I saw him lying facedown on the cavern floor, his killer now taking aim at me again. Blind rage took over and I propelled myself toward him so fast I don't even know if my feet touched the floor. The next thing I knew, my rifle was on the floor, and my hands were around the soldier's neck wringing the life out of this sorry excuse for a man with my bare hands.

His last breath had barely been drawn when I snatched up my rifle and surged into the cavern firing. Jacob was standing his ground, shooting point blank at the marines. The rest of our comrades charged with knives and cutlasses they had retrieved from our barracks. The aero rifle in my hand was all too soon empty, so I wielded it as a club by the barrel, smashing a man's startled face with its steel butt stock.

The American's rifles were empty as well, and my comrades fell upon them and engaged in hand to hand combat. Knives rose and fell. The cavern echoed with screams and oaths and the syncopated panting breaths of men locked in a desperate struggle for their very lives. And this is the moment when my men surprised and delighted me with the shear gluttonous, bloody glee with which they dispatched the intruders.

In awed silence I watched as they caught and slew every one of the invaders. Not a single man hesitated or showed any remorse or faintness of heart in this bloody task.

Two of the invaders nearly escaped and I was preparing to run after them, but it proved unnecessary. They were chased down as they attempted to flee this den of death, but they were no match for my enraged comrades and soon lay dead on the ground.

An echoing silence filled the cavern, as the men gathered around me, panting from their violent exertions, their clothes and faces blood spattered like Spartan hoplites after a battle. They raised their dripping knives and clubs high in the air and let out a cry– the cry of the savage triumphant over the tyrant. It was only then I understood that these were not just monks but warrior clerics who had guarded Father Blondeau as he went on his secret missions for Napoleon Bonaparte.

Jacob said, as if reading my thoughts, "We're holy men, but we're not saints."

I grinned savagely and clapped a hand on his broad shoulder. "Aye, and damned good fighters too." How could I possibly fail with such men as my comrades?

(Lacuna begins)
Note: Several pages are missing at this point, and it is impossible to say how many.
(Lacuna ends)

I stood in the Nautilus' salon guiding the large thick glass view port as it was lowered by the crane. "Move it two inches to the left!" I cried to Michael as he worked the crane's controls. The two big plate glass panels for the salon had been manufactured by the Corning Glass Company of New York. They were nine inches thick and completely devoid of bubbles and other imperfections. The same company had manufactured the portholes for the steersman cage, the glass shades for the various lighting fixtures, and the lens for the Nautilus' main navigation light. A series of drilled holes marched around all four sides of the glass plate. Michael pushed a lever and the crane head inched to the left.

I held up my hands then turned my thumbs down. With a growl the cable coming from the crane lengthened and the glass panel came down slowly, slidding smoothly into its bronze frame. I used a spanner to fasten it in place, tightening all the bolts.

The hull was almost complete. Only the top deck with its wheelhouse and lighthouse needed to be put in place. That would come last, after her engine was installed and the propeller fitted to its shaft. Behind me the starboard glass view port was bolted in place. The salon's iron walls were sheathed in rich oak paneling, as was the library in the next compartment with oak shelves rising from floor to ceiling, and thin brass chains running along each shelf to hold the volumes in place during rough seas. Gilded arabesque patterns of scrollwork and moldings on the wood paneling gave the salon and the library a regal look, as the décor of both of the compartments were in the tradition of Louis the Fourteenth, fashionable in continental Europe's finest palaces and hotels.

Inside the big ship I felt tiny. Overhead were steel and copper pipes; a network of them ran like a spider's web of arteries and veins throughout the ship. Some were for water, others for the electrical wiring that went to various devices including light fixtures; other special copper conduits terminated at the steel hull plates. The salon's ornate ceiling would conceal this maze of piping and half globe glass fixtures on the ceiling would house electric lights, for no oil lamps would be required on this thoroughly modern vessel.

I straightened, then looked around with a deep sense of love throbbing in my heart for this amazing vessel. The Nautilus was an evolution of hundreds of years of shipbuilding; the perfect ship in all aspects. All my experience of designing and building iron vessels, gained as Chief Naval Architect for **Her Majesty**, accrued over twenty years, was now crowned by this supreme achievement of naval engineering.

Frame by frame I had fashioned her, from stem to stern and plate by plate. Before my admiring gaze, she took on the majestic flowing lines that would allow her to slip through the water with unheard of ease. I watched her grow with the affection of a parent for a child prodigy, for this was my ship, my vision and my dream. Yes, I was building her for the good of our little band of brothers—but no one had put as much of himself into her as I had. I knew where every rivet was located; each steel plate's position on the hull was as fixed firmly in my mind's eye as the stars in the Heavens.

My Nautilus boasted amenities unheard of in even the most luxurious passenger ships: hot and cold water on demand, two flushing toilets, two showers, a galley with an electric oven of my design, and water distillation equipment so that we would never want for clean fresh water, and even cold storage for perishable food. Now, to be sure, some British navy ships and passenger ships had water distillation equipment, but none as efficient as mine. The Nautilus was my supreme achievement, and I had no doubt that when she was in the water she would do all I expected of her.

Mr. MacKay came into the salon and touched the brim of his black officer's cap emblazoned with a gold letter N. "Aye, she is looking more and more like a right proper ship, Captain Nemo," he said with a grin. "The last of the pumps was just installed."

"Thank you, Mr. MacKay." I liked the Scotsman. If Jacob was my right hand then Mr. MacKay was my left, and I therefore counted myself ambidextrous. "Tomorrow we shall install her engine and mechanical force transmitting device."

"I got them all nicely trussed up and ready to go," MacKay replied crisply.

Two men came into the salon carrying a fountain, a large bronze seashell with a bronze statue of Poseidon standing in the center of it holding a phial in his well-formed arm—it was from this that the fountain of water would pour—and a triton in the other. The men set the fountain down on the standpipe rising from the floor.

MacKay stooped to bolt the fountain in place. "Aye, this is as bonny a ship as ever it was my good fortune to set eyes on, Captain. You must be very proud of her."

"We should all be proud of her," I replied truthfully. "Without all of us working together in complete harmony, it would not have been possible."

"Aye, but she came out of your head, Captain Nemo," MacKay said, "and had you not come along we would all still be rotting on Belial Island."

The next day chief engineer MacKay and I were in the Nautilus' engine room with four of our comrades. Thundering like Hephaistos' hammer and belching clouds of smoke, the steam crane lifted the engine and its mechanical force transmitting device from the concrete floor then slowly swung it toward the Nautilus' gaping stern section. Four long hemp ropes dangled from the engine.

When the engine was directly above us the four men grabbed the ropes and waited for my command. I made a downward rolling motion with my upraised hands and the crane's steel cable slowly unspooled and the engine inched downwards. Then I thrust up my hands in a palm upwards motion, the non-verbal command to stop—it was pointless trying to be heard over a steam crane.

The engine hovered in the air just above our heads. I nodded to Mr. MacKay and he hastened forward to check that it was lined up properly with the mounting plates. He had two long iron dowels that were the same dimension as the threaded holes in the deck's steel plates and the engine's mounting holes. He stuck the dowels in the holes then looked up at the engine mounting holes. "They are off by three inches to the left, Captain," he yelled over the crane's noise.

I nodded then gestured to the men on my left to haul on their cables.

"That should do it," MacKay called out in his Scot's burr.

At my signal the crane lowered the engine and the iron dowels passed through the engine mounting holes. The engine crept down toward the steel deck then came to rest with a dull heavy clang, then we bolted it into place. The shaft that would transmit the engine's power to the propellers was already in place and it required only a small effort to bolt the propeller's shaft flange to the engine.

Or so I thought.

Bad language was coming from Mr. MacKay and the monks trying to get the propeller shaft flange to line up with the *mechanical force transmission device's* flange. I went over and said, "You need to pull this lever here to put it in a neutral gear than the flange will spin freely." I did so and, after a few minutes, there were grunts of satisfaction. The flange coming from the engine assembly spun freely. With the heavy bronze propeller mounted to the drive shaft there was no question of trying to move it.

Mr. MacKay's face was red to the hairline. "I dinna see how simple the fix was, and now I feel a complete dobber."

"You are hardly a fool, Mr. MacKay," I replied. "This mechanical device is, of course, unfamiliar to you since it is an entirely new invention."

I moved on and went about the engine room checking that everything was in order. Krupp's had indeed done a magnificent job of manufacturing this complicated machinery, faithfully adhering to my blueprints and specifications. I had not taken their quality of workmanship and adherence to my engineering drawings and formulas as an article of faith; I had disassembled the motor checking each part against my drawings, taking careful measurements of the parts. The engine rested in place, a concretion of brass and copper and steel.

My mechanical design was, like the vessel it would drive, an evolutionary step far and above what had gone before. An electric motor transforms electric energy into mechanical energy—in this case, the turning of a ship's propeller shaft. It accomplishes this amazing feat through the intercourse of magnetic fields and conductors that convey electrical current. My countryman Sir Michael Faraday had demonstrated the feasibility of this concept in the year (the exact date eludes me right now) eighteen hundred and twenty one or therabouts. William Sturgeon had refined this concept further and introduced a motor with commercial possibilities. Where the Nautilus electric motor differed was in the copper windings of the direct current armature, which were greater in bulk than any-thing that had come before—the copper wire if unspooled would have stretched twelve miles. The armature when connected to a source of electricity would spin at many thousands of revolutions per minute between two massive magnets.

Now mark this: even the most efficient screw propeller if ro-tated too rapidly will produce an effect called cavitation in which a sheath of air bubbles are created around the propeller blades causing them to lose the ability to propel the vessel through the water. Hence, the need for a *mechanical force transmitting device*, controlled by a series of levers that would use a system of gears of varying ratios to transmit and regulate the mechanical force emanating from the electric motor to the propeller, which was configured with blades whose pitch could be adjusted from within the engine room.

Ideally I would have been able to control the engine's func-tions directly from the bridge—but the complexity of that engi-neering problem exceeded even my considerable talents. Alas, the electric motor's controls would, like conventional steamships, have to be worked from the engine room. To be sure I would be able to send commands to the engine room via the ship's telegraph I had purchased from Hart Brothers of New York, and they had done a fine job. The *engine order* telegraph we received from them was polished brass with a nine inch round black dial emblazoned with command terms spelled out in bold Gothic white letters. It was connected to a companion receiver in the engine room.

I would enjoy yet still another advantage over other ship cap-tains. I could converse with my crew in different parts of the ship without resorting to the highly inefficient speaking tubes then used by surface ships. While in Europe procuring the components for my undersea vessel, I had become aware of the work of the celebrated polymath Innocenzo Manzetti. This urbane Italian gentleman had invented a speaking telegraph but had so far had little luck obtaining investors. Over espresso and biscotti at the Café Di Cesare in Rome he had told me about his wonderful invention. I at once saw a ready application for it on my vessel. For the tidy sum of five hundred pounds sterling, I had him construct half a dozen devices that would be situated at critical points around my undersea ship, connected by twin pairs of insulated copper wires. The three main areas of communication would be between the bridge, the engine room, and my humble quarters. This remarkable device consisted of an alerting device in the form of an electric brass bell, a transmitting micro-phonic device into which one spoke, and an electro-acoustic receiving device—cone shaped with a round magnet at the end—that would convert an electric signal into human speech.

(Lacuna begins)
Note: three pages hopelessly
water damaged.
(Lacuna ends)

The morning of the launch the sea outside our subterranean cavern raged and pummeled the island with fists of wind. Through the lava vent we could hear the ocean's roar and the shriek of the wind. Even the water in our subterranean lagoon was a bit restive. I stood at the mouth of the lava vent listening to the storm. It was mid morning and the storm had been blowing since the previous afternoon. Jacob and MacKay hastened toward me.

"Captain Nemo, Sir!" Jacob said, "We are ready."

MacKay added, "Your bonny ship is waiting to be brought forth, and I am certain there will nae be a lot o' birth pains."

"Then, Gentlemen, let us not keep her waiting!" I turned and strode back into the cavern, with my comrades following, our steps ringing on the tunnel's lava rock floor.

Everyone came to attention when I strode into the cavern. My comrades were clad in black uniforms, their flat caps sporting the name Nautilus in gold letters; and if they were officers like Jacob or Mr. MacKay, a bill cap emblazoned with a gold letter N.

"As you were, Gentlemen," I said. "This is a ship christening, not a funeral."

The Nautilus rested on the slipway, her steel hull gleaming. Even I was awed by her beauty. With her stubby steel spur and spindle shaped hull she looked more like a sea monster than a ship. Her square steersman cage with its inclined sides and four large portholes was set on the boat deck so that two of the viewports faced forward and two faced aft. We had greased the slipway in preparation of the launch, and just in case, mindful of the mishap with the HMS Warrior's problematic journey down her slipway, I had seen that the two steam tractors were fired up and ready to assist should the need arise. Electric arc lights blazed overhead. The dull roar of the sea rolled down the lava vent and filled the cavern. I felt a thrill ripple through my chest.

The Nautilus loomed over us, filling the cavern with her imposing presence. I could not suppress a dark smile, as I climbed slowly up the wooden steps to the tall makeshift podium near the bow. "Comrades," I began, "today, after many struggles and sacrifices, we enter happily into a life where tyrants can not follow, where the whim of the oppressor holds no sway over us. It is quite unnecessary to review what everyone here agrees on. Kings, Queens, and governments are to the physical world what monsters are in the dream world. The so-called law courts, held to be the home of impartial justice, are factories of crimes against the helpless individual, and the lair of petty be-robed and be-wigged tyrants with power of life and death over those before them. And the lawyers and bailiffs are naught but the ready accomplices in this odious joke against the fool who believes himself protected by laws. All here have seen firsthand what blood-stained civilization has to offer, and what it has taken. Many of us bear still the bitter stripes on our back of the lash, and the even deeper scars on our souls; have seen our families and our property wrested from us by cruel hands, and our liberty stolen. No more, I tell you, no more...." Every eye was locked on me as I spoke. "We go now to face a brave world unspoiled by the destructive hand of men, and we will rely on no man save ourselves." At this, a cheer rose from my comrades, but quickly died away as I continued, my voice rising. "To be sure, there will be dangers to be faced, obstacles to overcome, but I promise you this: We will never again face imprisonment or be forced to bow down to some god-rotting king, queen, or tyrant. The leviathans of the sea will be our companions, but never again will tyranny cast its black shadow over our souls. We may run afoul of our own short-comings but we will face them squarely and exorcise them boldly, and never again, my comrades, will we face the ignominy of involuntary servitude or oppression. The sea does not belong to despots. Upon its surface men may still exercise unjust laws, fight, tear one another to pieces like beasts, and be carried away with their terrestrial horrors. But just thirty feet beneath the waves, their reign ceases, their influence is quenched, and their power vanishes. There, we shall recognize no masters. There, we shall be free!" At this last yelled sentence, the men cheered again, but I quieted them quickly as I lowered my voice. "And I say this in conclusion: Any country that attempts to injure or impose itself upon even one of us will face the righteous wrath of all of us. We have, by the building of this undersea vessel, seized our precious Liberty in our hands, and woe to the despot who attempts to rip it from our grasp—for we will rise from the deeps like the Kraken in her terrible form and our vengeance will be terrible to behold." I paused then to quell the rising tide of anger taking hold of me as I spoke. "Join me now, my comrades, in casting off the shackles of so-called society—and enter into this new world beneath the seas, a world of just laws and peace and harmony. Let us claim our vessel, The Nautilus, as our home, for we are no longer citizens of a nation, or subject to its hypocritical laws. We are henceforth citizens of the seas and oceans."

There then rose from my men such a cheer as even now, writing about this glorious day many years later, makes my flesh prickle with excitement.

Jacob hauled himself up the steps and handed me a fine bottle of French wine. "Behold, I give you the Nautilus!" I cried, swinging the bottle against the lower bow plate just above the great keel. The bottle broke and wine red as blood spread all over the bow. Harrison Randolph Barrington's face flashed in my mind's eye. *A storm is coming for you Harrison, my storm, and soon it will be your blood I see on my ship's spur.*

Mr. MacKay and several men rushed forward with sledge hammers and knocked the blocks out of place on the slipway, and the long lean steel hull slid stern first into the water with a great splash. She would have kept going and smacked into the far side of the lagoon had not the great thick hemp cables and blocks done their job and arrested her movement. We used steam winches to haul her back to the dock.

```
(Lacuna begins)
Note: this may be an intentional
omission, as there is evidence
that two pages were carefully cut
out of the diary. We can only
surmise what wonders the missing
pages contained.
(Lacuna ends)
```

I stood before a tall iron pedestal in the engine room just in front of the electric motor. On top of the pedestal was a shiny brass container, an icosidodecahedron, a polyhedron shape with twenty triangular faces and twelve pentagonal faces. It's inside surface was coated with highly reflective mirrors on the twenty triangular faces, and magnets on the pentagonal faces. A medusa head of copper tubing was connected to this device. I was holding the *Atlantium* in its casket tucked under my arm.

I nodded to Jacob and he unlocked a panel at the top of the oddly shaped container, which I called the reactor grail, an appropriate name as what it would contain was the holy grail of limitless energy. The piece I had, small as it was, held enough power within it to vaporize an entire city if misused. For this reason, I will never write or reveal how I came to have it.

My eyes flicked to Mr. MacKay standing before the engine's shiny new control panel with its series of levers. "Is she in the neutral gear, Mr. Mackay?"

"Aye, Captain. She is in the neutral gear," he carefully repeated.

"Are the primary intake valves closed, Number Two." Jacob strode over to one side of the hull and checked a large valve in a red box-like device from which a steel pipe ran to the container on the pedestal. An identical one ran from the other side of the hull.

"Check the secondary intake valves, if you please, Number Two." He checked the valves on the same two steel pipes closest to the reactor grail.

His gaze never wavered. "They are closed, Captain."

I flipped open the casket's lid. A bright silvery light bathed the engine room. I removed the precious object, a perfect sphere of crystal throbbing with silvery light, as it had done for over thirty years. Ever so gently I lowered it into the reactor grail. Acted upon by the magnets, it floated in mid air and would have flown out of the reactor had I not held it down. I closed the reactor top and latched and locked it with a padlock. A small glass window in one of the pentagonal shapes gave off a soft green light.

There is nothing, nothing in the world, more frightening than attempting to put into practice what one has only worked out on paper—or on a small scale. As an engineer I was positive my calculations were correct. As a man standing in the engine room of an immense steel ship with an object the size of a golf ball in an unusual metal container that must provide unlimited electricity, I was bedeviled suddenly with doubts. What if I had been on a fool's errand all these years? I thrust the disquieting thoughts from my mind.

I said to Jacob, "Open the primary valves, Number Two." He went over to both sides of the hull and opened the valves. I heard the reassuring gurgle of sea water flowing through the steel pipes. "Open the secondary valves, Number Two."

"Opening the secondary valves," Jacob intoned, twisting the small valves on either side of the reactor grail. The reactor grail gave off a low vibrato hum and the pentagonal window glowed bright green. The copper pipes snaking from the reactor grail began to thrum rhythmically. I hastened over to the master control panel and threw a lever. The darkened engine room was suddenly flooded with light from above. I glanced up at the ceiling. The lights in their half-globe glass fixtures were working properly.

With a slightly trembling hand, I threw the switch that would activate the big electric motor. A steam engine when it first begins to run, once the minimum operating temperature of the water in her boilers is achieved, will start out slowly—the great walking beam moving methodically faster and faster as the water temperature rises. My electric motor emitted a high whine as its armature spun between the massive magnets.

I thought my chest would burst with pride. My ship, my love, was alive. I closed my eyes briefly, and I could feel her pulse, hear her heartbeat.

I opened my eyes then.

Mr. MacKay and Jacob were grinning like madmen.

"You did it, Captain Nemo! Look at that beauty go!" Mr. MacKay cried. Within its brass and steel housing, easily the height of a tall man, the armature was a blur, as we could see through a narrow glass view port. Fins rose from the housing and were bolted to the hull to dissipate heat in the seawater, an elegant solution, even if I say so myself.

"What's next?" Jacob was too stunned to say more.

I consulted a dial on the master control panel. "Gentleman, the Nautilus' electric engine is operating at five thousand revolutions per minute!"

I could scarcely keep the excitement from my voice.

"And no warm up time?" Jacob said, shaking his great bearded head.

"None is necessary with the dynamic force of electricity," I replied, proudly. Then I threw another switch and another set of copper pipes emanating from the reactor grail—these terminating at different parts of the hull – began to vibrate. The steel plates of the Nautilus's hull began to emit a high piping noise, like bell jars being played.

Mr. MacKay's head was swiveling around. "God's blood, what is happening?"

"Calm down, Sir, that is only the steel plates fusing. It is that that will allow us to achieve depths unobtainable with even the strongest of steel." The sweet bell-like tones tailed off into silence. "Ah, that took less time than I thought."

"It be the Devil's own magic," Mr. MacKay breathed.

I laughed outright then at such superstition from a somewhat educated fellow. "Have you gone soft-headed on me, man?" I asked baldly. "Listen. To the Red Indian, a locomotive is magic, as is the telegraph. This is but science of a type known only to me." *But it wasn't always so*, I thought, *but proving that thesis will take time.*

I looked around with an expansive sigh. The engine was running smoothly and so quietly that one could talk without shouting, something unheard of in conventional ships.

"How long will she go without refueling?" Jacob asked.

I gave a careless shrug. "How long will the sun shine?"

"Where did you get that…that….?'

I raised an eyebrow. "It's called Atlantium, Mr. MacKay, and I could tell you where it came from but then I would be forced, regretfully, to slay you." Then I smiled at him to show that I was only joking—about the killing part—and said, "As far as you are concerned, my friend, it came from out of the air from a world yet to come—or perhaps one that has already come and gone. I have always suspected that our concept of time is not nearly as linear as we think, but that is a conversation for dinner sometime."

My Chief Engineer looked apologetic. "It be better then if'n I doan know."

"Or even necessary," Jacob chimed in helpfully.

There was one thing left to do, and that was to fill the Nautilus' vast air reservoirs. I turned half a dozen knobs on the master control panel. At once there came the loud shrill whine of the centrifugal pumps working as they sucked in great amounts of air.

I gestured Mr. MacKay over and pointed to nine dials. "When the needles reach the end of the green zones, shut off the air pumps."

"Aye, Captain."

"Also, detail six men you think suitable to work under you, and divide them into two watches."

"But in the navy…" Mackay began.

"We are not in the navy, Sir. And the Nautilus will face far less perils than a surface ship. Two watches will suffice, unless I determine otherwise later."

By January third, eighteen hundred and sixty five, we were ready to get underway. My crewmates streamed across the gangplank carrying crates of supplies. The air guns and the diving suits were already onboard. The Nautilus sank lower in the water as supplies were loaded into her through the large main hatch on the boat deck.

I was supervising the loading of the steel launch in its special cavity on the deck. The launch was fully decked and watertight. A hatch in its side matched a similar hatch in the Nautilus's hull through which one could gain access by climbing up an iron ladder. The launch rose above the boat deck by about half a foot. To reduce drag I had placed it between two gently sloping steel bezels. A simple turn of docking bolts and the launch could be deployed from underwater. Then it would shoot to the surface, and we could either row or step a mast then hoist a simple lateen sail to get underway. I had devised a simple telegraph encased in India rubber connected with a thin insulated copper wire of ten cable lengths. When I wished to return to the Nautilus it would be a simple matter to send her a signal and she would rise to the surface to retrieve her launch. A retractable iron rail ran the length of the boat deck. It was in the closed position since we were about to get underway.

"Hurry up, Comrades!" I heard Jacob roaring through a bull horn. In the barracks some of the men were packing bags, others gathering boarding pikes and long-handled axes—not that I ever thought we would need them. All the same….

Then it was time to get underway. Every one was onboard. The steam tractors and crane were parked on the far side of the cavern. Jacob was with me on the boat deck, the outer hull plates slightly overlapping, which would give the ship when on the surface the appearance of big salt water crocodile from afar—this was not merely cosmetic though; the plates would lock even tighter together when subjected to pressure at great depths. And that was not laying aside the additional effects of the Atlantium on the hull.

"Is everyone onboard, Number Two?"

"Aye, Captain, and at his station."

I consulted my sterling silver Waltham pocket watch. It was three am in the morning. I did not want to risk a passing ship seeing the explosion that would blow open the side of the mountain and permit us to sail through—no, not sail, but *power* through.

"Come, Number Two. It is almost time." We hurried to the main hatch. I paused to peer over the side. Just as I had calculated, she was nine tenths submerged fully loaded.

I went down the metal corkscrew staircase quickly then hurried along the narrow companionway to another ladder which led to the steersman cage. The bridge was large enough for three men to perform their tasks without bumping into each other.

I picked up the speaking telegraph and turned the knob to the section that said Engine Room. I could hear the bell ringing in the metal handset.

"Engine room," I heard Mr. MacKay as clearly as if he were standing beside me.

"Are your men ready and at their stations?"

"Aye, Captain. We are all ready."

"Good. Stand by."

"Aye."

I hung up the speaking telegraph's handset. Michael was at the helm. Jacob stood at the ship's engine telegraph with a boulder-like hand on its handle.

"Comrade, I will take the helm," I said.

Michael moved away from the beautiful teak and brass ship's wheel.

My eyes flew to the electric clock on the wall. It was three twelve.

"Get ready," I called out.

At first it was a dull rumble. Then a roaring so loud that it penetrated our vessel's hull followed. A wall of water and earth rose before us. The Nautilus began to roll from side to side. A moment later there was another roar as the second set of explosives went off. Swirling clouds of dust obscured our view ahead.

Then I saw the gleam of water through a break in the swirling clouds.

"Ahead steady, dead slow!" I said, calmly.

"Ahead steady, dead slow!" Jacob gave the engine room telegraph a shove. I shot a quick glance over my shoulder. The big bronze screw propeller, three feet of which rose above the water, began to churn the water into a white froth.

I gave the wheel a turn to port and we headed toward the cavern's opening. A dense curtain of swirling dust had once again descended on the subterranean lagoon.

I stood on the bridge's steel deck with my legs planted wide apart trying to pierce the curtain of gloom as we headed toward the gap—or at least where I had last seen it.

Dark vertical streaks of varying widths appeared suddenly in the gloomy air.

Bang. Something slammed into the hull. I confess that I felt myself jump then.

Jacob cried, "The cavern is coming down on us!"

He was right. More boulders smacked into our hull with sledge hammer blows.

Bang...!

Bang...bang...!

I could not speak. My words were stuck somewhere just south of my Adams apple. I eased the wheel to port and she responded smoothly and precisely.

Bang...! Bang...!

Bang...!

I steered toward the gap's last known position with my pulse thundering in my ears, but I kept my face serene. A ship's captain cannot afford to display even the slightest trepidation before his crew or he will lose their respect as surely as the sun rises in the morning. And, once that respect is lost, he can never regain it. Coming from a family with a long naval tradition, a late father who had been a captain of a ship of the line, and a brother who had commanded a frigate, I was acutely conscious of this fact.

The hull resounded like a cathedral bell every time a rock hit. We pressed onwards and soon the swirling dust was replaced by the blackness of a tomb.

There was a slight grinding of steel against stone to starboard. I eased the wheel to the left.

Suddenly there was a grinding coming from below. It didn't require the well-tuned ear of a naval engineer to know what was happening. In a reflection of the starboard viewport, I saw Jacob and Michael exchanging worried glances.

Our speed began to decrease. "Increase to slow!" I cried.

"Increasing to slow." Jacob gave the engine room telegraph handle a sharp shove.

We pushed ahead with a grinding on our bottom, and my heart now in my mouth.

Then the grinding eased off and was gone and we gathered speed as the screw propellers bit deeply into good clean sea water, and then we were shooting into the lagoon. I gave the helm a sharp turn to port and we pivoted, no, it was more like the graceful pirouette of a well-trained ballerina, on our axis and I guided us toward the gap in the coral reef. Then a heartbeat or two later we were in the sea, and my heart lifted to the starry skies shining overhead.

CHAPTER 10

Mobilis In Mobili

"…Behold, thou art there.
If I take the wings of the morning, and
Dwell in the uttermost parts of
the sea;
Even there shall thy hand lead
me, and thy
Right hand shall hold me.
If I say, surely the darkness
shall cover me; even the night
Shall be light around me. Yea,
the darkness hideth not from
thee…

…or me…"

We were in open water powering along across a glass smooth sea when I saw the first blush of dawn on the horizon. I stared at it as if it was the first day of creation, and the thrumming deck plates beneath my feet the very motive force of creation itself. We were slicing through dark blue water that only lost its blueness when it broke into white froth on the gray steel brow of the fore hull.

"Well, what do you think, Gentlemen?"

"How fast are we going, Captain?" Jacob asked, staring out a viewport.

My gaze flicked down to the bank of dials on the console beneath the forward viewports at the knotometer's large black dial. "Twenty knots and holding steady."

"Sir, may I tell you that is….well…just amazing," Jacob said, shaking his head.

"Thank you, Number Two. Let's put her through her paces. Ahead half."

"Ahead Half," Jacob repeated as he moved the engine telegraph handle.

The Nautilus sped across the sea. My eyes flicked again to the knotometer.

Twenty five knots….!

My lips skimmed back from my teeth. She was already faster than anything afloat. My hands were rock steady on the helm. Michael's concentration was riveted to the console of gauges at the rear of the bridge monitoring the life support system, and the Nautilus' voltage levels. All the centrifugal pumps were working properly pushing air through a series of filters distributed throughout the ship to remove carbon dioxide from the atmosphere. We were sealed up in an airtight tube so this was of vital importance.

"There's an island ahead. Captain," Jacob announced.

"Where away, Number Two?"

"Two points to starboard."

I nodded. He was right. It was a very low lying island that would be difficult to spot even from the main deck of a sailing ship. We would have to use caution when powering through seas thick with islands and keys. I took us around the island for a look. There was a long white beach with three coconut palms and no gap through the reef.

We moved off from the island then were back in the open sea flying along, throwing up a rooster's tail of water behind us. I turned to Jacob. "Advise the engine room that we will be diving in five minutes. Bring us to dead slow."

I was staring ahead listening with only half an ear while Jacob relayed my message via the voice telegraph to Mr. Mackay. He shoved the handle on the engine telegraph and soon the trembling beneath my feet became almost imperceptible. We reduced speed to a slow crawl. "Comrade Michael, open valves four, five and six."

"Opening one, four, five, and six, Captain," Michael repeated.

I could hear the gurgle of seawater pouring into the main ballast tanks. The water rose around the upper hull as we sank and the sun climbed higher above the horizon. Then the water climbed up the glass viewports, and we found ourselves in a watery blue world with dazzling shafts of light spearing down all around us.

Endless schools of shimmering fish performed an intricate minuet seemingly for our benefit as we moved among them. We saw jelly fish swimming beside us, their large bell-like structures expanding and contracting. I eventually identified more than two hundred varieties of them! They are just astounding to watch in their natural habitat, and skillful predators, as my careful observation later found. I stared in wonder at my first look at the swarms of jelly fish. Some were the size of a lady's thimble and others larger than a man's head.

I consulted the dial of the manometer on the main console under the forward viewport and almost gave a war whoop like a Red Indian on a raid.

Two meters!

That was good but I wanted to take my undersea ship deeper. To my left, right across from the engine telegraph was another brass console with two large levers used to adjust the angle of the hydroplane's control surface. A device that looked like a brass ruler ran alongside each lever and indicated the angle the hydroplanes were set. Now, I never revealed this to that imbecile Pierre Arronax, and had he not been such an unobservant ass, he would have noticed, but at the stern of the Nautilus were another set of hydroplanes perpendicular to the rudder. The forward hydroplanes made it possible for us to dive, but it was the rear hydroplanes that, although much smaller, controlled the overall attitude of the ship as she was underway. Without the aft hydroplanes my beautiful ship would have been difficult to control under less than ideal conditions.

The first lever controlled the aft hydroplanes and the second one controlled the diving hydroplanes located just forward of amidships. On top of the console in low flat brass framed glass case were two glass tubes with spirit bubbles set perpendicular to each other. The one running parallel to the ship's long axis allowed me to see whether we were running on an even keel. The

other glass tube orientated port to starboard would advise me in
no uncertain terms as to whether we were listing or rolling from
side to side.

But my Nautilus would not be subject to severe rolling even
in the roughest seas since she had a very low center of gravity,
and as an added precaution I had provided her with bilge keels,
two long fin-like structures that ran either side of the length of
her lower hull, and three small antiroll tanks—internal tanks
with baffles on either side that would retard the movement of
water from the port side of the tank to the starboard side when
we were surfaced. This last device would prevent every captain's
nightmare and every naval engineer's shame, for it would coun-
teract the *free-surface* effect that could cause a ship to capsize.
Under ordinary circumstances, a ship rolling from her perpendicular axis, for instance in a heavy sea, will right itself—we
naval engineers refer to that as a *righting moment*—this happens
when the increased volume of water on the ship's lowered side
acts to push it upright. But if there has been a shift of cargo or
armament during the roll then the ship will go into a terminal
roll from which she cannot recover. We on the Nautilus had no
need to fear such a calamity, as I was relying on the three different strategies I mentioned above to maintain the Nautilus' sta-
bility.

And I was confident that they would work superbly.

Ah, but how to know what direction to steer for? Compensated compasses using a series of magnets had been in use for
the last twenty years with the advent of iron hulled ships, but
they were still unreliable in certain situations. I needed a way to
find my bearing under any circumstance, and since I might find
myself navigating between undersea mounts of volcanic and

hence highly magnetic rock, I came up with the perfect solution. Oh, to be sure, I had a conventional binnacle with a compensated compass right in front of the steering wheel, but it was the device spinning in a glass case on top of the forward control console I would most rely on—a directional gyroscopic compass.

It looked like a child's toy top but was a sophisticated navigational tool that would always point my way as clearly as if Poseidon himself was pointing his finger and saying, "Get thee hence…" The gyroscope had been invented by a talented German gentleman named Johann Bohnenberger in the year eighteen hundred and seventeen. A French mathematician, Professor Jean Leon Foucault working at the Ècole Polytechnique had refined the design to the extent that for nine minutes, it would indicate direction of geological north, the topmost axis around which our earth rotates. But it was I whom devised a further refinement that turned it from a mere curiosity in a university laboratory to a useful tool: a small electric motor operating at a constant speed to keep it spinning. As long as the motor turned, the gyroscopic compass worked, and I knew our true heading with a precision that would have been the envy of any mariner.

Outside our viewports, schools of silvery fish surrounded us. A grouper fish with a stout body and large mouth came up and inspected us as we slid through the deep. He moved off rapidly and I soon saw why. A swarm of white tip sharks in great numbers raced by as if in pursuit. Thousands of small fish awed us as they turned and flashed like burnished silver in the bluish light.

I smiled to myself. Here was an opportunity for a lifetime of study. I checked the dial connected to the manometer. We were still at two meters, and the water was clear and blue and clean. The only sound was the hiss of the water sliding around our spindle-shaped hull, and the ticking of the chronometers, one mechanical and two electric, on the bulkhead walls along with the gentle whirring of the gyroscopic compass.

"I wouldn't believe it if I were not seeing it with my own eyes," Michael said in hushed tones. "We are actually sailing underwater!"

"Not sailing, Comrade," I corrected him gently, "but driving beneath the Pacific Ocean under our own power. Now let us plumb the abyss to see what marvels of nature await us!" We were in a state of neutral buoyancy, a condition whereby the Nautilus' ballast tanks were filled, and the ship equaled the mass of the water it was displacing, obviating the force of gravity which would otherwise serve to cause it to sink. If I left the hydroplanes as they were we would neither sink nor rise to the surface.

"Comrade Michael," I called over my shoulder, "Would you kindly take the helm, Sir?" He came forward and I let the young man take the helm.

"With pleasure, Captain Nemo."

"Stay on the current heading."

"Aye, Captain. The helm is in hand. Course is steady as she goes."

I lay my hands on the two levers and gave them a slight push upwards, and the Nautilus descended at a slight angle. As we plunged deeper into the Pacific the sunlight began to fade. My eyes were on the manometer dial. We were now at sixty meters and dropping deeper by the moment. It was black outside our viewports. I turned around and went to the back of the bridge to the console Michael had been monitoring and turned a large knob. Suddenly we were enveloped in a pool of green light. I closed the black curtains over the rear view ports to keep the light from blinding us in the bridge.

Deeper and deeper we went, the Nautilus's screw beating the water steadily. My heart swelled with pride and I don't think I had ever known a happier time in my life.

Then the bow with its steel spur suddenly pitched downwards sharply.

"What's happening, Captain?" Jacob cried.

Michael was practically lying on the wheel, too frightened to utter a word.

I stared at the manometer dial in horror, my eyes wide. We were falling in an uncontrolled dive with our angle growing steeper by the moment.

The needle on the manometer kept climbing even as we were falling. I heard things crashing in the hull. The voice telegraph rang. Jacob answered it.

"Captain, its Mr. MacKay. He wants to know if we are in danger."

I stared wide-eyed at the depth gauge. One hundred meters… . One hundred and fifty…. Two hundred meters…. My mind was racing. Two hundred and fifty meters… What could have caused her to pitch forward so sharply? Three hundred me-ters….

"Captain…!" Jacob's voice was throbbing with rising panic.

"Tell him I said to stand by for my orders!" I whirled around and fought my way up the steeply slanting deck to the console at the rear of the bridge where the ship's various systems were monitored. My eyes flickered over the ballast tank gauges.

Of course! That's it. The forward trim tank was full. What a blind fool I had been. We fell deeper still with clouds of fish scrambling to get out of our path.

"Number Two," I called out in my clear tone, "engine to Astern Slow!"

I turned the knob that controlled the forward trim tank's pump. The great four-bladed screw propeller stopped, and began to churn the water in the opposite direction. I heard the great whooshing sound of the pump emptying the bow trim tank. We began to slow then crawl backwards with the bow rising steadily. I rushed over to the hydroplane levers and set them at neutral. The Nautilus leveled off.

"Thank, God!" Michael cried, "We are saved."

Jacob asked, "Are we out of danger, Captain?" I nodded. "It was a simple mistake. The forward trim tank, tank One, is only to be used when we are employing the spur against a foe and need to control the depth of the bow."

Michael whirled on us, his face aghast. "My God, I could have destroyed us!"

"Consider it a good learning experience," I replied, going up to him and patting him on the back. "Now that I think about it, you called out the names of the tanks you were filling. It was my job as commander to correct you, so let us all earn from this."

"How deep are we now?" Michael asked.

"Four hundred meters and running level," I replied.

      (Lacuna begins)
      Note: The next seven pages are
      hopelessly water damaged.
      (Lacuna ends)

I had just completed an enjoyable repast with my Number Two, Jacob, and a tableful of my companions in the dining room. It was furnished with a fine Louis the Fourteenth table, long and elegant, with legs carved in the likeness of nymphs and bolted to the deck to keep it from moving; elegant plush chairs marched around it. The side boards were equally recherché; and the lovely ewers and plates and utensils were all in hall-marked English silver (and therefore unbreakable) and gleamed in the bright light cast by the glass half globe set in the ornate ceiling.

The dining room's dark wood walls were covered with French tapestries and paintings I had purchased during my sojourn in Europe. I and my comrades would have access, not just to the wonders of the sea, but a library, and many fine rare paintings to enjoy when not on duty. I was meticulously dressed in my neatly cut black uniform, my beard trimmed; a heavy gold ring with an emerald sparkled on my ring finger. My men were all in their black uniforms, a color they much appreciated, being monks.

"Thank you for building us a chapel," said Brother Laurent.

I inclined my head. "Father Blondeau would have wanted me to." Adjacent to the crew quarters was a simple little chapel with an ornate altar, a wood cross with a gold statue of Jesus, and on a pedestal to one side, an antique statue of the Virgin Mary.

"Will you conduct Sunday services?" asked another monk, a man named Girard.

I shook my head emphatically, "It would not be appropriate."

"But you are the captain," Jacob said gently, "and by the law of the sea it is the job of the captain to conduct Sunday services for the crew."

I looked up then, conscious of my comrades' eyes on my face. I was conscious of something else, too: their desire to save my immortal soul. A soul I did not believe I possessed, any more than I believed in the God who was said to have created it. No God worth believing in could have created the world from which we fled. I was certain of this.

I turned to Jacob, "Why don't you conduct the Sunday services, Number Two?"

"I am not the captain," he replied stubbornly.

"Gentlemen, I will consider your request, and let you know when I have made my decision." But I had already made my decision. A captain can captain a ship alone but he cannot run it alone, and they had so far proved a loyal and able crew. Reading a few scriptures to them once a week seemed a small price to pay to keep them content. The conversation turned to other subjects and I fell silent and let their talk swirl around me.

I was brooding about my former best friend, the pox ridden Harrison Randolph Barrington, the villain who had first deprived me of my liberty, then my wife and children. He was much in my mind these days. Oh, how I pined to meet him on the open sea and slay him. The seed of a plan had taken root in my breast and blossomed into a plausible scheme. I believed it would accomplish two things at once. It would instill a deep fear of the sea in the hearts of men (no one would ever willingly attempt to venture beneath its surface after I was done), and it would bring him—who would quickly ascertain the truth— out to sea hunting for me.

I was counting on his arrogance—and the certain knowledge that he could not pass up an opportunity to seize the most advanced ship ever constructed. What a prize to tow home to **Her**

Majesty, and just think of all the endless honors and fetes it would win him. I was easy in my mind about **Her Majesty's** government not revealing the existence of my undersea boat to other nations. That would set off still another arms race they could ill-afford, even with their lucrative opium trade in China.

And there was something else: with the exception of my comrades, I had come to believe that most people were little better than vermin. And what was the best way to rid oneself of vermin? Drown them. I harbored an especially deep dislike of warships, and of how powerful nations used them to bully and ultimately overcome weaker nations. If I could throw a lever and make the whole human race cease to exist, I would not hesitate to do so. From the loftiest royal to the lowest waterfront hooligan, I loathed them all.

Thrusting my dark thoughts aside, I rapped the table top with my knuckles to get my fellow diner's attention. "Consider this," I said, holding a fine Venetian glass filled with an especially fine sherry. "No one has ever lived in such a place. We are one hundred meters beneath the sea with a storm raging overhead and we feel it not. Who knows how many ships above us are even now fighting for their lives."

"It pains me to think of the lives that might be lost this night," Michael said.

I gave a careless shrug. "I am done with caring about what happens up there."

MacKay hoisted his glass. "You did all you said you would."

"We did," I replied generously.

"Well, it was your excellent scheme that started the idea," Michael pointed out, "without you, we would still be slaving away on that hellish island."

I rose from the table. "Gentlemen, follow me, if you please." I lead them into the darkened salon and threw a small lever near the doorway. There was a hiss as steel panels opened on both sides of the room. The elegantly furnished salon with my beloved pipe organ at the far end was flooded with light. Everyone headed for the starboard viewport.

There was a chorus of startled gasps for a magical transformation had taken place.

I felt a stirring within my depths. The reef was so lovely, so pristine.

"Behold our realm, Gentleman," I said proudly, "a paradise that will never be lost or taken from us!" The men crowded around the big oblong view port. Outside was a lacy living wall of many colors. Swirling masses of small metallic blue fish filled the water. A silvery barracuda swam by. Most of my comrades had supported their monastery by working as fishermen so were not strangers to sea life. But they were seeing wonders no living man had ever beheld. Everyone in the room seemed to be holding their breath.

We were anchored just off the Great Barrier Reef.

I nodded toward the viewing port. "I estimate that there are as many as fifty different types of coral just within our view." It was true. Some looked like small terrestrial bushes or shrubs, but instead of being green, were red or orange or blue or yellow, while others looked like low, wide-spreading trees. "If you will direct your attention to the very bottom left of the view port, you will see what I will wager is the largest clam anyone of you has ever seen." A dozen faces were pressed against the glass.

The massive bivalve lay on a ledge on the reef, its shells parted slightly.

(Lacuna begins)
Note: four pages hopelessly
smudged.
(Lacuna ends)

It was a moonless night when we surfaced to recharge our air reservoir. We were in the Torres Strait, a body of water between Australia and New Guinea. It is a maze of reefs, islands and dangerous rocks, and not more than twenty meters deep. Jacob and I were on the boat deck. Number Two was taking our bearings with a sextant. We were riding against the current with our screw propeller beating the water just enough to keep us on station. There was a light west breeze blowing and the sea was flat and calm.

I looked around trying to pierce the dark. In the distance I could make out the low masses of small islands. The sky above us was covered with an icy rime of stars. It was as if some old Olympian God had reached into a black velvet bag and grabbed great handfuls of diamonds and gemstones of various colors and flung them across the heavens. The sea rippled with the faint reflections of these heavenly lights.

I could hear the pumps sucking great draughts of air into the reservoirs where it would be stored under pressure. I called out to Jacob. "I have noticed that the crew rarely come on deck when we surface to recharge our air reservoirs. Why is this, Number Two?"

His back was to me and I saw his large squat form give a shrug. "When we lived at the monastery on Helena we slept in a communal sleeping room and passed our time studying scripture and discussing Father Blondeau's sermons when not working."

"Is that why you wanted communal quarters?"

"We are used to one another. And on the island we were separated from one another by being locked in individual cells. It was very hard on us, Sir."

"You and the men are happy then?"

Jacob lowered the sextant slowly then turned to look at me. "How could men who have regained their liberty after many years of hard living not be happy, and grateful?" After a pause he added with a chuckle, "We are not nearly as complicated as you, are we?"

I laughed. "I have been called a lot of things and thought a lot of things about myself, but I have never regarded myself as a particularly complicated man."

"Try stamping your boot to see what complicated sounds like," Jacob laughed.

I went astern to examine the lighthouse. Like the pilothouse, it was a low square structure with sloping sides. Two thick glass lenses facing the bow protected the powerful lighting apparatus and its reflectors within the thick steel housing. Back in our island lagoon, after the lighting apparatus had been installed, I had swung a sledge hammer at the housing many times to see if it could be broken, and not once did the lights even flicker. It didn't even dent the armored steel housing.

I leaned against the lighthouse and withdrew a cigar from my coat pocket and was about to light it with a Vulcan matchstick, when something made me look to my left.

At first I thought it was a trick of the eyes, another island, only taller, with a few dirty gray clouds crowding around its peak. Then I saw the bow wave, white and foamy, heard the chuff of steam engines and saw the orange sparks flying like sprites in the air.

All the blood drained from my face. I surged to my feet with a jolt and raced for the hatchway, calling out to Jacob, my voice raw and harsh, "Get below!"

Number Two whirled around and saw what I saw. And even as he ran toward the hatchway I saw his swarthy complexion had taken on an unnatural pallor.

Bearing down on us, seemingly oblivious to our presence, was a steamship with her sails full bellied. They would be on us in minutes. I closed the hatch and dogged it, then we pounded along the companionway for the bridge.

I shot up the ladder to the bridge with Jacob on my heels. Michael was checking the gyroscopic compass. He whirled around. "What's wrong?"

"We are about to be rammed," Jacob hurried to the wheel.

It was true. By then I was standing at the engine telegraph. I looked out a view port. The big black hull blocked the sky. I gave the engine telegraph a hard shove to the words that Mr. Hart of Hart Brothers in New York had found so curious—*Crash Dive*.

In an instant the big screw propellers went from lazily beating against the current to churning the water into a foamy froth. I hurtled over to the hydroplane console and gave the two levers a sharp shove upwards.

We slid beneath the waves.

But not fast enough—or deep enough....

There was a loud grating sound of metal against metal. The steamer's copper clad keel grated against our boat deck. The sound was loud but the actual force not enough to cast us off our feet. Then we were entirely clear of the steamer. She passed overheard with her paddle wheels churning the black water just a few feet above us.

I threw on our light, rushed over to the helm, and elbowed Jacob aside.

We went down lower and lower. Then I gave the wheel a sharp turn and the Nautilus went into a tight banking turn such as one sees a raptor do when it is after prey.

"Michael, go see if we are taking on water!" I cried over my shoulder.

"Number Two! Get ready to set our diving planes to neutral!"

Michael bolted from the bridge. I heard him take the ladder three rungs at a time then pound along the corridor. Jacob had rushed over to the port console and had his boulder-sized hands on the hydroplane control levers.

When we came out of the turn, I cried, "Now, Number Two!"

We leveled off at a fathom beneath the waves. I pointed the Nautilus' spur at the retreating ship, a steamer of about three hundred tons and making about eleven knots. We closed the distance in minutes. She was so close that had we been on the surface I could have exchanged greetings with her captain without a speaking trumpet.

"Captain, do you think they tried to run us down on purpose?" Jacob was now at his usual post beside the engine telegraph.

"I don't know. Our light was off and they may not have even seen us. But I want to see if it is a warship. Ahead One Half!" I cried. I gave the wheel a slight turn to starboard. We pulled away and surged ahead from her a little, just far enough for me to see dimly the pale faces of passengers at her rails pointing at the strange sea monster.

"It is a passenger ship. They may go in peace," I said evenly. "Take the helm, Number Two!"

"Captain, look!" Jacob cried. I peered through the viewport.

In her mad dash to escape the *sea monster* the ship had struck a submerged rock and ripped her bottom out. Before our startled gazes, she was sinking fast. We saw men and women fighting to get into the one boat they managed to put over the side. Other men, all fine gentlemen I am sure, elbowed women in hoopskirts out of the way as they took to the ratlines to escape the rising water.

Just like vermin...rats fighting to escape their doom...their imminent death revealing their true nature...The sharks will dine heartily tonight...

Jacob turned to me. "What should we do, Captain?"

I blinked at him. "Do? We will do nothing since their fate is of no concern to us."

(Lacuna begins)

Note 1: This incident may refer to the loss of the PS Mary Jane, 325 tons. Reportedly out of a crew of sixty and a hundred and twenty passengers, thirty survived and were picked up by a passing Brig, the HMS Fowler.

Note 2: The next two pages are severely water damaged.

(Lacuna ends)

Then I wearied of the south and I decided to go north. I had onboard dozens of crates of glass jars of various sizes filled with alcohol to preserve the specimens I intended to collect. In my salon were wood and glass display cases such as one would find in a museum, divided into compartments; hand crafted of oak and brass.

We had to pass through the Coral Sea to get to the Pacific. We skirted the Vanuatu Islands, discovered by Louis de Bougainville, a thoroughly wretched place where the natives had been forced into virtual slavery by European planters, living in abject squalor while their European masters lived a life of luxurious comfort. The island reminded me of all that was wrong with the human race. We bore past this island quickly, going north by west, traveling at forty knots.

Some days we rode the surface but most of the time we traveled submerged. I had devised a means of trailing a large net from a metal boom sticking out from the side of the hull to capture sea creatures, not only for our dinner table but for analysis. And soon the sample jars in the salon had such rare specimens of fish and mollusks and corals of many varieties that would have made any museum curator bang his head against the wall in envy. For the whole ocean was my laboratory. The Nautilus had temperature sensors on the outside of her hull connected to thermometers in the salon that allowed me to take very accurate readings, which I entered into a special log book, one of many I kept. We utilized everything we caught. Our chef, Michi Shichirōma, continued to tantalize us with a seemingly endless variety of delicacies from our harvest. This grave Japanese lord and I had many interesting conversations about food preparation.

"The presentation is every bit as important as flavor," he said to me one day in the galley. I had stopped by on my way to the engine room to say hello. He was a cultured man of great learning to whom I never tired of listening. "Is this not so in your country?"

"The Oceans are now my country," I replied with a smile, "but to answer your question, the quality of the food in England I find, in general, inferior to that of France, which I had thought to be superior to all others until you introduced me to Japanese cuisine." We spoke in ArtLang, as he did not speak any European language and I did not speak his. In fact, I had instructed my comrades that, as we were no longer citizens of any nation, we would henceforth speak exclusively in the artificial language the gentle Father Blondeau had developed. Even casual speech amongst us was conducted in Artlang.

Our sample taking did not slow us down much, and our ship was so fast that we had gained the mid pacific in a short time and I found my glass trained on the rake-masted clipper ahead of us. She was charging east under full sail with her square sails and gallants and royals and topgallants full-bellied—her rigging taut against the stiff wind. I saw the Union Jack at her mizzen. She was on a port tack with a broad reach and her bow wave looked like charging white horses against the green of her hull and the deep blue of the ocean.

I sucked at my teeth as I studied her through my glass. As a naval engineer I thought how beautiful she was with her bow lightly raked forward, her low freeboard, so she could clip easily through the waves. I had designed a few clipper ships during my former career. It was her cargo I was pondering. What did her holds contain? I was certain I knew the answer: Opium, a pernicious drug that instantly robs men of their souls and women of their virtue. My former country had built its empire on the back of Chinese opium addicts, by cultivating the wretched plant in India and forcing China to buy it.

In my lifetime two wars had been fought between England and China over the lucrative opium trade—on unfair terms to be sure: lumbering Chinese junks with small cannon against British frigates with mouths bristling with deadly eighteen pounders, and the ability to sail in any wind; running circles around the smaller junks.

I turned to Michael and Jacob. "As I am not sure of her cargo...."

"Could be tea," Michael offered.

"Not going to China." I saw my dim reflection in the glass of the forward viewport. I looked as ferocious as an offended sea god about to visit doom upon some fishermen who had forgotten to make an offering before casting their nets. My eyes were wide black disks, teeth bared in a humorless grin, nostrils flaring; my countenance wrathful and filled with an unquenchable bloodlust.... I realized my hands were clamped to the spokes of the helm like a vise. "Number Two, Ahead Full...."

(Lacuna begins)

Note: one page missing. We simply do not know if Nemo in fact sunk the clipper ship. It was not uncommon for them to be lost to storms and pirates. That year

> alone, two dozen vessels were
> lost on the China run.
> (Lacuna ends)

One day we raised the Sandwich Islands, named thus by the explorer, James Cook, in honor of the man who financed his voyage: John Mantagu, Fourth Earl of Sandwich. The natives referred to their island kingdom as Moku ino o Hawai `i. The celebrated James Cook, and I say this with more than a little sarcasm, justly lost his life by treating the peaceful natives in a most injudicious manner, and it pleases me to recount the tale of at least one man whose unjust acts were visited back upon him. Polynesians, like most primitives, have no concept of ownership of property so they thought nothing of helping themselves to one of the captain's longboats. To get it back, Captain Cook attempted to kidnap their king with a view to holding him hostage until the longboat was returned—this resulted in him and four of his men being slain by the outraged Hawaiians. How much simpler and civilized, in the proper sense of the word, would it had been if he had simply let them have the longboat. Even a brig always has several of them, and the Hawaiian ruler had generously allowed his guest to replenish his water and resupply his vessel with food. Alas, that is not the way of so-called civilized men, and now the archipelago, while still nominally independent, is crawling with missionaries who teach the natives to feel shame about their nakedness, while doling out medicine to treat the terrible diseases visited upon them by Europeans. It's a sickening story and I shudder to think of how it will end. May these good people one day rise up and drive the Europeans from their midst and return to their ancient ways.

It was this man's untimely end, which I was dearly hoping had been none too short, which was on my mind when we rose to the surface at night to replenish our air supply and take our bearings. A nearby island, volcanic in origin as they all are in this region, was erupting in god-like hellish beauty. I studied the lava pouring down the flanks of the largest volcano I had ever set eyes on. It came down the side of the mountain like one of Hell's rivers and where it reached the sea, tall clouds of steam rose into the night air. The sheer destructive power awed me and I ruminated that the planet was perhaps as piqued by its human vermin as I.

We passed as near as we dared between the big island and its smaller neighbor to the north. The water was certainly deep enough to submerge, but I wanted to study this stirring phenomenon as I had never seen a live volcano, and there were no ships in the channel, except for a few native outriggers which probably did not note our passage.

```
(Lacuna begins)
Note: two pages carefully cut
out. No clue as to what was writ-
ten on them, and the following
page and a half are water dam-
aged.
(Lacuna ends)
```

And so three weeks later, we found ourselves entering the Bering Sea. That day, October the twelfth, eighteen hundred and sixty six, we rose to the surface with our pumps throwing two tall geysers of water into the icy air from our ballast tanks. For the last two weeks we had been the beneficiary of a most curious escort. Bowhead whales, perhaps seeing in us a kindred creature, had accompanied us for many leagues. Some days we had a whole pod of them surrounding us, their great dark eyes, ageless and filled with a wisdom we can only guess at, locked on us, and their songs to one another a frequent beautiful accompaniment to our engine.

As I steered my Nautilus beneath the waves, I could not restrain myself from giving them a warm smile and a friendly wave. I do not believe any naturalist would have hesitated to join our band of brothers—even if it meant that he could never again set foot on land—just to have the opportunity to see these gentle creatures in their element.

We had powered along at a leisurely rate of twenty knots and a depth of forty meters. These waters were quite cold and I was happy that I had thought to use the engine to heat air which was then forced with fans throughout the ship's air vents. We couldn't have been more comfortable anywhere. As the Nautilus drove deeper into the Bering Sea these amazing creatures stayed with us, and I spent many hours in the salon observing them through the great viewports.

Whales are mammals, of course, and must periodically rise to the surface to replenish their air supply, and they would often rise with us as we replenished our air together. We were lucky enough to witness the bowhead, like most baleen whales, feeding in a manner similar to a basking shark with its large jaws agape, sluicing water through flat flexible plates with frayed edges arranged in parallel rows from its upper mandible scooping in dense clouds of krill and small fish. I had observed that the whale would then partially closes its jaws to expel water and thus sieve out the food which it would then swallow.

I discovered a most amazing fact one night as I was in my salon with the panels opened. I was in a fuliginous mood as I played my pipe organ. I was playing a rather intricate piece by the Italian composer Frescobaldi. It was the night and no one disturbed me as my fingers danced along the keyboard and my feet pumped the pedals, filling the salon and indeed the entire ship with the strains of *Il Primo Libro delle Fantasie*. I was increasingly overcome by the feeling that someone was watching. I paused and looked over my shoulder. My gaze went to the starboard viewport and I saw this enormous eye staring in.

I rose slowly and went to the viewport and stared out. The beautiful creature did not move away but continued to stare at me intently. I had the distinct impression that it was waiting for something. We stared at each other through the glass. I was hit by an inspiration and turned away to go back to my pipe organ when I heard a melodic sound. It was a gurgling "ah ooogla..ahh...urrrpph....uuurrrgh..urp."

I stood there utterly entranced, as more calls came from it. Then I hastened back to my organ and played another piece. Soon another whale was at the other viewport looking in. Beyond them I saw an entire pod of whales swimming with us. He had called his companions over to see us strange humans in our undersea ship! Over the next few days my crewmates came to the salon and watched and visited with our new friends.

It was only a few days later when the whales' songs changed and they seemed to be agitated. We rose to the surface to take our bearings and replenish our dwindling air supply and I saw ...saw with ineffable horror off in the distance, whaling ships at their grisly task.

—No not saw only, but smelled the unmistakable stench of burning whale flesh.

"Those dirty bastards!" I murmured to myself. All around us were whaleboats in pursuit of bowheads, their task brutal and gory. Once a victim was sighted, the crew took to their whaleboats and rowed after them with the harpooner standing in the bow with his harpoon, a nasty barbed weapon held aloft ready to be thrown. Whales have to come up for air eventually and when they did, the harpooner launched his weapon with deadly accuracy and the whaleboat was treated to what was, I found out later from that scoundrel Ned Land, called a 'Nantucket sleigh ride' as the poor animal, in agony, losing blood, and towing the full weight of a heavy whaleboat loaded with overfed men, tried to make good its escape.

Meanwhile, other boats would row up and, as the whale tired, hurl their lances into it and soon instead of clear vapor, a bloody geyser would shoot from their blow holes.

I don't think I have ever seen anything so monstrous in my life. Worse still, I thought of my past mindless complicity in this horrendous trade. Had I not often read by the light of lamps fueled with whale oil? Had I not often enjoyed seeing my former wife in nothing but her whalebone corset as she crooked her cheater's finger at me from our big four-poster? Had not the fat of whales greased the slipways of ships I had built for the little old fat lady named Victoria that we silly Englishmen style **Her Majesty?**

I swept the scene before me with my glass. I counted three whaling ships, belching thick clouds of smoke from their kettles where the blubbery flesh is boiled. Each of them had the carcasses tied alongside. There were about a dozen whaleboats chasing after whales or being towed pell-mell across the frigid sea by their terrified victims.

I felt something then I had not felt for a long time: tears rolling down my cheeks. Such barbarity could not go unpunished. I whirled around to Jacob. "Prepare to submerge at once!"

In a few minutes we were on the bridge, and had submerged to just below the level of the sea. I took the wheel myself. Michael was at the hydroplane controls and Jacob was at his station at the engine telegraph. Whaling ships are slow sailors at best and are wooden hulled, and completely unprepared for what was about to befall them.

"Ahead full," I cried. The Nautilus surged forward and I felt my hands tightening on the wheel, as we ran full tilt at the first whaling ship. At fifty knots we crashed through the hull. There was a splintering of wood and the ship broke into two pieces and sank. I swung the helm and took the Nautilus into a long curving turn. The second ship had seen what had happened to the first. Through the view ports I could see the sailors busily hacking at the ropes and chains securing carcasses and their sails being set.

But it was too late for them.

Their doom was foreordained from the time I first set eyes on them.

I sliced through them like an iron fist smashing a child's toothpick house. As I bore down on the third ship, I could see men running along her deck. There was another splintering crash and her back was broken too, but she caught fire, likely when her rendering kettles and the fires beneath them were knocked over.

Oh, how she burned even as she sank! "Prepare to surface!" I said, "All hands to deck with aero guns!"

And for the next three hours as Michael steered the Nautilus, with me perched before the steersman cage, giving hand signals with an aero rifle in the other hand, we chased down every god-damned whaleboat. And when we pulled alongside, my men and I leveled our rifles and killed every one of those accursed, hell-bound savages that dared to call themselves civilized men – and I was glad to help them to their final destination.

"Gods Above, Captain, look!" I jerked my head up. I had just expended my last round on a dirty faced boy who had held up his hands and pleaded for his life, even with his harpoon still stuck in the calf of a bowhead. I followed Jacob's pointing fingers with my eyes. Warships! Three of them…! And they were racing our way.

"Get below!" I shouted to my comrades.

In moments we were submerged and streaking underwater toward the shelf of ice that was the beginning of the Arctic Circle. As soon we were under the ice I switched on our light. A dazzling world of stark blue and white opened up before us. We were in uncharted waters and as far as we could see there was nothing but ice. Not just ice, but great inverted mountain ranges of ice whose blue white surfaces shimmered like diamonds or sapphires as the Nautilus' light played across their faceted surfaces.

"Ahead half slow," I called out.

"Ahead half slow," Jacob repeated as he gave the engine telegram a shove.

We reduced speed and gingerly picked our way around inverted peaks of ice that would have shamed the Alps. We were moving through a world of stark whites and blues. I edged the helm to the right and we slipped around a peak and up into a valley.

Michael was at the console at the rear of the bridge monitoring the ship's systems.

"Captain…" he began.

"I know…"

"What…?" Jacob asked, looking from me to Michael.

"Well, you know why we surfaced in the first place?" Michael asked.

"Shit!" Jacob cried, "I almost forgot….to replenish our air tanks."

"How much air do we have?" I asked, guessing the answer.

"Six hours at best."

His words tolled in my head like a death knell.

"Why don't we just reverse course and slip by the warships?" Jacob asked.

I shook my head. "I am certain they will loiter there to see if we reappear, and when we come up for air." I gave a shrug.

On and on we drove under the ice mountain, our screw propeller beating the water. I scanned the shimmering surface above us for a sign of a lake or thin ice.

"Look out!" Jacob cried. A massive wall of ice appeared as if from nowhere.

"Astern, Full! I cried.

But it was too late.

CHAPTER 11

White Death

"Michael, slam those levers up as far as they'll go!" I swung the wheel hard to port. To Jacob: "Ahead, Full!" I was breathless with panic and struggled not to jeopardize my comrades' good opinion of me by showing it.

That long spindle-cone bow pitched straight down; the propeller blades lashing the water, as the hydroplanes and the rudder moaned in protest.

We went into a half roll away from the ice cliff. I watched helplessly as these few seconds of time seemed to draw out into long eons wherein our fate was undecided.

Jacob held on to the engine telegraph, staring wide eyed out the viewport.

"I am coming over, Sir!" Michael flung himself from the hydroplane controls to the helm and bore down on his side while

I shouldered mine up, both of us lying on our bellies. It was one wild hair-raising ride that I feared was about to end in disaster. As the seconds seemed to draw into hours, my heart ached over the possibility that my beloved Nautilus would be destroyed before she had had a chance to experience all the wonders that the oceans had to offer her. But my heart also raged with the realization that if I died here the injustices that had been visited upon me would go unpunished.

I pulled my need for revenge and my love of my ship and comrades out of the depths of my soul and roared, "Hold fast!" Even as my arms began to tremor, not from timidity of spirit, but from shear exhaustion, I imagined that my drive of purpose alone could hold my ship and my men in safety. Perspiration ran down my face. True, we were pointing straight down, but momentum was working against us. Ice filled the starboard viewports as the huge inescapable wall of ice rushed toward us. My heart was in my mouth– we wouldn't make the turn in time. The Nautilus slammed keel down onto the cliff and went into a long, bone crunching slide down its vertical face.

I stared wide-eyed out the forward viewport, as we sped down the wall, our keel one long steel ski. Every steel plate and rivet in the hull screamed in protest as we cut a furrow through the ice. Suddenly, over the shriek of tortured metal, we heard the skirling notes of music, a sweet rising and falling piping, coming from the ship herself. All around us, hull plates buckled then sprang back to their former condition. The spider web of copper tubing that ran from the hull plates and converged on the reactor grail was pulsing as if made of India rubber. I was looking around wildly, my eyes hazy with wonder.

Of course, of course…it had to happen this way…So I could see how amazing you are…My One True Love, My Nautilus…I hear your voice…

"God above! Will you look at that!" Michael gave voice to the awe and utter disbelief that I'm sure was evident in all of our faces as he stared at the rippling steel plates. Before our startled gazes large bumps appeared in the hull's surface then vanished without a trace, like pressing a fingertip against a sheet of rubber then removing it.

Jacob reached out and laid a hand on the hull and stared at it with undisguised wonder. He was a cool one that Jacob, which is why I had chosen him for his position, answering to none but me. He turned his head and yelled at me over the din, "May I say, Sir, that this is yet another example of astonishing engineering." Still looking at the hull, he added as if discussing the weather, "By the by, Sir, do you know how deep the water is here?"

"We'll find out soon enough! Gentlemen, brace yourselves!"

And we were flung downwards into a black abyss, but I could not resist a quick look over my shoulder at the retreating cliff and our long swirling silvery wake.

Looking forward again, I shouted at Jacob for *Astern Full*. I still don't know how he did it, but he somehow got a ham-like hand on that long brass handle and gave it a pull that would have made a giant proud and the engine telegraph's bell sang out. I looked at Michael fighting to hold the wheel down. "Get back to the hydroplanes and set…

(Lacuna begins)
Note: next few lines water
smudged.
(Lacuna ends)

We sliced straight down through the water still going much too fast, gravity seeming to have a magnetic pull on us as we attempted to slow. A long sinuous line of blackness appeared before us, blacker than its black background. Then I saw the muddy tan strip on either side of the jagged line, and the image resolved with terrible clarity.

We were hurtling toward a crack in the ocean floor.

The black line grew in breadth by the moment.

Michael was sprawled across the panel wrestling with the levers.

We arrowed into the yawning chasm, and steep rock walls flew by on either side.

Michael was gritting his teeth as he bore down on the levers. I could not leave the wheel or the Nautilus would go out of control—I mean out of control worse than we were presently experiencing, which was bloody well bad enough.

Then the bow began to rise, slowly at first, and then came level, and we raced along the chasm at sixty knots an hour, the extra ten knots a dubious gift from angular momentum and our recent struggle with gravity. The bow climbed steadily until we surged out of the chasm and leveled off. The adjustable pitch propellers spinning backwards slowed us down and the Nautilus settled into a leisurely pace. It took a moment for me to overcome the hammering in my ears.

But we were by no means out of trouble and I had to think fast.

"Take the Helm, Mr. Moreau," and I do not think he missed the tone of respect in my voice. I stumbled over to the control panel at the rear of the bridge. Although we had, by my reckoning, been but two hours under the ice pack, our collective exertions in the ship had resulted in a steep reduction of our remaining air. According to the dials, we had exactly fifty minutes of air left in our reserve tanks.

I returned to the helm. "I will take the wheel if you please, Mr. Moreau." I was speaking in an even tone, but my heart was still racing. I cast my eyes down to the binnacle. The needle was spinning because we were close to the pole, and the gyroscopic compass was lying on its side in its case.

We rose up from just above the seabed floor with the vortex from our screw churning a tall brown cloud of silt and sediment in our wake, and climbed toward the pearlescent sheet and leveled off a safe distance below it.

I had no idea where we were. Three pairs of worried eyes stared out the viewports for an opening in the ice. We pressed onwards with the air growing staler and staler.

A massive black and white shape appeared off our port bow. A big eye regarded us solemnly through a viewport. I had a vague sensation of recognition, but was too preoccupied to pay attention to it. The creature dropped back and bumped against the hull. The ship shuddered and yawed to starboard, but I gave the wheel a turn and resumed my earlier course, which was no course really. My head was spinning. The air was thickening. My throat and lungs were on fire. Another bump sent us briefly off course. The big eye reappeared in our port viewport then dropped back. My vision had narrowed.

There was another sharp bump from the side. Then a long line of massive bowhead whales cut across my bow and I was forced to turn sharply to keep from running into them. Then I understood. They were trying to lead us to air.

And in moments the white pearlescent ice sheet gave way to a great dark gray oval. I tried to speak but could not. But Michael and Jacob had seen it too.

Jacob sent an order for *Reverse Full* to the engine room, and Michael threw the emergency switch that would purge all ballast tanks at once. We rose at an angle and burst through a thin rind of ice into a twilight world, with the nozzles on the boat deck throwing two geysers of water high into the air.

Whales surfaced all around us, sending up tall misty fountains of vapor and water, their flukes slapping the water playfully. One of them was treading water so that it stood on end out of the lake with an eye turned toward us. It was the bull that had nudged us toward the lake, and before that had kept station with the Nautilus peering into the salon while I played my pipe organ. I waved at him and he dove into the water and slapped it with his flukes. I owe you thanks, and more than thanks, I thought. You are a good friend.

Moments later, all of us that could stood on the boat deck heedless of the freezing wind howling from somewhere on its way to somewhere else—with the magnetic and gyroscopic compasses inoperative there was no way of telling direction.

I was stooped over with my hands on my knees sucking in great draughts of air. I looked over at Jacob when he came on deck. "The injured…"

"Six with cuts and bruises, one with a broken wrist…two with concussions…"

"Any dead…?"

Jacob shook his head. "We were lucky."

"It's a miracle that we made it," Mr. Mackay said.

"That was no miracle." I jerked my chin toward the whales. "They saved us." I straightened and then surveyed our surroundings. We were floating in a black pool of water surrounded by about fifty bowhead whales.

The sun was no more than a soft roseate glow on the horizon, dazzling ribbons of greenish light shining overhead. An icy wilderness surrounded us, jagged ridges and hummocks of ice marched off into the gloomy distance, and a heavy blanket of snow covered everything. Our exhalations came out in great swirling white clouds. Over the great whoosh of the pumps filling the Nautilus' depleted air reservoirs I heard the loud cracks and groans of ice moving. An unrelenting wind raked at our exposed flesh, and I became aware of the first signs of frostbite on my nose, and my hands tucked in my armpits were numb. "Get the men below," I ordered Jacob.

When the last man was in, I followed but left the hatch open.

Jacob, Michael and MacKay were waiting for me in the companionway when I came down the ladder. Even with the ship's heaters running, an icy blast came through the open hatchway, searching throughout the ship with icy tentacles.

"Gentlemen, the first order of business is to discover how much damage the Nautilus has suffered." I looked at MacKay. "We'll start with the engine room."

All that day the wind increased, and even after we secured the hatch, we felt its buffeting blows. Through a glass window in the engine housing, I saw the massive armature whirling between the two huge magnets. Then I went over to the reactor grail, and pulling on a pair of goggles, peered through the viewport. The *Atlantium* was suspended in midair, held in place by the force of the magnets lining the inside of the reactor grail; spinning in the seawater washing over it with bright bands of red, violet, blue, aquamarine, garnet and citrine crisscrossing its silvery crystal surface. It filled my reality until I felt myself merging with it as I stared unblinkingly. I forced my eyes away from it, removed the goggles, rubbed my eyes, and met MacKay's amused stare.

"It be like going eyeball to eyeball with the Devil, doan it? Aye, she has the Devil in her—and no doubt about it. No ship could a done what she did and come out all right."

"That is superstitious thinking. It is eighteen hundred and sixty seven, Mr. MacKay. We have electricity and steam power and industrial machines. Mr. Darwin in his *Origin of Species* has shown that men are the product of millennia of natural selection, and not the creation of some capricious divinity. The time for talk of demons and boogey men is long past. We live in the age of science and reason."

"That may be so, Captain," MacKay replied obdurately. "But steel doan be giving in like rubber then return to all normal and such like."

"Yet it did exactly that," I replied evenly.

"Aye, but it nae be natural."

We were walking back toward the engine, our voices echoing in the cavernous engine room. I paused and looked at him, and in my head was the sweet piping melody coming from the ship's steel hull and bulkheads. I felt that my eyes hardening into black disks as I looked at MacKay. "She doesn't like it when you speak about her like that."

We stared at each other.

"Begging your pardon, Sir?" His small blue eyes were studying me. With the sweet music singing in my ears, I gestured to the ship around us. "Can't you feel it, MacKay...? The Nautilus is alive in a way no ship has ever been alive. If we treat her with respect—honor her—and take care of her, she will look after us."

There was a long echoing silence.

At last, MacKay pulled a wry face and said, "Aye, that be true enough of any ship, and perhaps this one more than others, given how different she be." He was staring at me closely. I turned and moved onward with him in my wake.

We lifted a steel deck plate, and I dropped down into the crawl space then reached up for the electric torch he handed down to me. The torch's cable added to the difficulty of moving through the crawlspace. I went on all fours the length of the ship, directing my light into every nook and cranny. Removing another panel, I wormed my bulk down into the bilge where the hull plates met the keel, between two ballast tanks five and six, and pressed reverential fingers against the steel. It was cold to the touch from the near freezing seawater. Then I backed out and continued on my way, closely inspecting tanks, pipes and hull plates. Not a single buckled plate, not so much as a cup of water was to be seen. Never in all my years of experience with ships had I ever seen this. All vessels ship a certain amount of water, and with iron or steel hulled ships, there was still a need for a bilge pump. But the Nautilus' hull was truly watertight; her air and ballast tanks had not been damaged by our unfortunate encounter with the underwater ice wall.

As I crawled back to the engine room, I could feel through the palms of my hands the steady pulsing of the propeller as it slowly beat against the current to keep us in place.

I paused, with my eyes shut tight, feeling her pulse.

There was a slight off-kilter trembling.

"We have to check the propeller," I said to MacKay as I hauled myself up from the crawlspace. A moment later, I pressed my face against the rubber eyecup of the telescopic viewer and studied the slowly revolving propeller. The telescope was in a fairing that ran from the hull. There was another fairing right above it with a small light at the end of it behind six inch glass with the diameter of a coffee mug. The purpose of this equipment was so that the propeller could be inspected without having to send someone outside or dry docking—an option unavailable to us in any case.

"Reduce revolutions to twenty per minute," I called over my shoulders.

Mackay was at the main engine control panel. He turned a knob and the propeller slowed. I peered at it through the telescope. Yes, there it was, the number three blade was slightly bent at the tip. It would have to be changed.

Everyone stiffened when I came into the salon. I looked around with a sigh. It was a mess. Broken specimen jars lay everywhere; the rich Persian carpets on the floor were soaked with water that had sloshed out of the fountain. Heavier furniture like sofas, divans, display cases, and tables had been bolted to the floor, or it would have been so much worse. Likewise, my valuable paintings had been fastened at all four corners to the walls so they wouldn't move in heavy seas, but several bore stains from God knows what. And the library beyond was in worse shape with nearly all twelve thousand volumes lying in heaps on the floor.

I looked at my comrades. "At ease, gentlemen," I said quietly. "I regard this incident as but a test of our Nautilus' capabilities. While not indestructible, she will clearly take a lot of punishment. No other ship in the world could have withstood the violent physical shocks she did and still remain afloat. But the fact remains that one of the screw propeller blades has been damaged and will have to be changed before we can get underway. I need a volunteer to help me change it. Beware though: This is a hazardous undertaking. We will be working in freezing water, in near dark conditions. One misstep could result in injury or death."

A dozen hands went up. I pointed at one, a middle aged man with a thick cap of salt and pepper hair named Jean-Luc Poitiers, for I knew he had some knowledge of ships and had been part of the team that had installed the propeller. "Meet me in the airlock."

MacKay stepped forward. "Captain Nemo, Sir. I canna in good conscious let you go without taking me. I am the Chief Engineer."

"I need you to monitor our progress from the engine room in case something goes wrong," I said with a shake of my head.

Then I looked over at Jacob. "How is work on the gyroscopic compass?"

"We should have it back in place and running in a couple of hours."

"If it can't be fixed we have a spare, and we still have the ones in the auxiliary bridge in the engine room, and in my cabin. Those are working perfectly well."

Jean-Luc and I stepped into the airlock. The Nautilus still rode the surface of the Arctic lake, but we were by no means safe. Earlier, when I had gone topside to supervise the installation of the boom and block and tackle from the aft boat deck, I had become aware of another danger. The bowhead whales were gone and the lake had grown noticeably smaller. The icy shoreline was now only about two cable lengths on all sides from us. Several of the crewmen had hauled the replacement blade up onto the boat deck while I stared at the lake. At the rate it was shrinking, I estimated we would be trapped in the ice in less than four hours.

"I will go first and then you follow," I said to Jean-Luc.

"Right behind you, Captain."

We each had a rope tied around our waist as a safety harness while we used handholds on the hull to work our way toward the stern. I had two spanners on my belt.

A crewman helped us put our helmets on. Then he left the airlock, closing the door behind him. Soon there was the gurgling hiss of water and I felt a sharp coldness climbing up my body. As the water reached our shins, it was so excruciatingly cold that I had to fight the urge to yell to be released from the airlock. It felt like a slow death as the water climbed up my legs and, as it gained our torsos, a sharp intake of air and an arching back were our involuntary responses. We looked at one another and I could see my wide-eyed concern mirrored in Jean-Luc's eyes until we were all too soon submerged.

With a quick nod to my brave companion, and a look that I

hoped was bracing, as if to say, "We'll be fine," I turned a wheel on the hatch leading to the outside and shoved it open. Stepping halfway out, I reached over and grabbed a handhold. Underneath my diving suit were several layers of clothes but the cold still turned my bones to rods of ice. My hands felt like numb knobs on the end of my arms as I swung from handhold to handhold, with the device that regulated my air supply click-clacking in my ears. The handholds were slippery and icy cold, even through the thick gloves.

When I got to the stern followed closely by Jean-Luc, I scrambled onto the horizontal hydroplane, switched on the light hanging from my belt, and grabbed onto the damaged propeller blade which was pointing nearly straight up at one o'clock so it would clear the rudder assembly when it was pulled. A weighted cable dangled from the surface. With a joint effort, we wrapped it carefully round the blade, knotting it in place.

After tapping him on the arm as our previously agreed sign of what I was about to do, I swung over to the starboard side of the propeller with one hand on the boss, and the other gripping a spanner. I placed the u-shaped end of the spanner on a bolt and pushed up on it while Jean-Luc looked on.

Nothing…it wouldn't budge.

Jean-Luc clambered up to the top of the propeller boss, sat astride it, and reached down and grasped the spanner. While he pulled, I pushed. Rivers of sweat ran down my face and into my eyes as we loosened first one, then the other nine bolts on the propeller boss. The round bronze cover came off and I thrust it into a pouch hanging from a belt at my waist then peered inside at the three bolts securing the blade root to the driveshaft mounting collar. These bolts were smaller and hence the reason for the second spanner I had brought along. I reached inside with the spanner and tried to loosen them.

They were frozen in place.

No amount of pulling and swearing would make them yield.

I felt a hand on my shoulder and I leaned back at the waist to look up.

Jean-Luc gestured for me to switch places with him. While he slid down from the propeller shaft housing I pulled myself up on to it. He stuck his spanner in the boss and pushed up on it. I heard a thin clink of metal on metal just as a shadow fell over us and a sense of deep primeval fear overtook me. Inside my helmet, my head was swiveling from side to side trying to identify its source when abrupt movements caught the corner of my eyes and I turned to Jean-Luc just in time to see him falling away from the propeller, his arms and legs wind milling.

I grabbed for him, but it was too late. He sank before my gaze. As we were each tethered to the Nautilus with a long safety rope, I did not fear overly much for his safety. When I next looked down he was hanging by the waist with his arms and legs akimbo, his face hidden by his helmet. Then from the corner of my eye, through the side viewport, I saw something big and black flick by below. The Nautilus' stern dipped sharply and I had to grab hold of the propeller to keep from being pitched off.

I looked down again.

Jean-Luc was gone.

At first I thought it a trick of my eyes. Perhaps he was still there but hidden by the murky black water, but then I saw the ragged end of the rope. A killer whale had been unable to resist the tempting treat dangling at the end of the line. I stared hollow-eyed at the end of the rope drifting with the current and shuddered at my comrade's gruesome end. Gathering my courage, I sidled down from the driveshaft housing and went to work with renewed force, loosening the blade's mounting bolts. When the last one was removed, I gave the rope tied around the blade a sharp tug. It was hoisted to the surface.

Just moments later, the replacement blade was lowered down. With difficulty, I manhandled it into the slot in the propeller boss. With my fingers trembling whether from the chill of the Arctic Sea or trepidation, I cannot say, I bolted the new blade in place then replaced the boss cover. I had just stuck the last of the mounting bolts in place when something struck me violently on the shoulder, knocking me from my precarious perch.

I fell toward the seabed with my arms and legs flailing, all the while stubbornly holding on to the huge iron spanner. I came to a stop with a sharp painful jolt and swung in a lazy arc about a hundred feet down, staring up at the dark silhouette of my ship's cigar shaped hull. Then something made my eyes flick to my right.

A black and white shape filled my vision. I lashed out desperately with the spanner, swinging with all my might, and felt it land with a solid thud on flesh. The killer whale turned sharply and raced away. Then I was being borne upwards toward the light, toward the place of my safety, my love and my home—the Nautilus.

When I stumbled from the airlock, MacKay and Jacob were waiting for me.

Jacob removed the heavy helmet. "Where is Jean-Luc…?" he asked.

"Dead…" I somehow got out through chattering teeth. With

the help of my comrades I peeled off the diving suit and they wrapped me in warm towels. I was filled with mind-numbing remorse for Jean-Luc. 'Take care of my flock,' Father Blondeau had begged me. Yet, since our escape from Belial Island, three men had died on my watch. I searched my companion's faces and saw no hint of blame, but that did nothing to stem the rising tide of grief. I had given the old priest *my word*. I felt my face grow long and troubled like a rising sickle moon, suffused with the pale light of sorrow.

MacKay handed me a tankard of rum. "This'll warm your bones. What happened out there?" I told them. When I was done, MacKay said, "That is a hard blow, but at least you got the new blade in place, saving us all."

"I couldn't have done it without him." I replied, with a heart brimming with deep bitterness, "I should have thought to bring an aero rifle with me."

Jacob looked at me shrewdly. "Captain, would it have made a difference?"

I stared down into my tankard. "No, no it wouldn't. It happened so fast."

After a pause, Jacob said, "There's more trouble ahead for us, Sir."

"What trouble?" My eyes snapped away from the tankard.

Jacob fished his pipe out of his coat pocket and lit it. "I'll show you."

An icy blast howled in our faces when I stepped out onto the boat deck with Jacob, but I was still warmer than when I had been underwater. We were in heavy seaman's coats, with knit caps on our heads; scarves doubled around our necks, and wore thick gloves against the cold. The lake was gone, and snow covered ice surrounded our ship. Whether or not we could break free depended on the ice's thickness. Even the strongest hull will succumb to the relentless pressure of ice. My Nautilus' steel hull was strong but it could not withstand such pressure indefinitely—in time it would crack like an egg shell and then we would all be lost.

"Prepare to get underway," I hollered to Jacob over the wind's banshee howl.

I was at the helm on the bridge. "Fill ballast tanks four, five and six!" I ordered.

"Filling four, five and six," MacKay repeated turning knobs on the control panel.

As the ballast tanks filled, I felt my excitement rising. The ship settled a little then stopped. Through the hull we could hear the cracking and groaning of ice.

We were held fast in an icy grip.

"Fill trim tanks one and two," I called out.

"Filling trim tanks one and two..."

The Nautilus' bow suddenly pitched downwards, but the ice still held us in its viselike grip. "Empty trim tanks one and two."

"Emptying trim tanks one and two…" The bow pitched back up.

"Fill trim tanks seven, eight and nine," I ordered.

Michael repeated my orders as he turned another set of knobs. The stern dipped below the ice and we slid stern first beneath the waves. "Ahead, half slow!" I called out.

"Ahead half slow!" Jacob gave the engine lever telegraph a

shove. A moment later the screw propeller began to lash the water and we were underway.

With my eyes flicking between the whirling gyrocompass and the ice above us, I guided my ship through inverted valleys and mountain ranges, moving slowly so as to avoid another brush with death, and more than a little nervous about what we would see as we continued to move forward. I do believe I had developed a fear of icebergs, and all I wanted to do was get out of this place. We had a full supply of air and thanks to Jacob's expert use of the sextant I had a very good idea of where we were. We had been two miles from the North Pole. At another time I would have wanted to plant my flag on it. Now, all I wanted was to be quit of that frozen Hell.

CHAPTER 12

Prise de Fer

We passed by England like an evil shadow, quietly slipping into the English Channel at the Strait of Dover, Pas de Calais to the French, cruising at a depth of six fathoms—no reason to cause **Her Majesty's** knickers to catch fire over the presence of a sea monster in her bathing pool (I wanted her to worry about a much more dangerous possibility)—and shimmied like a sea serpent around Brest to enter the Bay of Biscay.

Above us, dirty green waves with long white streaks rose and fell whipped by a thundering wind coming down from the Arctic. Hail fell on the sea and I have no doubt it made those sailing on the surface anxious and miserable. Not us. We glided in tranquil waters well below the roiling mess above. I have been on that bay dozens of times—*on it*, not beneath it. We saw pods of Minke (small baleen whales), harbor porpoises, and bottlenose dolphins frolicking and herding rich schools of fish. Further out, the continental shelf suddenly ended in a steep cliff and the depth increased from hundreds to thousands of meters. It was here that we encountered beaked common dolphins, and fin whales who were clearly taking advantage of the prey that had congregated at the crown of the upwelling currents rising from the mountainous seafloor. Roaming with a stateliness that one has to see firsthand to appreciate, we encountered sperm whales, a few killer whales, and many striped dolphins. The hull plates were singing, a high piping song that rose and fell as the pressure of the water on the hull increased.

As we neared the Iberian Peninsula the continental slope began to rise and we nosed gingerly through a surreal world of submarine canyons that rose around us like great Gothic cathedrals. I had with me a set of professor Arronax's works and was not surprised to discover how wrong he was about some things while guessing correctly about others—a not inconsiderable feat considering that prior to our ill-fated encounter he did not have the benefit of direct observation, which is the only viable way to study a marine environment. Even here, man left his dirty boot print on an otherwise pristine seascape. One wreck after another leaped out of the gloom as we glided through the bay. I was not merely indulging my curiosity. It was of paramount importance that we understand our new home, so in all our travels we pursued detailed observations of everything around us.

After our narrow escape from the North Pole, I was determined to put my ultimate plan into action. My confidence was high; my shipmates had displayed a fierce loyalty to the Nautilus and to me personally, and were utterly ruthless when necessary. Our next objective had been agreed upon even before constructing our ship. But to *say* a thing and then to *do* a thing are entirely different—especially when it comes to vengeance.

Traveling south after our narrow escape from the ice, I sat in my cabin with my elbows propped on my desk and my hands clasped before my face, studying a nautical chart while the deck thrummed comfortably beneath my feet. Jacob had assigned a man named Tyrrell to be my steward. A former butler to the royal family, he was a gangly white haired man with an expression as somber as he was silent. His silence was only partially due to a reticent nature. While performing his duties in Buckingham Palace, he had witnessed something no one except the parties involved should have seen. As payment for his many years of loyal service, he was carried away in the night and, much like myself, subjected to a quick conviction for spying. His tongue was cut out and he was sentenced to Belial Island. He was a gentle soul and had it not been for the kindly priest he would not have survived his stay on that brutal penal island.

The door opened and Tyrrell came in and made it known with hand signs that the men were assembled in the Grand Dining Room. He understood Artlang, but without a tongue could not speak it. I thanked him, then rose from my desk and headed for the door and went down the companionway, my boots' heels ringing on the deck plates.

Taking my seat at the head of the table on that day, I felt every eye in the room on me as I got right to the point. "Comrades, the next bit of our journey will take us away from the studies, whimsical scientific observations, temperature measurements, and discoveries that we have come to cherish. We are bound by our regard for Father Blondeau to carry out his wish that we aid the Greeks on Crete in their fight for liberty against the Turks. Therefore, I am bringing them bullion to finance their bid for freedom. This will be the first of two deliveries I intend to make to them. I needn't tell you how vital it is that we support these men who yearn for that which was taken so cruelly from us. And…." I paused here and cast my eyes down at my hands clasped on the table. "When we began this journey, I made no secret of my intention to hunt down the evildoer who betrayed me. This is still my objective but I feel constrained to advise you this undertaking will be both dangerous and harrowing. As this is my fight, I do not expect any of you to participate, unless you desire it. I call upon any man that wishes to leave to signify his desire by raising his hand. I will take you to a country of your choosing and provide you with enough bullion to live out the rest of your days in comfort. But before any of you agree, one way or another, know this: Admiral Barrington will come after us with everything he has; our success is in nowise a foregone conclusion. But there will be no peace for me until I have slain him. And that is not all, comrades, for I intend to be a terror and a nightmare to those who sail the world's oceans; it is only a matter of time before some man of business discovers a pecuniary advantage beyond simple fishing and whaling in plumbing the Ocean's depths. On that ill-starred day the last pristine frontier on earth will be ravaged like a Sabine maid in the name of mammon. Listen! Have we not already come across great swirling swatches of garbage in the Pacific? Can we not tell when we are drawing near to a busy port or crowded coast by noxious islets of refuse surpassed only by the stench of rapacious capitalism?

We are not just fighting for our hard-won liberty but for the preservation of our home beneath the waves."

A hand went up. It was a compact older man named Henri. I nodded at him.

"How long will we go on sinking ships?" he asked shyly.

"Whenever we are attacked we will defend ourselves, Brother Henri. Other than that, I plan to sink every British warship I come upon until the right man comes after us. And, as a concession to you, my gentle brothers, I will merely injure passenger ships. There will be exceptions to this guideline, of course: ships carrying opium to China, whaling ships, and slavers." The war between the states in America had ended recently but slavery was still common in other parts of the world.

Jacob, in a fulsome tone, said, "The British Admiralty will guess rightly who and what they are dealing with and think they can crush us like cockroaches." He was in his black officer's uniform, his blue eyes blazing. "But we won't let them."

"No," I replied evenly, "No, we won't. And their hubris will be their downfall."

Mackay was sitting in a chair near the opposite end of the table. "I canna tell you this, lads: the Lord help humanity if this ship ever be captured. Nothing a float canna withstand or outrun her. A world in which underwater vessels be common would nae be a good place to live. So doan be forgetting there be those who would like to get their hands on our Nautilus, and would sleep better if we was again in irons on Belial Island."

"Mr. MacKay is correct." I raised a finger. Up there— " Our shorthand for the surface—"are any number of so-called civilized men butchering each other for queen, god, country or personal gain. They must know a terror of the Ocean depths or it too will be only one more battleground for them. There is only one way to deal with those carrion eaters up there. We must make them afraid, very afraid, of what lies beneath the ocean's surface."

"Why not bring the admiral to battle here, and get it over with?" Suggested an older man with a receding hairline in his sixties named Fredo.

"I don't care to allow other people to choose my battles for me nor the place where they will be fought. I will not fight Admiral Barrington in European or Mediterranean waters—where he could have a hundred warships and all Britain's industrial might at his disposal. I want to lure him far away then kill him."

Henri said. "Because of you we are free men. I for one want to stay that way."

There were nods and assents and positive affirmations from all the men.

"Thank you, Brother Henri." My eyes went to the others. "So there you have it. Who wants to be put ashore?" And not a man there raised his hand.

That conversation set us upon our course and we soon found ourselves off the Coast of Northwest Spain sweeping back and forth along the bottom of Vigo Bay.

Michael was at the helm and Jacob was at his post beside the engine telegraph with a weather eye on the control panel that monitored the ship's systems. For a mile around, our light played over the sandy bottom. "Slow to *Half Ahead*," I called out.

"Aye, aye. Slowing to *Half Ahead*." Jacob shoved the engine telegraph handle and the telegraph bell sang out. He looked over at me standing at Michael's elbow. "May I ask what are you looking for, Sir?"

Still looking intently through the viewport, I explained, "In seventeen hundred and two, a Spanish Treasure fleet set their own ships aflame rather than see their treasure fall into enemy hands. We may have need of such treasure in the future."

A moment later, a blackened hulk emerged from the gloom, then another and another. "Behold, gentlemen, before us lies the lost treasure fleet." Sure enough, the vessels had the high ornate sterns and long low beaks characteristic of seventeenth and eighteenth century warships. Coral encrusted cannons and barrels and crates littered the seafloor. I turned to Jacob and said...

(Lacuna begins)

Note: Severe water damage for the next seven pages, and two pages carefully cut out from the diary. We do not believe that Captain Nemo stopped at this time to remove the treasure from the sunken Spanish Galleons. We believe that he noted the sunken fleet's position and returned while carrying Professor Arronax and his companions to obtain the treasure. This is hardly surprising as he was already the wealthiest man in the world, thanks to the lost treasure of Napoleon Bonaparte which he had already acquired.

(Lacuna ends)

We were in the Atlantic off the Grand Banks prowling the sea lanes. It was my intention to let my enemy know in no uncertain terms that I was there. I gave the command and we rose at an inclined angle to the surface. Oddly enough, the sea was calm and only a gentle breeze ruffled the surface. The sun shone above the western horizon like a bloody fist and the ocean's hue was crimson in the afternoon light. Michael was at the helm and Jacob manned the engine telegraph. The only sound on the bridge was the whir of instruments and the hiss of water caressing the hull.

In the distance was a steamer traveling under a full spread of canvass, her paddlewheels slapping the water into a white froth. I glanced up to the sun before I raised the glass to my eyes. The optics brought the steamer leaping almost to the end of my nose. Ah, I knew this ship well—the RMS Scotia, a large passenger ship operated by the Cunard Line. She was heading east toward Cape Clear and thence to Liverpool.

I grinned wolfishly. An attack on a Cunard passenger ship would not go unnoticed by the Admiralty. I lowered my glass and turned to my comrades. "Prepare to submerge."

We slid beneath the waves and followed the steamship on a parallel course six cable lengths off her port quarter. "Left Standard Rudder," I ordered.

"Aye, Sir. Left Standard Rudder" Michael replied.

We went into a long banking turn beneath the waves.

"Ahead Full!" I called out, my voice throbbing with excitement.

"Aye, Sir. Ahead Full!" Jacob swung the engine telegraph lever to the indicated command. An instant later we were surging through the water just below the waves.

As we raced full tilt at our target, I held my breath in antici-pation. The ship's bottom loomed ever larger in our viewport. My spur slammed into her iron flank just aft of her port paddle-wheel, knocking us all forward then back with the sudden stop.

I turned to Jacob. "*Astern Half,* Number Two."

"*Astern Half!*" We backed away and I could hear our steel spur grating on the ship's iron plates as it was withdrawn. It was not my intention to sink her. I knew that she would be hauled into dry dock when she returned to Liverpool. The shipyard workers would not know what to make of the neat isosceles-triangle-shaped hole, two meters wide, but one man would figure it out – Admiral Harrison Randolph Barrington.

He would hear about how easily the sea monster's spur punched through the four centimeter thick iron plates, and he would know—know that it was me and he would not be able to resist my siren call to his doom. We powered away from the steamer which was now dead stopped in the water, the dark form of her hull receding into the gloom.

"Will she flounder, Sir?" Michael asked.

I shook my head. "She has seven watertight compartments and I poked her in the next to the smallest one near the stern, well behind her engines. She'll make it home." We turned away from the New World and returned to the waters of the Old World.

We skirted Tangier Bay and entered the Strait of Gibraltar at thirty fathoms. The land closed in on either side as we pow-ered through the long funnel between Spain and Morocco. A mere seven miles wide at its narrowest point, the strait was enclosed by two great rocks known since antiquity as the Pillars of Hercules—the Rock of Gibraltar to the north, and Jebel Musa to the south. Even for a modern steamship with paddle-wheels or screw propellers, the straits can be difficult to navigate. A strong current draws water in from the Atlantic along the surface, and a cooler submarine current runs outwards to the west. On the surface one is bedeviled by gale force winds that build up in the high walled strait. The engines have to strain to push a steamship through, and sailing into such a wind entails much tacking. None of this applied to us as we arrowed through the strait with a pod of Atlantic bottlenose dolphins as a playful escort.

Gibraltar was **Her Majesty's** largest overseas naval base, the linchpin of British hegemony in the Mediterranean, and it was the most heavily fortified stronghold on the planet. Deep galleries had been excavated on the rock to serve as artillery casements. Hundreds of cannons could be brought to bear on enemies approaching by sea. And there was no question of taking *The Rock* by land, as the fortress could only be reached by long, dangerous, steep switchbacks. But it was what was in the harbor that concerned me most. Warships, hundreds of them—both steam and sail. I stayed submerged for the run through the strait and did not rise to the surface until we were well inside the Mediterranean and then only at night so we could replenish our air supply.

We passed the Balearic Islands famous for the quality of their Slingers during ancient times. Off Sardinia we accidentally collided with a P & O steamer while cruising just below the surface. Happily, the steamship suffered a slight wound to her hull and she was able to limp into Olbia. From then on I maintained a depth of one hundred fathoms.

```
(Lacuna begins)
```
Note: the text is much water damaged here. We were able to recover part of it from two pages.
Six pages are still stuck together and the ink has run.
```
(Lacuna ends)
```

I was standing easily in the prow of my cutter, my hands thrust deep in the pockets of my black sea coat, my billed cap pulled low, with a Navy Colt revolver tucked into my belt. My men were rowing, each armed with an aero rifle, each tense. By prearrangement with the contact I had while in Europe, the man I had come to talk to was at the beach with a small knot of armed men. Behind me the sea was deep blue and calm and a cheerful sun shone on the white buildings with their blue tiled roofs that glimmered on the bluffs above the beach. The Nautilus was submerged waiting for our signal to return. Crete is the largest of the Greek islands and was currently a possession of the despot who ruled the Ottoman Empire. Many churches and synagogues had been converted into mosques and the pious Greeks forced to convert at the point of a sword. As mentioned previously, it had been Father Blondeau's wish that some of the bullion go to the Greek freedom fighters. We had a large chest of bullion in the cutter—more than enough to buy guns, ammunition, and supplies of all kinds.

"Oars Ho," I ordered as we came up to the beach.

```
(Lacuna begins)
```
Note: Two pages missing. We do
not know the identity of the man

> Nemo met on the beach, nor the
> exact beach.
> (Lacuna ends)

I peered ahead at the Gibraltar strait. Directly ahead, spread out against the horizon, was a menacing flotilla of British warships. The entire horizon, as far and wide as I could see, was covered with vessels, their masts and funnels as thick as a forest.

Jacob said in awe, "Quite a display of power, Sir. They are probably after us."

"You are no doubt correct, Number Two."

"Those bastards mean business, Sir," Michael added. "God's blood! Look at what they are doing!" I trained my glass on the ships and grinned through my beard. I had to hand it to whoever had come up with this scheme. They were spreading purse seine nets, long deep nets, weighted at the bottom and with floats on top. There was no doubt in my mind that the nets would pose no danger to the Nautilus but they could fowl our propeller, and that would be a problem. I could feel my heart pounding so hard I thought it was going to burst through my mouth. We turned away and ran back into the Mediterranean at one thousand feet at forty knots and our foes were soon left behind.

We went back and forth along the coast of Egypt's Delta, concentrating our efforts near the new Port of Said where Monsieur de Lesseps of the *Compagnie Universelle du Canal Maritime de Suez* was busy digging his canal—with thirty thousand Egyptians who had been forced to work as virtual slaves. Thousands died every year in this monumental task that would ultimately benefit only the European moneymen. The thought of such oppression, such wanton racial arrogance, sickened me.

Father Blondeau and I had spent many hours during our time at Belial Island discussing the possibility that a submarine passage connected the Mediterranean and the Red Seas somewhere near Suez. We crept along the coast searching for it.

One night I could not resist attempting to enter Alexandria's Eastern harbor. I hoped to locate the great Cleopatra's palaces which had sunk beneath the waves, and to look for the remains of the Great Lighthouse which had been toppled into the harbor by an earthquake ten centuries earlier, but I soon discovered that the harbor was too shallow for the Nautilus to safely navigate. We continued up the coast toward Sinai and arrived there just as the day dawned with sudden brightness. There the drop to the seafloor is steep, and almost appears bottomless. Here we were greeted by a submarine garden of exotic shapes and colors, rich swirls and intricate shapes of coral that was the home to brilliantly colored fish of such variety that it was dazzling. And the sea was that good clean turquoise hue and lit up in all its glory—not by our great light but by a dazzling bright Mediterranean sun. Even as I searched for an escape route, the sight of this lush variegated underwater Garden of Eden enthralled me.

At Suez I found it, a large round opening in the cliff face about the size of two railroad cars, more than enough room to enter. A strong current issued from it, a current so strong that one could almost see it. We were pointed bow-on at the tunnel mouth.

"I will take the wheel, Mr. Moreau." Then I called out over my shoulder, "*Ahead Slow, Number Two!*"

"*Ahead Slow,*" came the acknowledgement from Jacob. As I guided us into the tunnel, a large submarine gallery opened up before us. All my concentration was focused on avoiding a collision. The current was running against us but we cut through it with our screw propeller beating the water. I noted that the rock here was entirely sandstone.

Jacob standing to my right at his post beside the engine telegraph commented, "Sir, it occurs to me that we are in more than a little danger."

"Perhaps a great deal if we get wedged in somewhere," I replied. "But take a look at our escort." Dolphins tumbled playfully through the water as we glided along. Some even nudged our hull and seemed to feel a connection to the giant steel fish in their midst. "They are clearly not strangers to this passage."

"But a dolphin is a lot smaller than the Nautilus," Michael said.

My eyes were locked on the forward viewports. "There is not enough room to turn around so we have no choice but to forge ahead. If we succeed, we will have the means to rapidly enter European waters from the Indian Ocean." I added dryly, "And we won't have to pay the toll to travel on the canal being excavated on the surface. I suspect that it looks worse than it really is." As soon as the words left my mouth there was a scraping sound as our hull brushed against a stone outcropping. The hull plates emitted their surreal song, low and sweet. Then the scraping stopped as we cleared the outcropping. Our light turned the tunnel into a blue world. Another hint that my suspicions would prove to be correct was the volume of fish in the cave. Not dwellers of the tunnel but, like us, travelers through it. There were several species that I knew were not native to the Mediterranean and that I suspected came from the Red Sea. All around us were fish of every shape and hue, a dizzying array of marine life.

We slowly worked our way through the tunnel; it was a tight fit at times and I would not have dared to attempt it without our powerful light. When the tunnel began to rise I did not panic. Father Blondeau had advised me that Napoleon's surveyors had determined that the Red Sea was actually thirteen feet higher than the Mediterranean.

That would explain the rise of the tunnel, I thought. "Hydroplanes, up five degrees." The repeated command came back from Michael as he worked the levers. And we inched our way past fantastical formations of water sculpted rock.

Five hours later, we slipped out of the Suez tunnel into the Red Sea.

"My God," Michael exclaimed. "We actually did it!"

"Now let us rise to the surface. I have always wanted to see the Red Sea," I said with a tight grin. As I write this, my anger at Arronax is rekindled over his exaggeration about the shortness of the journey. Of course, it was faster going the other way at three hours with the current pushing us but the knave said in his memoirs that it took only half an hour. What nonsense! And really the truth was just as amazing as the lie in this instance. Before my discovery, I would have had to somehow slip through the Gibraltar Strait and sail the length of Africa and double the Cape of Good Hope to reach the Indian Ocean. With the discovery of this tunnel we shaved several weeks off our voyage.

We rose to the surface and were greeted by a cheerful afternoon. I grinned at the idea that Harrison Barrington would search the Mediterranean in vain for us. What would he make of our presence in the Indian Ocean when the sea monster was undoubtedly sighted by some steamer or sailing ship? Perhaps it was not his old enemy after all but a new species of sea monster or a giant narwhal. There would be confusion at the Admiralty. Fear would run rampant among seafarers and merchants.

We proceeded steadily toward our destination—the Indian Ocean.

(Lacuna Begins)
Note: 1. Text severely water damaged for next three pages. This portion of Captain Nemo's memoir is in very poor condition, and we are not hopeful that we will ever be able to recover the lost text.
Note: 2. Captain Nemo's belief that the Admiralty at the highest level would suspect the true nature of the creature they were dealing with turned out to be correct. As a result of Freedom of Information act filing with the British government, we were able to determine that the admiralty suspected they were dealing with a "submarine boat" constructed by the fugitive Jonathan de Chevalier Mason. To avoid a new arms race with their French,

German and American rivals, this knowledge was treated as top secret.

Note: 3. The use of weighted nets was in fact the brainchild of Captain's Nemo's nemesis Admiral Barrington who wanted to capture the Nautilus so it could be studied.

(Lacuna ends)

We were running on the surface of the Indian Ocean at forty knots. I was making for the South China Sea. In the Bay of Bengal I sank every outbound clipper ship I came across, as I knew their holds most likely contained opium. To quell any lingering doubts, after the ships sank, we donned our diving suits and inspected the wrecks. True, there were often passengers onboard that went down with the ship, but I thought it only just that they also pay the ultimate price for supporting this vicious trade by booking passage on these vessels with their cargo of death. My conscious is clear. In the South China Sea I sank more clipper ships, and several whalers. We often fished newspapers out of the water or retrieved them from the wrecks of ships we sank. News of the terrible sea beast had apparently seized the public's imagination. Debate raged in scholarly circles, confirmed later by that knave Arronax, as to whether we were a species of giant narwhal or some type of sea monster. These accounts warmed my heart. Yes, land dwellers. Fear me at all costs and be you warned that the depths of the world's oceans and seas belong to me and my comrades.

And now it was time to hurl my gauntlet at Admiral Barrington's feet, curse him to Hell. And I got the opportunity to do so in the South China Sea near the new British colony of Hong Kong.

We rode the surface on a fine morning while my Number Two took bearings. It was then that we spied the warship, the Union Jack fluttering from her mizzen mast.

Silently, Jacob and Michael and I watched the warship. She was a steamer but also carried sails which were now set. We saw her turn and beat toward us against the wind under sail and steam power. I studied the ship through my telescope. She was lean and black and sharp-bowed with three sharply raked masts.

"Gentlemen, we are about to sink our first warship," I said evenly.

"That will get the Admiral's attention." Jacob returned his sextant to its case.

We went below. We did not submerge. For three hours I played with the warship, circling her at high speed, rushing at her and then veering away at the last moment.

Then I tired of the game.

My mind was working coldly, dispassionately, without rancor, but with a surfeit of contempt for the frigate and the hated tyrannical government it represented. I grasped the spokes and gave the wheel a turn. The steel ram came starboard and I locked it on the frigate's stern quarter. She was steaming away to the north with every bit of sail crowded on, and then some trying to flee. The Englishman came suddenly about and let loose with a broadside. Oh no you don't, you bastards!

At fifty knots we flew across the surface of the sea.

Geysers of glassy green water suddenly towered on either side of us. I glanced over my shoulder through the rear viewports. Our huge four bladed screw-propeller was throwing up a rooster's tail of water. I smiled at the irony of the splendid rainbow arcing high in the clear blue sky, shimmering with jewel-like colors, while the Nautilus' long steel spur cut through the water like a spear hurled by Poseidon himself. The next thing arcing into the sky would be a tall cloud of steam and coal dust, and a couple hundred British sailors and their officers. It would have been prudent to dive sooner but I wanted to see the terror on their faces as they realized what was about to befall them.

At the last moment, I gave the command to drop down to three meters. The sea rolled up the long hull and then we were racing beneath the waves. Even so, there was still good light transmission at this depth. I peered through the two large brass-rimmed viewports. I don't think I breathed or even blinked. I felt suspended in a green world - and in my head was the sweet piping coming from the Nautilus.

I could not make a word in my mouth.

Not until I saw the brown shape of a long narrow hull. Its two-bladed propeller was leaving a long loose silver corkscrew in its wake as she made a turn away from us. I touched the wheel just a hair. The spur shifted a bit to port and I bared my teeth at the fleeing warship. Oh you won't be putting into port, my friend. Not unless Hell has one.

The sunlight was very bright at this depth and the water was as clear as the emerald sparkling on my finger, as clear as the hull with its churning propeller growing larger and larger while the green world surrounding it shrank within the view ports.

I shouted. "Gentlemen, brace yourselves!" And then there was a tearing crash of steel into copper sheathed wood and a heavy grinding on the upper hull as we tore through the other ship, and then we were through.

CHAPTER 13

The Sea Serpent and the Prince

I was standing at the pulpit in the Nautilus' little chapel. My comrades sat at their pews watching me intently. "Almighty and most merciful God, of thy bountiful goodness keep us, we beseech thee, from all things that may harm us; that we, being ready both in body and soul, may cheerfully accomplish those things which thou commandest; through Jesus Christ our Lord. *Amen!*" I paused to clear my throat. "We beseech thee, Almighty God, look with favor upon thy humble servants, and stretch forth thy majestic hand against all our enemies; through Jesus Christ our Lord. *Amen.*" That was the best I could do – protection and (in my mind) retribution was bound to be part of my prayer, and I could not change and would not apologize.

The church service was painful for me as I did not believe in a divine being—and if there was a God then in my view he had made a very poor showing of running things. The evidence was all around and as plain as day. Human history was one long catalog of horrendous act upon horrendous act, and in our own time entire swaths of the planet had come under the iron grip of despots of one sort or another. In my former country, children and women labored in unspeakable conditions in great mechanized factories from sunrise to well after sunset to enrich the overfed moneymen in their grand salons. And this was the least of the heinous acts that humans committed upon one another. No loving god could look upon such atrocities and stay his outraged hand—unless he didn't exist. And as for the glorious afterlife, it was notable only in that none had ever come back to tell of it.

The men rose and began to file from the room.

I called out. "Shipmates! Wait!"

Those that had left returned and they all looked at me. Jacob and Michael were in the front pew with Mr. MacKay, who was impudently grinning at me, as if he could see the unbeliever writhing uncomfortably behind the mask of the pious ship captain. But I had not concealed my disbelief in god from them—but nor did I attempt to meddle with their spiritual beliefs, as I believe that every man must chart his own course. Some of us steer by Polaris and others by Southern Cross, and it was not for me to say which was correct. But, as for me, I could not place my faith in any god or man. I was trying to do my duty, no matter how painful, and tend to the spiritual needs of the pious monks who were my comrades.

Stepping down from the pulpit, I said, "We are close to the place of our sorrow—Belial Island. You recall as well as I do the suffering inflicted upon us in that hateful place, day after miserable day. I intend to land there and destroy the place and free its inmates. Will you join me in this undertaking to do for others what no one did for us?"

Jacob stepped forward. "We are all with you, Captain Nemo."

"Then let's make our plans."

That moonless night, the Nautilus rose to the surface of the sea and rode at anchor, a cable's length from Belial Island. In silence, we slid the cutter from its bay on the boat deck into the water. In silence, my comrades took their places on the bench and began to row, quietly and deliberately.

"The beach north of the guard tower," I ordered, automatically checking the lie of the Nautilus as we set off. She rode low in the water with her light extinguished, looking like a saltwater crocodile with her overlapping steel plates. The sea was calm but I could smell a storm brewing. Maybe it is your storm that is coming, I thought. And there was reason to believe this, as I knew that the time of my reckoning with my former friend was drawing nigh. My comrades and I were armed with aero-rifles, cutlasses, and explosives, and carried many spare rounds, as we expected much killing.

We pulled strongly for the island looming ahead, reaching it without detection. I leaped out into the surf with my men right behind me. Fighting on the seas, I was closed up in the protective steel hull of my ship. On the beach, a long bare dull gray strip in the black of night, I felt naked as a corpse laid out for embalming. It was then that I knew this would be the last time I would ever willingly set foot on land.

"Five to midnight," I said in Artlang, consulting my pocket watch. In my black officer's tunic, sea boots, and billed cap, I felt more a creature of the sea than the land, making an excursion onto land only to exact retribution.

I looked at my comrades. "No one is to be spared."

Many of my men sported beards. One of the tallest of them grinned at me, his teeth shining in the dark through his gruff, bearded face. "Do not fear, Captain. We intend to send these sinners to their just reward." There were amused grunts and much head nodding from the others, and they had the look of vengeful dark angels come down from Heaven to right a grievous wrong with sword and fire. I bared my teeth in the dark. My shipmates were men who, like me, were utterly fearless and would not hesitate to act where others would only ponder and complain about injustice. Not we brave souls. Slaying the agents of despotism and exploiters of the weak who dared to venture onto our element was for us a holy crusade, an ironic term perhaps in view of my atheism.

I turned to Michael. "Mr. Moreau, you take your men and circle round the camp and come in from the jungle. Wait until after you hear the explosion to commence your attack. You have fifteen minutes to get into place. Let's synchronize our watches."

We did so, then he moved off while we advanced to a pile of boulders beside the stone jetty. One of the men had a rucksack which he handed to me.

A moment later, I was crouching at the bottom of the guard tower. I opened the sack and removed the bundle of dynamite, tied it to one of the tower's wooden supports, and lit its long fuse then bounded back toward the rocks, my head twisting every way to see if we had been discovered. No shouts, no gunfire, just the cemetery sound of a penal island at night. "Let's go!" I hissed to my men behind me.

A guard a hundred meters ahead appeared out of the shadows, but didn't notice us until someone behind me coughed. The guard whirled at that unexpected sound and I cut him down with my aero-rifle. I used hand signals to indicate that we were heading toward Merrick's fine plantation house, where still more guards patrolled. As we headed toward the white two-story house there was a huge explosion to our right and the guard tower toppled over and burned. Ghurka soldiers tumbled out of the barracks, confused and partially dressed with guns in their hands and surprise on their faces, as if still dreaming, only to find themselves caught in a deadly hail of electric pellets.

The soldiers caught on quickly and bullets sprayed past, bitting into the ground around us and kicking up divots of earth around our running feet. One of my comrades crumpled to the ground and was pulled to cover by two others, groaning but alive. My comrades shot back at the guards as I bounded along toward Merrick's house with an escort of two men, bent over to make ourselves as small a target as possible.

Some of the guards threw down their weapons when they saw the strange men in black uniforms rushing at them, firing weapons that didn't make any noise other than a phssst. They watched in horrified confusion as their braver comrades inexplicably contorted like a child's rag doll and dropped to the ground. The men without arms looked into the eyes of their attackers but found no mercy in this onslaught of Hell's angels as they were immediately relieved of their worthless lives, surprise evident on their dead faces.

I pounded up the veranda steps and kicked the front door open, then rushed inside. At the top of the stairs leading up to the second floor stood Colonel Merrick in his nightclothes. His eyes boggled in his deep angry red face when he saw me. The one-armed bastard gripped a revolver in his one hand. "You!" he cried, raising his weapon.

I dropped and rolled to the right. The two men with me had taken revolvers from the dead guards and entered with them. One was thrown to me as they fired covering shots over Merrick's head and around him so as not to kill him. In the confusion of exchanging gunfire with this admittedly brave martinet, for he stood his ground without flinching, I was able to shoot him in the leg and he fell, dropping his gun and cussing.

"Get it over with and kill me! Kill me, you bloody sods!" he screamed.

I raced up the stairs and jammed the tip of my cutlass against his throat, "You will not escape so easily, Merrick. You have much to answer for." Then I dragged him down the stairs by the collar like the sack of refuse he was and out the front door.

Michael's men, as planned, had gone immediately to the barracks and had killed the guards that had remained inside then released the prisoners known to them and armed them. Those freed were now joyously finishing off the last of the guards and the gunfire was beginning to die down; the job of overtaking the island nearly finished.

Heedless of the bullets whizzing past me, I dragged the wretched Colonel Merrick across the square where he had often made us stand for hours in the hot sun.

"You can't do this!" he screamed.

"It's over for you," I said, as if talking to an imbecile.

I tied the now babbling Merrick to the flag pole in the center of the compound and left him to his fate. I will not describe it here as it was a particularly gruesome scene that we witnessed from afar as we left the men on that island with the means to liberate themselves with the next supply ship that would return in two weeks' time.

While my comrades hoisted the cutter back into its bay on the boat deck, I dipped my bloody cutlass in the sea and cleaned it. On the island, the camp commandant's house and the barracks were on fire. I could see the figures of prisoners clearly outlined against the inferno running back and forth, laughing and discharging the firearms they had obtained from the armory. When the cutter was secured I ordered the men below and we dropped below the waves and sailed away, our dark hearts well-satisfied with the night's work. Not only had we destroyed that place and paid back the man that reveled in tormenting those unfortunates condemned to toil ceaselessly there, I was certain that word would eventually get back to England about what had happened on Belial Island, and one there would become cognizant of my deadly intent against his country. Only one man of our party had been shot. While his wound was serious, it was thought that he would recover.

And then I waited impatiently for Harrison Randolph Barrington to come for me. And while I waited, I prepared my ship, myself, and my men, and made a nuisance of myself whenever possible so as to state through direct action my intentions clearly to him – *I will terrorize these waters, kill your men, sink your ships, and make the seas unsafe until you come for me, my old friend and blood for blood enemy.*

With every sighting and every attack, those known to the press and those unknown because the Admiralty did not wish to divulge the secret of the undersea ship by revealing the true count of the British ships I injured or sank, I yelled out my position and challenged him. And then, finally, he did come. With fire and brimstone he came for me—the terrible sea monster of the deep, finding me just after the next dark moon.

For several days I had been working on a device I believed would aid us in avoiding collisions with surface ships while cruising at shallow depths, and aid us when we were attacked. As mentioned earlier, the Nautilus' engine room had a machine shop that would rival any on land. Taking a spare speaking telegraph unit apart, I placed the hearing apparatus at the bottom of a sealed brass tube. Sound moving through water alternately compresses and relaxes due to the water's density, like a sheet of rubber alternately stretched and released. I had discovered that whales and other submarine mammals routinely communicate with each other even over great distances. I believed that if I placed a speaking telegraph outside the hull and amplified the sound waves, we would be able to hear more clearly, not only the sounds of the sea but the approach of propeller or paddlewheel driven ships.

Over the period of several weeks after our liberation of the poor inmates of Belial Island, I experimented with this device. I found a young monk among our band of brothers with uncommonly good hearing named Alexis Boutin. I bolted the *submarine hearing device* to our boat deck and placed the receiver in a cozy little chamber below the bridge at the foot of the bridge ladder. For this purpose, I thought it best if monsieur Boutin was seated, as he would have to spend many hours listening. The youth was enthusiastic about his new duties. I also installed a spare gyro compass in the listening room so he could determine the direction the sound was coming from.

Other than royal navy warships, the south pacific at that time was still sparsely traveled by steam propelled ships, as it required a surfeit of coal to get there. True, my countrymen, ever efficient, had located coaling stations throughout the pacific as they continued to bind the globe to their ever-widening grip. But the fact remained that for shipping cargo and transporting poor Irish emigrants and English convicts and low value cargo, sailing ships prevailed in those seas. So I headed toward the China Seas where I knew the Royal Navy had a strong presence to try out my new invention.

In the South China Sea we had ample opportunity to try out the *submarine hearing device*. I confirmed my belief that a sailing ship could not in fact be detected by the device as it makes little or no noise as it moves through the water; a paddlewheel ship sounds like a child's hand playfully slapping a tub of water, and a ship driven by a screw propeller makes a swishing sound that increases as it draws near. We lay submerged outside the mouth of the harbor at Hong Kong listening to the traffic. Brother Boutin claimed to be able to distinguish individual ships by the sound of their propellers and the clanking racket of their inefficient and noisy steam engines.

During our investigations and travels in the South China Sea, we took the opportunity to ratchet up our attack on British ships. At every opportunity, we nudged, attacked, hit, and punctured opium ships and even a few small British warships, sinking some and injuring many. Our goal was not to sink them all, but to proclaim to Admiral Barrington, *I am here, you dirty Son of a Bitch! Come and get me!*

I quit those waters then and headed north to the seas off Japan, leaving a trail of damaged ships in my wake. Here we came across steamships of the American Navy, and Boutin claimed that the American steamships sounded different than their British cousins. This was a very useful tool since we carefully avoided attacking these ships. I admit that despite what I had witnessed during my stay in New York that I harbored a certain amount of admiration for the American Republic where a war had been fought to abolish slavery, and where each man was his own master and bowed down to no despot. American ships need not fear the Nautilus or her wrathful commander. I will contradict myself here and say that this forbearance did not apply to whaling ships. I saw myself as the protector of these magnificent intelligent creatures. Whaling being a barbarous and unconscienable practice.

I steered North by West ghosting through the green deeps of the Formosa Strait desirous of not being in waters dominated by my countrymen when the encounter I had craved—that I had wanted more than anything in the world—actually happened. I baited him well. So well, in fact, that he came unexpectedly quickly and caught me off guard.

Jacob, Mr. MacKay, and I were in the salon discussing which of our men could serve in the capacity of listeners to provide for a 24 hour watch, and eagerly looking out the salon window. I admit that my mind was elsewhere. It was on Admiral Barrington, as if just by hating him enough even in my thoughts I could pull him to my side as a moth is drawn to a flame. Outside, two cable lengths away, was one of the most spectacular reefs I had ever seen, but its beauty could not touch the cold burning hatred in my heart.

Jacob was saying, "That would be the perfect job for a couple of the elderly brothers and they would be thrilled to have something to do that was not beyond their capabilities. That would certainly take the pressure off Brother Boutin."

I only half heard him, but the importance of maintaining a proper twenty-four hour watch on our ship broke through my dark reverie, and I readily approved his choices and asked that he proceed with haste so that we would not be caught unawares.

Changing the subject, I said, "It pains me that Father Blondeau is not here to witness our many triumphs. He would be astounded by our Nautilus, would he not? Besides the obvious fact of her being an undersea ship, she is not like other ships, as I am sure he would readily agree."

"But what do you mean by that?" MacKay asked with a quick glance at Jacob.

I twisted the slender stem of my wine glass in my hand and looked at the tawny liquid in its bowl, an unbidden thought rising to my mind that I would love to see it filled with Barrington's blood. Without thinking, I replied, "The Nautilus is alive in a way that other ships are not. You gentlemen have heard her singing and seen how she behaves. She regards us at once as her wards and caretakers." I fell silent then. I had said more than I intended, and felt at once foolish and perilously exposed before my comrades, as my fingers idly twirled the glass. There was a long drawn out silence in the great salon. From the corner of my eye, I saw Jacob and my chief engineer exchange looks.

The speaking telegraph mounted to the wall rang suddenly, allowing me to escape the shame of my carelessly exposed feelings. I rose to pick up the handset and was walking toward it when there was a loud explosive crash and my undersea ship gave a violent shudder. I was flung off my feet with the unexpected movement of our normally peaceful ship. There were more hammer blows, one, two, three.

I pulled myself to my feet.

"Jacob…"

My words were cut short by six more hammer blows in quick succession, each one seeming more powerful than the last.

Tension was at a peak. My nerves were frayed as I threw myself in disbelief at the speaking telegraph, which was still ringing on the wall.

It was Michael on the other end. "Brother Boutin was on a break and had just returned when the pounding started. He says he hears steamships. He is certain they are English warships."

I felt strangely light-headed as I ran from the room.

As I gained the bridge with Jacob another explosion rocked the Nautilus, slamming us to the deck plates. A second detonation burst amidships moments later.

"Seal the salon viewports!" I cried.

Jacob staggered over to the console at the rear of the bridge and pressed a button.

"Viewports sealed, Sir!" he called out over the hammer blows of still more explosions that grabbed the Nautilus and flung her from side to side.

I peered out the window. Steel barrels were falling from the surface. I saw one explode and the force of it nearly hurled us from our feet. "Extinguish the light!" I yelled.

Jacob turned the knob and our great light winked out.

I poked my head down the deck hatch and called down to Boutin.

"What do you hear, Comrade?"

"One screw propeller to port and a paddle wheeler coming from astern."

"Can you tell how far away they are?"

"No, Sir, but they are getting close. The sound is getting louder."

More violent concussions rocked our ship.

I surged to my feet. "Hard right rudder! Ahead Full!" The giant screw propeller began to lash the water and we went into a tight turn that took us away from the ship to port. With our light extinguished, there was no question of them knowing our position, but we were sailing blind. The water against the viewports was black as ink.

Two more charges erupted in our wake, flogging us like a giant cat o nine tails.

The Nautilus' steel hull plates began to emit its sweet melodic piping, and not only that but the glass viewports in the bridge took on a faint glowing violet hue which I prayed was not bright enough to be seen from the surface.

"Take us to the surface, gentleman." And the Nautilus rose from the depths of the sea. We were three miles off a small volcanic island. It was 2100 hours and the moon was an orange sickle over a black sea. I swept the horizon with my glass through the viewports, which had thankfully resumed their normal hue-less transparency.

I saw two low shadows to port with running lights on about nine cable lengths away. Even as I vowed that the bastards would pay for their impertinence I could not withhold my admiration for the ingenuity behind the underwater explosives, which they had apparently packed into steel drums with some sort of clockwork detonator.

I trained my glass on the two warships. Two steam sloops: one paddle wheeler and one screw-driven. "Left rudder, twenty degrees." I called out.

"Left rudder, twenty degrees," Michael acknowledged.

The Nautilus came around on her axis and raced toward the ship I had marked for death. I could see orange embers like sprites dancing from the paddle wheeler's funnel.

We pointed our steel spur at the paddle wheeler.

"Do you think they know we have surfaced?" Michael asked.

I twisted my mouth wryly "They will find out soon enough. Two points to Starboard!"

"Two points to starboard!" Michael called.

"Steady as she goes." I checked the attitude of the ship. She was riding level, knifing effortlessly through the water.

"Captain Nemo, Sir, look!" Jacob pointed toward the rear viewports.

The screw-driven sloop had made a long swooping turn and was positioning itself to fire a broadside. "Make your depth three meters!" I called out.

"Making my depth three meters!" Michael replied briskly.

We slid quickly into the water like a sea serpent and arrowed through the water at fifty knots. We turned on our light which lit up the sea for a good mile around us in a great bright green luminous oval.

The paddle wheeler's hull loomed ahead.

"Brace yourselves gentlemen!" I cried but I need not have bothered. We slammed into the wooden hull just behind her bow. There was a great tearing crash of steel against wood and then we were through and the paddle wheeler died with her back broken.

We went into a long arcing turn and raced toward the screw-driven ship which had turned away and was fleeing toward the island at fifteen knots. We overtook her in minutes and I circled her three times at fifty knots before I rammed her. She went up in a great ball of flaming wood and sank with all hands.

"Take us to the surface!" I ordered and we rose with our pumps throwing two tall silvery fountains of water in the night air. The paddle wheeler was just slipping beneath the waves and the screw-driven ship was nowhere in sight.

And then a huge shadow slid slowly from behind the island. Even in the dark I was able to make out the two funnels I knew as well as the back of my hand—saw the long black iron hull with its thick belt of armor. It was the HMS Black Prince, sister ship of the HMS Warrior, that I had designed for **Her Majesty** Queen Victoria.

The warship pulled well away from the island, seemingly unconcerned by us, then came to a full stop. I turned and ran along on a parallel course and slowed to a stop too.

The warships lights were extinguished. I swept the darkened ship with my glass.

Suddenly there was a flare of light on her bridge and I saw by the crimson flames the flag being waved with my former friend's distinctive coat of arms, a rearing griffin holding an anchor in one clawed hand. Indeed it was Harrison himself waving his flag, like an armored knight on his steed challenging an opponent.

My lips skinned back from my teeth in a death's head grin. My former friend wanted me to be in no doubt as to whom I was now facing. Here was a challenge that could not be ignored by an honorable man.

And in response I switched on the bridge light and moved to the forward viewports. I could almost feel my former friend's cold green gaze on my face.

I took the helm myself, for this confrontation was too personal to simply stand back and give orders. Killing the man who had robbed me of my wife, my children and my liberty had been the mainspring that drove me all those long bitter years.

I gave the command and we leaped forward. The Nautilus' engine went into high gear, our screw-propeller churning violently as we raced for this big black monster, one that I had created for the fat little old lady that held sway over millions of human beings around the world, whose livelihood was derived from opium and the subjugation of the darker-hued races of the world. Red tongues of flame lashed out from the tall sides of the great iron warship. Tall geysers of water bracketed us as we raced toward our target. Beyond a certain point, her heavy 100 pound rifled guns and 68 pound cannons would be useless as they would not be able to drop their barrels low enough to reach us.

Broadside after broadside raked the waves on either side of us.

"Sir, should we not submerge?" Jacob asked, his voice throbbing with panic.

I said nothing in reply as I gripped the spokes of the wheel so hard that my knuckles were white. My eyes, black as death, were locked on the behemoth ahead.

More geysers erupted on either side of us. I gave the wheel a little turn and steered between columns of water. A shell hit just aft of our wheel house. The Nautilus' plates sang out a dark anguished note, as the ship rocked violently, but the steel plates strengthened by the unique properties of the Atlantium held.

"Make your depth six meters!" I cried. I do not recall whether the order was acknowledged but we slid beneath the waves as we hurtled toward our objective.

We slammed into the warship's iron side below the waterline. The impact was so violent the wind was momentarily knocked from me as I was thrown against the wheel. The bastards above us began to drop iron hand grenades and those infernal torpedoes that caused our ship to twist and writhe with every explosion. The Nautilus' voice called out in plaintive tones, her hull rippling with each explosion.

"*Astern Slow!*" I called out.

"*Astern Slow!*" Jacob called out, as more explosions rocked us.

But we did not move. We were held fast in the side of the great warship.

"Astern Half!" I cried, fighting a rising tide of panic.

Jacob worked the engine telegraph and I could feel the deck plates trembling, but we did not break free. We were as stuck as if we were a part of the warship's hull.

I knew it and apparently Harrison did too because the Black Prince began to move forward dragging us with her. When I designed the Nautilus, I had not been overly concerned about shear forces acting on her spur. We would punch through our foes, withdraw, and then leave them to flounder. Now, I was worried as we were dragged along by the five hundred foot long monster with our propeller lashing the water impotently. Would the spur hold or would it be torn off leaving us defenseless?

The piping coming from the hull's steel plates was tortured. On and on we went.

"God's blood! Look!" Jacob pointed out the viewport.

The Warship had swung around and was heading straight for the little volcanic island. Harrison was going to smash us against the rocks!

More bombs rained down on us.

I reacted at once. "Ahead, full!"

Jacob slammed the engine telegraph forward and the propellers reversed direction. Slowly, ever so slowly, the Nautilus began to drive the much larger HMS Black Prince sideways, as the adjustable pitch screw-propellers bit into the water.

But we were still firmly locked in her iron hide. "Reverse, Full!" I cried.

Then we popped out. We shifted to *Ahead Half* and increased our depth to forty meters and passed underneath the warship. My mind was racing. Dimly I was aware of a great swishing from the warship's two-bladed propeller as we passed underneath her hull.

We doused our lights and increased our speed and steered by gyrocompass. It was out of the question trying to hole the warship and sink her. She had thirty seven water tight compartments. I had hoped to disable her engines but had missed the mark.

But I knew of one place where she could be hurt and hurt badly. A place that no one in the Admiralty thought would ever be vulnerable.

I took the Nautilus into a long sweeping turn then climbed back to three meters. We surged toward the warship at top speed, throwing up a rooster's tail of water. She was crossing our bow at her maximum speed of fourteen knots.

I gripped the spokes of the wheel hard. I said aloud, "We are not done yet, Harrison." And in my head were the lines from the novel *Moby Dick* that I used to keep on the desk in my study before my life was wrenched from me. *To the last I grapple with thee; from Hell's heart I stab at thee!*

We raced through the black water. The hull grew larger and larger in our viewport. My eyes were locked on the one place in the hull I knew she was vulnerable.

We slammed into her magazine below the waterline; under the armor belt.

There was the grating crash of tempered steel (strengthened by the unholy properties of Atlantium) ripping through mere iron and teak. A massive explosion enveloped both ships and I knew no more.

When I came to a moment later I was sagging against the wheel.

"Take us up!" I cried. We rose to the surface and I fixed my startled eyes on the sight I had prayed to see for all those years. The warship was broken in two, split in front of her bridge. Another explosion and the forward half began to blow herself into flaming pieces. The pressure wave raced across the water buffeting the Nautilus. Chunks of iron and wood rained down on an otherwise placid sea. Some clanged onto our hull.

Three sets of shocked eyes looked at the huge dying warship, thought by the world to be invincible. The second half hung vertically in the air like a barrister pointing the finger of doom. Sailors clung to the railing and the masts. Then the HMS Black

Prince slid beneath the waves and the suction took them all down with her.

And we turned away from that place of death and its bitter-sweet victory, for suddenly instead of Harrison R. Barrington the arch villain, I saw the face of my childhood friend—and I wept bitter tears for the loss we had both suffered.

And for three days I remained in my cabin. Poor Tyrrell could not coax me to eat, and I did not sleep. I lay in bed staring out the little porthole, the one luxury I permitted myself in a Spartan room. On the third night, the door to my cabin opened and Jacob came in. "Sir, there is an American frigate in pursuit of us! What are your orders?"

I sat up and shoved my hair from my face. "What is our position?"

"Two hundred miles east of Japan."

I let out a long ragged breath. Now the Americans were in on the hunt for the *sea monster*. I pulled on my clothes and went up to the bridge. I ordered us up to just below the surface to have a look. I had seen this ship in New York being built and had read of her launch while in Panama City. It was the USS Abraham Lincoln. I could not bring myself to sink the American, so I took out her rudder to frighten her officers and crew.

(Lacuna begins)
Note: Text severely water damaged for one page.
(Lacuna Ends)

I do not know what mad impulse seized me but I took onboard three men I found stranded on the back of my Nautilus as we rode the surface. A Frenchman who claimed to be none other than Pierre Arronax, his manservant Conseil, and a Canadian fellow named Ned Led. At the time I did not know whether I had made the right decision. I did not know if I was inclined to spare their lives because, at long last, I had wearied of inflicting death. And then began another journey, one that stretched for Twenty Thousand Leagues, crisscrossing the globe from pole to pole.

Epilogue

O430HRS: The Pacific Ocean

Jacob Ballion leaned against the rail and pulled deeply on the unfiltered Camel cigarette. The Pacific was oddly tranquil these days. Had this been a dive to the Titanic in the Atlantic, he would have been lucky to stay on station four days without problems from the weather. They had been here for two weeks with a perfectly calm sea—very strange.

The largest body of water on earth was the graveyard for countless ships—some lost to accidents, many sunk in the course of all the wars that had been fought on and below her surface, but most had been taken by the terrible storms that could arise seemingly out of nowhere. He wondered if this could have somehow been the cause of the demise of the Nautilus.

It was dark and the moon was low on the horizon. The history of submarines would have to be rewritten now that they had found Captain Nemo's Nautilus. He could hardly wait to share their discovery with the world. There was much excitement at The Pacific Oceanographic Institute over this latest discovery, and he was at the head of it, participating in history as it was being written. Other than the enquiries to the British government, they were keeping this one close because they didn't want the area to be inundated with every thrill seeker with a boat until they had had time to fully examine the site themselves.

But what was the Atlantium? Ballion wondered. They were only three hundred pages into Nemo's eight hundred page diary. It was slow going because the large book had suffered a lot of water damage. He hoped Nemo would disclose more about the mysterious Atlantium and where it came from later in his journal.

Ballion's mind went back to the Atlantium, a crystal of some sort that could apparently provide unlimited electricity, strengthen a steel hull (and its glass viewports) enough to allow a nineteenth century submarine to attain depths only reached by a handful of small research submersibles. Getting a hold of something like this, he thought, would be an earth-shattering discovery.

He was about to flick his cigarette overboard when he saw a long low black shape suddenly rise from beneath the waves about a thousand yards off their port beam. He was just leaning forward and squinting into the darkness to get a better look – it almost seemed that the Nautilus had raised herself – when he heard the quick rapid steps of men running along deck.

He whirled around just as a fist smashed into his face.

When he came to, he and all the expedition members as well as the ship's crew were on the deck near the fantail. Men in black wetsuits and ski masks stood guard with machine guns trained on them. He could hear more men moving around inside the ship.

"Are you all right, Sir?" Brierly whispered. The young man was sitting to his left.

One of the guards barked. "No talking!"

Ballion stared hard at the man. "This is a civilian research vessel. What right does the US Navy have to board us?" Silence was the only answer he got. From the corner of his eye, he saw that the others were in a state of shock. He puzzled over what was happening as he looked around. More Navy SEALs were going in and out of the superstructure and their quarters carrying empty boxes in and full boxes out. A small pile of boxes was being stacked on the foredeck. When Ballion saw Nemo's iron bound chest being carried out, his evaluation of the situation came to a halt and he surged to his feet.

"What the fuck do you bastards think you're doing? That is the property of The Pacific Oceanographic Institute!" He wasn't the only one who had shot to his feet. James Dunham, the archeologist doing the transcribing, pointed at the iron chest. "That book is very fragile," Dunham said. "If it isn't handled properly it will fall apart! At least let me look at it to make sure it is properly packed."

One of the Navy SEALs standing near the confiscated research material strode over with his hand on the holstered pistol on his belt. "Not any more. It is the property of the United States government," he said flatly. The masked head turned to Dunham. "Sit your goddamn ass down and shut up."

Ballion's eyes flared as he stared up at the tall SEAL. "This unwarranted search and seizure is tantamount to piracy on the high seas. What's your name?" he demanded.

"You don't need to know that," the man behind the ski mask said. "What you *do* need to know, Dr. Ballion," —here he raised his voice—"and this goes for the rest of you, is that this wreck site and everything pertaining to it is now a matter of national security and top secret. We are confiscating all that we need and will leave you as soon as our job is done. But know, all of you," his eyes swept past all the crew sitting on the deck, but landed on Ballion, "that I *will* do my job and have been authorized to use force should the need arise."

Ballion continued to stand, nose to nose, with the masked intruder, but knew that he didn't have a chance of changing the outcome of this day. He stepped back and sat down as ordered.

The man continued, "If any of you are feeling like moaning about this to your friends or family, or trying to get word out on the web, let me enlighten you. What you have witnessed here is top secret and therefore leaking word of this in any way – verbal, written, or otherwise – is a violation of the Patriot Act. We are only letting you leave this site by the good graces of your government which doesn't wish to cause its citizens any harm. But if any word of this gets out, you can count, as sure as death and taxes, on growing old in Leavenworth prison. Do you understand me?" The ski masked head turned slowly to look at the prisoners sitting on the deck. When no one answered, he thundered. "I said, do you understand me?"

Ballion's teammates and the ship's crew knew better than to say anything other than "yes, we understand". While they were held under guard, the confiscated diary and all their records of the expedition were loaded onto a zodiac and taken to the submarine which was more than twice as long as the RV Antediluvian and then the SEALs left—and Ballion slowly got to his feet and thought that perhaps Nemo had been on to something, after all. The world is run by despots.

From: Jacob Ballion

Subject: Nautilus lost!

Date: August 19, 2011 12:07:53 PM
PDT

To: SBrockton@PACOCEANINST.org

Sherrie Brockton, Director

Pacific Oceanographic Institution

Dear Sherrie,

This will be the last of my re-
ports to you in regards to the

Nautilus and her famous Captain
Nemo. At 0430 this morning we
were unexpectedly and forcibly
boarded by Navy Seals who had advanced on us stealthily in the
early morning hours while most of
us slept. They confiscated all
our computers, hard drives, flash
drives, all our files, pictures
and videos, and took Nemo's chest
and diary as well. We have nothing left of our discovery and research and are under penalty of
prosecution if we make our knowledge public.

We are all much shaken and outraged by what happened. Imagine
such a travesty being committed
upon Americans by their own government! The last word we had
from the commander was that we
were to vacate the area immediately under penalty of government
sanction and possible prison
terms. So as you read this, we
have turned for home and will be
in San Diego soon.

We are all mad as hell here and

don't want to take this lying
down. We have been discussing
some options and potential plans
of action, but I will not write
to you of these now. As soon as
we land, I will fly out there to
discuss this with you in person.
If there is anyone from the legal
department that you can have on
hand for that meeting, it might
be useful. There are some bits of
information that aren't all bad,
and I look forward to telling you
the whole story in person.

Sincerely,

Jacob Ballion, PhD
Expedition Leader
RV Antediluvian
Pacific Ocean